# *Carl Weber's*
# *Kingpins:*

# Detroit

# Carl Weber's Kingpins:

# Detroit

*Ms. Michel Moore*

URBAN
BOOKS

*www.urbanbooks.net*

Urban Books, LLC
300 Farmingdale Road, NY-Route 109
Farmingdale, NY 11735

Carl Weber's Kingpins: Detroit

ISBN 13: 978-1-64556-144-6
ISBN 10: 1-64556-144-5

First Mass Market Printing January 2021
First Trade Paperback Printing August 2019
Printed in the United States of America

10 9 8 7 6 5 4 3 2 1

Distributed by Kensington Publishing Corp.
Submit Orders to:
Customer Service
400 Hahn Road
Westminster, MD 21157-4627
Phone: 1-800-733-3000
Fax: 1-800-659-2436

# Dedication

*MW-MW*
*12/28/15*
*LONG LIVE LOVE – WHAT WAS STILL IS*
*BIG AS THE WORLD IS ROUND*

# Acknowledgments

As I have crafted numerous novels throughout the years, the list of people that support me has continued to grow. I'm so very thankful. And beyond all, I'm often humbled. Sometimes being blessed to do what you love all seems like a wonderful dream. My husband, best friend, and rock, author *Marlon PS White*, you've been holding me down behind the scenes since 1999. Now you have stepped out of the shadows and are doing ya own thing in this book industry. I love you big as the world is round and support your endeavors, just as you've done mine. What was still is.

My mother, *Ella Fletcher*, has had my back in each and every way a parent should. She has stood by me and supported my dreams. She believed in me even when I didn't believe in myself. I know I don't say it enough, but I love you. My daughter, author *T. C. Littles*, has been here to see my visions and assist me in making them reality. We have spent countless hours on the phone, plotting and scheming about how we can take over the world. One day we just might make it happen (smile). Thanks for my grandkids, *Jayden* and *Lil Ella*. My brother *Dwayne Fletcher* and my cousin *Othello Lewis*, it's always love. *Rita Fletcher* continue to RIP. I miss you still.

At Aretha Franklin's funeral, Jesse Jackson was posted from beginning to end and never left the legendary singer's or the family's side. At one point I remarked, "I wish I had a friend like that." Truth be told, I do. My best friend, *Dorothea Lewis*, has been my road dawg for decades. I love ya, sis! Even when you clown, I will pull out my red nose and clown with you (smile).

There are several folks in this industry who have made my journey more than interesting, and each one I hold in high regard. *K'wan Foye* is the first author that I considered my friend. He is also the first author to sign his novels at my bookstore. *Nikki Turner* prayed for me when times were hard. *Carl Weber* blessed me with a deal and constant advice. *Karen Mitchell* and *George Denard* are like true family. *Jeff Dumpson* and *Jewels*, *Chelle* and *Jada's* cousin (smile). When the chips were down, *Faye Wilkes*, *K'wan*, *Danielle Green*, and *Blacc Topp* stepped all the way up. I will never forget the love you showed me and mines. We appreciate you. Nothing but respect and gratitude. People talk shit all day long, but these four backed it up. If you want to know the definition of *loyalty*, look no further.

Monique Hall, Margret Waleed, E. Williams, Lissha Sadler, Racquel Williams, Spud Johnson, Eureka Jefferson, Ebonee Abby, Nika Michelle, JM Benjamin, Shannon Holmes, Brenda Hampton, Amaleka McCall, La Jill Hunt, Ty Marshal, Danielle Bigsby, Avery Goode, Joe Awsum, Linda Brickhouse and, of course, my li'l hometown soul sista for life, India-Johnson Williams, collectively, y'all have had my back, shown love, and been nothing short of a hundred since day one. In this industry, that's rare.

I still thank God for Sidi, Oumar, Mustafa, Henry, Porgo, Akieon, and the list goes on of street vendors who showed me love when I first started. Blessings always to my friend Hakim (Black & Nobel Books). A special thank-you goes to Tonya Woodfolk, Johnnay Johnson, Stacy Jabo, Papaya, Jenise Brown, and Ne-c Virgo for always traveling to my events. And, Qiana Drennen, you created something great. DRMRAB was legendary. That book club and all its chapters impacted the paperback world in ways that were unimaginable. I salute you for that. To the other Detroit-based book clubs that rock with me, The Plot Seekers and EYE CU, thanks for the continued support.

Major respect to all who have supported my bookstore, Hood Book Headquarters, located in Detroit; my clothing store, Talk of the City Xclusive, in Oak Park; and my husband's barbershop, Talk of the City. And thanks go to those who have supported the Detroit Hustle and Grind Book Fair. Lastly, I wish to express my appreciation to the Hood Book Ambassadors—Trina Crenshaw, Yolanda McCormick, Nia Smith, Krystal Robinson, Jay Knox, Desiree Bailey, La Kiesha Wright, Renita Walker, Kenya Johnson, Chanelle Patton, Eurydice Lofton, Martha Falconer, Tina Brown, Vickie Juncaj, Candance, Passion Beauford, and T.C. Littles. You are the greatest book club and moral support a girl could ever have. I salute you all. We stay rocking that blue and orange. Ain't nothing betta than my HBA family!

God bless you for reading this. Make sure you check out the titles listed below.

# Chapter 1

The sun had yet to rise. But that didn't matter. Life and death stopped for no one. Neither man nor beast, neither the truth nor a lie. A disturbing sneer graced Kalif's face. He glanced over at the clock. It was now 5:11 a.m., the perfect time to pray and the perfect time to kill. Having no remorse, he had three bodies this month by his own count. The young king knew that more were easily in his near future. Their final destination would be the Wayne County Morgue. He'd been through hell and back this year. He'd borne witness to the most unholy, unspeakable acts, and he was still standing. He couldn't be broken, physically or mentally, or so he believed.

Despite pleas from those around him, he hadn't taken his longtime prescribed meds since the beginning of spring. Even though he refused to admit it, Kalif Abdul Akbar, adopted son of Rasul and Fatima, was out of control. Damn near out of his mind. But the confused man-child was still a soldier for the cutthroat game in the streets and the will of Allah.

His sacred Koran was in plain sight. As he stood there, Kalif placed his open palms to the sides of his ears. "*Allahu Akbar*," he chanted out loud before crossing his arms. Closing his eyes, he lowered his head. By religiously going through all the steps of Fajr, he was able to focus his often tormented mind. "Allah is the greatest," he repeated before dropping to his knees. Touching his forehead to the top portion of the rug, he praised Allah once more. When he neared the end of this morning ritual, Kalif turned his head toward the right, then the left. Eyes still closed, he prayed for God's ultimate blessings in all he did. Afterward, he sat silently for a moment, and then the devout Muslim finally stood. He was at peace.

After rolling up the multicolored prayer rug, he placed it next to the holy book. Kalif was now ready to start his day. He walked to the other side of the room, then sat on the couch. After reaching down and grabbing his wheat-colored Tims, he put them on. Then he tossed his kufi on the coffee table, grabbed his gun, and double-checked to see that one was up top. Satisfied, he dipped off into the kitchen. Kalif tucked the firearm in his rear waistband, and then he opened one of the kitchen drawers and quickly retrieved a huge deli-style meat cleaver. With determination on his mind and malice in his heart, the street warrior headed down into the basement, cleaver in hand.

His anxious crew members had gathered together in the basement and were passing around a gallon of Hennessy. Kalif watched them as he took out his cell phone and waited patiently to receive a text. Several hours ago he'd received word that their sworn enemies were posted at a certain stash house located near the old Kettering High School, so he'd sent a throwaway worker named Dennis to the other side of town to make sure the information was indeed true. Not trying to tip his hand, he couldn't run the risk of being made.

Even though everyone that worked for him was capable, Kalif didn't have to ask for volunteers when this kind of job needed to be done. When dealing with dummy missions like this one, he always sent half-witted Dennis, because he was expendable. Given all the pills he popped and all the lean he drank, if Dennis got caught by the police or even killed by the other crew, then so be it. It'd be no great loss to the organization. This time around, Dennis's task was fairly simple: creep on the address he was given and take pictures of all the vehicles in the driveway and parked out in front of the house. All he had to do then was text the photos to the Obama burnout, nothing more and nothing less.

It was 5:23 a.m. and still no word from Dennis. If they wanted to make an early morning move, Dennis would have to get at them sooner rather than later. Yet while the others remained restless as they finished their community bottle, Kalif was patient. The crew had been down at Greektown Casino all night long, keeping their "go time" energy up. But Kalif's energy had been up for trouble ever since his homeboy's murder. But now he continued to be calm. He'd prayed this morning to be protected from all his enemies and to be granted grace. So of course, he moved differently than the nonbelievers that surrounded him. His need for revenge and his taste for blood would come on Allah's time, not on his own.

Seconds soon turned to minutes, and then Kalif finally received the notification he had been waiting for. He downloaded each picture, and the reality of the situation quickly became evident. The informant was telling the truth. The vehicles with custom paint and expensive rims that were posted up at the designated address were easily recognizable and all too familiar. They belonged to several members of the infamous Black Bottom Mafia, otherwise known as the BBM and named after a neighborhood on the Near East Side of Detroit. They were Kalif's main competitors in the drug trade in the Midtown area of the city and in other illegal activities.

Detroit, once home to the Motown music dynasty, was divided into two major sides—the East Side and the West Side—by Woodward Avenue. This landmark avenue ran from the Riverfront and Hart Plaza across the town limits and clear up to Pontiac, a nearby crime-ridden city. Kalif and his band of killers held a tight grip on the West Side, particularly the Dexter-Linwood neighborhood. Brutus, who was on the East Side, was their main leader but was seldom seen. He and the BBM claimed the same area. For years, Midtown had been a neutral playground of sorts. That was until the financially strapped residents of Detroit elected a Caucasian mayor. An all-black city with a white overseer had all the makings of a perfect storm. Most knew early on that all hell was going to break loose. And the ongoing deadly war proved them right. Both squads seemed to have outgrown their inherited territory. They had a thirst for more power in the streets, and if they took control of Midtown, they would have exactly that.

"Okay, my niggas. Dennis's ass done fucked around and got every picture we need. Not only are Cutt and his boy Mutt posted up there, but East Side Randy and his people too."

"What up, doe? Is them bitches some faggots or something? They having a damn sleepover like some li'l pussies." Amir shook his head.

Kalif and the others laughed at the first lieutenant of the group of the childhood friends now turned notorious. Amir was Kalif's right-hand. Their fathers had both been highly respected when they were alive. They'd led the Islamic underground's assassins, who had never been caught or charged with any crimes. Kalif was focused. He followed the rules of Islam like his pops, Rasul, and Amir's dad had. But his homeboy had been raised Baptist, like his mom, which was something Kalif had never understood or accepted. Nevertheless, Amir and Kalif had been linked up by force as kids and had remained tight as grown men. Whenever Kalif was in one of his weird zones, a result of being off his meds, Amir would step in and make sure things on the streets continued to run smoothly.

"Yeah, no doubt they some straight-up bitches. And before daybreak, they gonna be some dead bitches," Kalif vowed before stepping over to the washing machine. Ready to put in even more work, he snatched up the meat cleaver that was lying there and wrapped his fingers around the dark brown handle. With the meat cleaver down at his side, he felt like the angel of death was speaking to him. *Fear not being in the land of the living. But fear the painful scorch of hellfire that awaits you.*

In a show of respect, the members of the nine-man crew, who had been handpicked to murder when need be, backed up toward the walls of the basement. Kalif slow strolled along the path they had made for him. He then focused on the man they had duct-taped to an old lawn chair, and the next play was obvious to everyone present. As he got closer to the visitor, Kalif's grip tightened on the handle of the meat cleaver. When they were only two feet from each other, they locked eyes, the predator and his prey. A stone-faced Kalif was not bothered by the other man's gaze. He knew the tortured BBM member wanted mercy in return for snitching. And even though he had ratted out his own people and had put Kalif and 'em up on game, unfortunately, there would be no mercy.

Retaliation for being on the wrong team and for killing Kalif's homeboy would be swift.

They were working against the promise of daybreak. After thanking the BBM member for his service, Kalif raised the meat cleaver. There was no hesitation on his part. The future was now. With one strong swing of the blade, it was done. Kalif hit his mark. Blood splattered on Kalif's face and forearm and on some parts of the wall. When he looked down, he saw an open wound on the man's neck, a wound so wide that the man's head was left dangling on the side, much to his executioner's delight. Kalif showed no remorse, and neither did the others in the basement, who'd been down this deadly road before. For them, it was business as usual. After watching the man's body slump over, Kalif dropped the bloodied meat cleaver to the floor and proclaimed victory. Surrounded by his loyal, devoted henchmen, he smirked with satisfaction before launching into one of his famous "Damn, why don't he take his meds and chill?" rants.

"Do you motherfuckers know what it's like to be me? Do you? Hell naw, you don't," Kalif asserted. "I was born with less than nothing. Shitted on, fucked over, and damn near left to die. I did what I had to do to survive. And now society out here judging, acting like they better than my black ass. I'm the bad motherfucker around these parts. I been labeled a child of God, a shepherd for Satan, and now a goddamned king! And y'all think this shit easy, a game." With stern conviction and a clenched fist, he beat on his chest.

He went on. "Y'all see all this jewelry, them cars, and these thirsty bitches hanging around, and you think it's gangsta. It's a headache! These hoes is some straight-up headaches, always wanting, always needing, always begging with they hands out, feeling entitled. Niggas trying to come up when I ain't looking. My own team trying to kill me." He scanned the faces in the basement for signs of any more weak links, but thankfully, he saw none. "My brother and my people done turned they back. The shit don't ever stop. Kalif this. Kalif that. A nigga get tired of it all. And now, with old girl about to give birth to the heir to all this madness, I'm back at war. But yeah, I'm good. I'm built for this shit. My real old dude was a true soldier, so I was told, and that legacy is blood deep, and so the fuck am I."

"Hell, fuck yeah. We all is," said one of Kalif's henchmen, strongly cosigning on their joint thirst for the game and their loyalty to living life.

"So, like I said, if y'all rolling with me, suit up and let's hit the block. We got work to put in," Kalif told them. "Amir, you already know I'ma need you to stay behind and make sure this rat bastard piece of shit is taken outta here."

Kalif's best friend agreed, knowing there was no sense in arguing about this direct order, which was what most of them considered it. When they began this journey of mayhem, nonsense, and murder, Kalif had vowed that he and Amir would never go on missions together. Although he'd been ostracized by his family and by the majority of the Muslim community after his father's disappearance, Kalif's bond to his father mattered. If both he and Amir got knocked off, their fathers' longstanding legacy in the game would run the risk of being nothing more than history and a cautionary tale warning others to leave that lifestyle alone.

"Yo, I got this down here. Y'all go do what ya do." Amir nodded toward the deceased mess of a man in the corner.

Kalif had his squad's undivided attention now, and they did as he requested and suited up for battle. After washing his victim's blood off his face and hands, Kalif, the calculated master of slaughter, stood in the doorway, adjusting his vest. He knew his destiny was waiting.

"All right, y'all. We out," he told his men as he grabbed his AR-15 from behind the door. Kalif, a tattoo-covered, tan-skinned menace, was mentally prepared for whatever was to follow. Today was that day.

It was still rather dark outside, but that didn't slow down Kalif. And the normal busy traffic on Davison was not a factor, either. Kalif looked over at the passenger seat, at his high-powered weapon and the 9 mm that was keeping it company. In true gangster fashion, he had filed the serial numbers off both weapons. Unlike his boys behind him, Kalif had opted to ride alone. Always in deep thought, he had tunnel vision for what was about to take place. Concentration was boss as he drove through the city, heading east. Since there was no music playing to distract him, his adoptive father's final words before his untimely death ran through Kalif's mind.

*Born to die. The angel of death is certain. Allah, spare me long dwelling on the threshold of final judgment. Take me quick. Do with my soul what you see fit. I'm not worthy.*

He couldn't come to terms with the fact that the man he had once looked upon as his hero was gone. The only man that Allah had put on this earth to believe in him was no more. Kalif would forever be plagued with guilt over Rasul's ultimate sacrifice. From the moment he had witnessed his father take that fatal bullet to the head, and had realized his own life had been spared, Kalif had been no more than a shell of a man, one of the walking dead.

But for what? Kalif knew he didn't deserve having been conceived, let alone having a life. That thought haunted him and always would.

Navigating around countless potholes, he and his squad kept the vehicles tight, as if they were in a parade. As they jumped onto the Lodge Freeway, then connected with 94 East, it was almost "go time" for the band of would-be assassins. After they exited at Harper Avenue, the blue-colored metal K greeted them. They made a few right turns, passed a cluster of vacant lots, and then made a sharp left at a huge abandoned house. The clock was ticking.

When the ill-intentioned caravan reached their destination, Kalif's heart raced. Not out of fear, but in anticipation of snatching the next man's soul. After he came to a stop, Kalif flung the driver's side door open. One foot on the ground, then the next, he took a deep breath, ready to do battle. His team did the same. Like a boss, Kalif was the one to lead the charge. And like a warrior, he was prepared to die first. As he let off a barrage of bullets, the street-ordained kingpin of Detroit mumbled his earlier thoughts with each step he took.

"Born to die. The angel of death is certain. Allah, spare me long dwelling on the threshold of final judgment. Take me quick. Do with my soul what you see fit. I'm not worthy."

Kalif prayed for the best but would bravely accept the worst. This madness was the world he had been born into and the life he embraced.

# Chapter 2

*In the beginning God created chaos . . .*

Brother Rasul was a proud black man. Tall in stature, his mind occupied by Islam, he was easy on the eyes. Any single woman or otherwise would be proud to claim him as her own. He was well known and extremely respected wherever he went, and his word was his bond. But now he stood speechless on many occasions. Now he felt defeated. Everything he had wanted to go right had in fact gone wrong, very wrong. His strong foundation had been shaken. The man who was sometimes loyal to the supreme word of God had been left fighting with his own demons.

Stunned at the bizarre, deadly turn of events, Brother Rasul had to remain on point. He had no choice. He now had an extended family and one on the way. He knew they were counting on him to make things right, even if it hurt to do so. This was the game he had chosen. This was the lifestyle he'd embraced. Though he was recognized by his peers as a ruthless street soldier, ironically, his daily fate had become a routine of cold sweats, paranoid thoughts, headaches, and sleepless nights. Repeatedly, he had tried to reason with himself that he'd made the correct choices in the months prior. Yet this hadn't absolved him of guilt. The pain of his past mistakes was still present.

As much as he'd attempted to hide his true feelings, the love he had for his friend couldn't be denied. Discovering Kenya James bleeding to death in the rear of his truck replayed in his mind. The vivid flashbacks were a constant. Days, weeks, and months had gone by, but to Brother Rasul, it was as if the callous murder had just occurred. As he had held Kenya in his arms, begging Allah to spare her life, his prayers had been denied. Just like that, she had slipped away. His longtime secret love was gone. He wanted to believe they'd meet again in paradise, but her sinful actions had definitely dictated that hellfire would be her final resting place. Brother Rasul was caught up in his emotions. Reminiscing on the bullshit he was now facing and how it had jumped off, all he could do was shake his head. With chills running down his spine, he stared out the window. It was like it was just yesterday.


"Oh my God! I made it. I finally fucking made it back home." Hysterical, Kenya turned the car engine off. In haste, she flung the driver's side door open and exhaled. After slamming the door behind her, she ran up onto the porch of the small framed bungalow. Tears now streaming down her cheeks, she practically collapsed in Brother Rasul's arms.

Sensing whatever it was she was going through was deeper than he had first imagined, he held her tightly. Then he took a good look at her, and seeing that she looked a mess, he reached back and twisted the knob on the steel security gate. Knowing he had nosy neighbors, Brother Rasul led her inside the house so they could have some privacy.

"Damn, Kenya. What is it?" he asked her once they were inside. "What's wrong? What has you so spooked? And why you couldn't tell me over the phone?"

Kenya grabbed ahold of his arm. Cautiously, she peeked around the corner of the living room. "Wait a minute. Who here with you? Is anybody else here?"

Brother Rasul raised an eyebrow and sighed. He was trying to be calm but was running out of patience. As he led her into the living room, he said, "Look, I told you nobody was here when you called earlier. Now sit down and tell me what the deal is. What's so urgent that you drove damn near across the country to get here?"

Paranoid, she continued her impromptu quiz as she took a seat on the couch. "Well, first off, did ole boy call you? Have you talked to him in the past twenty-four hours?"

"Kenya." Still standing, Brother Rasul towered over her. He placed his hand reassuringly on her left shoulder. He was done with the games. "Real talk. You can miss me with all this secret-squirrel bullshit you taking me through. You acting like the damn police. Now, what the fuck done jumped off? Why you here? And don't leave shit out."

Burying her face in both hands, Kenya was silent for the first time since she arrived. Seconds later she slowly lifted her head. After taking a deep breath, the self-proclaimed drama queen started in on her rambling, tear-filled confession. Brother Rasul tried to follow the chain of events she described the best he could. The part about her suffering a miscarriage was indeed sad. He sympathized by nodding his head. That revelation was followed by another. Storm had gone behind her back and had got life insurance policies that named her twin as the beneficiary. Sure that was odd to Brother Rasul, but that didn't elicit much of a response from him.

However, when Kenya disclosed the next item on her growing list of reasons why she'd fled her home, he was shocked. Her scattered details of hearing gunfire right outside the front window of her condo made normally even-tempered Brother Rasul take a seat. Rubbing his beard, he could easily tell that Kenya was not even halfway finished with her wild tales.

"It all happened so fast. One minute I was coming down the stairs to tell that snake London to leave my house, and the next minute . . . *bam*. I swear, I just wanted her to leave, that's all."

Confused, Brother Rasul wasted no time flipping the script. It was now his turn to ask more questions. He leaped back up to his feet and said, "Hold up. What your sister got to do with somebody outside your crib shooting? I don't get it. Was London shot? Please don't tell me she hurt. What in the fuck! Stop playing with me."

Kenya knew he was fed up with her reluctance to divulge the truth. There would be no more stalling. She felt a lump develop in her throat. She knew her sister had not been fatally struck by one of those random bullets. It was a lie, a major one at that. However, London's fate had still been the same—death. Exhausted from the long trip, Kenya just wanted to blurt out what she'd done. Although the thought had been tormenting her for hours on end on that highway, she couldn't speak the truth. Once tough as nails, Kenya could not seem to get the words out and bring herself to confess just yet. "Naw, the major shooting outside the crib was just that, outside. I mean, a few bullets did come through the walls, I guess. And one of them did kinda hit London."

"Kinda hit her? What in the hell that mean, kinda? I mean, was she grazed or took one?"

Kenya cleared her throat before she continued. "Yeah, she got shot in the shoulder. But O.T. took the rest of it."

Brother Rasul, always wise beyond his years, was confused by the twisted tale Kenya was laying out. "So wait a damn minute. O.T., Storm's brother, got shot too? Fuck. Is he alive or what?"

"I guess he is. Well, yeah. That's what Storm told me."

"Wasn't you there? You said it was just outside y'all condo, if I heard that part correctly."

"It was, but I didn't go outside." Kenya wiped her tears with the sleeve of her sweatshirt. "I don't know why, but I didn't. I just didn't go."

Brother Rasul paced the living-room floor as the story he was hearing got stranger and stranger. He tried to make sense of the twisted tale. Finally, he stood still. "So hold up. Your pregnant sister got shot. Your man's brother got set down too, and you bugged out that bad? I mean, what in the entire hell! That made you get in the car and leave your own house and drive across the country? I mean, I'm sorry, sis, but I don't get it. You gotta break this bullshit down a little better."

Kenya stood up. Walking over toward the window, she tried to gather her composure. Her mind was racing. However, remorse was not a thought. It was too late for all that. Besides, remorse wasn't in Kenya's heart, as she felt she was blameless. After moving the curtain slightly, she peeked out the window. She wanted to check on her vehicle, which just so happened to be where her innocent nephew was sleeping. "Listen, Rasul, I don't know why I did it. It just popped off before I knew it. I was so fucking mad at how they had played me. Not just mad, but *mad*!"

"Come on, girl. Don't start on that again. Mad at what or who exactly?"

"What the fuck? London and Storm, that's who. They pushed me into all this bullshit!" Kenya replied in an even harsher tone. Balling up her fist, she marched over to the other side of the room.

"So let me get this straight. Your sister got shot. Storm's brother got shot. And you just up and left both of them and came back to Detroit, just like that? Kenya, don't you think Storm probably needs you to hold him down? And isn't your sister, no matter how angry you are at her, ready to deliver?"

"Please, Rasul, you gotta know I didn't mean it. You right. She was my sister." Her expression started to change. Reality was starting to set in. Now in a panicked, remorseful state, Kenya walked up to Brother Rasul. She dropped her head in shame.

He knew Kenya. He knew her when she was calm, but he was also no stranger to her other side. To her "act a fool" alter ego, Tastey, who used to dance at the strip club where he was once a bouncer. Those days seemed so long ago, Brother Rasul often forgot. But as he stood face-to-face with Kenya now, he knew she had definitely done some irreversible bullshit. He roughly grabbed both her shoulders and shook Kenya. It seemed to him that the room and the space between them started to get smaller, but he wouldn't stop until he got answers. "What in the hell you mean, was my sister? Why you say, was? Kenya, sis . . . where is London at? What did you do?"

Kenya pulled away from his strong grip and gave him an evil stare. "Bottom line, I did what I had to do. She's back in Dallas."

"Okay. And?" He raised one of his eyebrows.

"She's at the condo, in the walk-in freezer."

A weird silence filled the room as he tried to absorb what she'd just said and what she possibly meant. "Kenya, I'm confused. The freezer? What in the hell is you trying to say?"

"Man, you from the streets, like me. You know what it means. I let London die. I watched my sister have that damn bastard baby, then let her selfish ass bleed out."

"What?" he yelled, praying to Allah that he'd heard her wrong.

"Yeah, then, after I told her about herself, about her thinking it was all good to have a baby by my man, I grabbed her feet. I dragged her across the living-room floor into the kitchen." Kenya's lips quivered slightly as she recounted out loud the horrible act she'd committed, supposedly in the name of love. "Then I hid her body in the rear walk-in freezer. So, um, yeah, that's about it. Yup, that's what happened and what I did. London is back at my condo."

Holding his head with both hands, Brother Rasul couldn't believe what he'd definitely just heard. *Did she just say what I think she said?* As he moved erratically from one side of the room to the other side, his heart raced. No stranger to murder and mayhem, he normally brushed the grisly parts off. He'd been around death plenty of times, had even put in work to send a few niggas to the upper room, but this right here was some kind of different. This right here, what he'd just heard Kenya cop to, was beyond sinister and twisted, to say the least. Stunned almost to the point of denial, Brother Rasul was hesitant to ask any further questions, in fear of what she would say next.

But he had to speak. "Kenya, sis, please tell me you lying. Please tell me you didn't. Where is your damn sister at, Kenya?"

Kenya was motionless. Her face was blank. She did not answer him.

"Naw! Naw, sis. Naw!" Brother Rasul pounded his fist against the wall, causing it to shake.

That loud sound seemed to bring Kenya out of her silent trance. Hysterical, Kenya dropped to her knees. Tears poured from her eyes as she screamed for God to help her and forgive her sins. "I'm sorry. I'm so sorry," she shouted, having an all-out hyperventilating fit. "Please, please bring her back. Please. Oh God. Oh God. I'm sorry. Please."

Brother Rasul, although still in disbelief, regained possession of his thought process. He went over to Kenya, and then he crouched down on the floor. He grabbed her forearm and tried to pull her back up on her feet. "Listen, Kenya, listen to what I'm telling you right now. You gotta tell me what all went down so I can try to make some sense outta this madness. Damn. First off, where is Storm at? What did he say? I know it can't be good. I mean, that girl was carrying his seed."

Hearing her man's name instantly made her infuriated. The repentance and the tears stopped. "Fuck Storm's no-good, cheating ass. She thought it was all good to have a baby by my man. And before you start judging me some more, let me tell you what all happened. Let me tell you how they both played me." Kenya wiped her face, then gave him a rundown of what had made her go what could only be called crazy. "So it was like this . . ."

***

After making sure the gunfire had ceased, Kenya peeked her head out, in total disbelief. She was in shock that this type of madness was happening in her always quiet community. Normally, if there was any type of small disturbance going on, it involved her and her household. But this chaos seemed to be a couple of houses down. While still holding some smoking-gun paperwork and her cell phone, Kenya tiptoed down the staircase. It wasn't hard to hear all the commotion people outside were making. When she got to the front door, she opened it a crack and peeked out, but Kenya didn't dare go outside. She didn't want to get involved, considering all the illegal firearms they had stashed throughout the condo, so she being extra nosy would have to wait.

*Damn. I wonder what in the hell he did.*

Then, as she peeked some more, she saw the legs of a man who was facedown in the driveway of her neighbors' house. Several landscaping workers, who were obviously quite rattled, had gathered around him. Kenya shook her head. She had been raised in the heart of the hood in Detroit. The coldhearted diva had learned early on that if shit didn't concern you, you didn't let it concern you. Especially gunshots. Since her brother-in-law, O.T., had parked several houses farther down the block, Kenya couldn't see his car from where she stood. That being said, Kenya had no way to know that it was Storm's little brother who was badly injured or, worse, dead.

"Help me. Please help me." Kenya heard the faint cry coming from her living-room area.

Kenya had forgotten about her sister, who was the main reason she had started coming down the stairs in the first place. She followed the sound. When she reached her sister, who was lying on the living-room floor, she said, "Girl, is you still pretending like you in pain or what? With ya good punk, fake ass. I'm about tired of all this showboating you always doing."

"Please, Kenya. Help. I need you." London reached out her hand to her twin.

"Oh, so now you on the floor, huh? What the fuck is wrong with you? You going way too far for me. And what's the deal on this bullshit?" Kenya held up the papers she was holding.

"Help me, Kenya." London barely raised her other arm. That was when her twin noticed a hole, almost the size of a quarter, in London's upper shoulder blade. The hole was bleeding.

"Damn!" Kenya panicked and threw the papers she was holding on the couch. Instinctively, she quickly glanced to the right and saw the broken window on the far right side of her living room. "A stray bullet must've came through here. Damn white people in this neighborhood ain't no better than us."

"For some reason, my shoulder is hurting so bad, Kenya. And I think the baby is about to come. Will you call an ambulance for us?"

"Us." Kenya rolled her eyes and said nothing, knowing that her twin sister was referring to that grimy, troublemaking bastard in her stomach.

"Yeah . . . Or can you call O.T. back and see what's taking him so long?" London screamed out in agony as she took short breaths "Argh!" She had to be in shock and delirious if she did not even realize that she had been shot. "I love my baby, I love my baby," she whispered in between panting and desperately trying to catch her breath.

As the blood soaked through her shirt, London kept rambling on about her and Storm's baby. Kenya was pissed, agitated, and cold. One part of her wanted to do the right thing and immediately get her sister some medical attention. However, the other part wouldn't allow Kenya to do it. *Look at this silly-ass backstabber. She's lying there like shit's all sweet.* With a revengeful demeanor, Kenya stood there, indecisive, contemplating what move to make next. Tragically, her twin was bleeding to death on the floor in the middle of her condo living room, her big belly ready to pop.

"Why did you have to fuck my man? That shit was foul. Huh, why?" Kenya barked, really expecting to get an answer in the middle of everything that was happening.

Hearing ambulance sirens in the distance, London mistakenly thought they were for her. With all her power, the pregnant female struggled to get off the floor. Staring at the papers on the couch, Kenya felt her fury take over. With her foot, she pushed London back down on the floor and held her there.

"My baby, my baby, my baby," London kept repeating while holding her stomach.

Kenya saw her sister's body start to shake. Obviously, she was in excruciating pain. London's voice got loud as she yelled for someone to help her. Not wanting anyone to overhear her twin's desperate cries for help, Kenya went over to the CD player and turned on some jazz. The music drowned out the noise, and Kenya grinned with satisfaction. After getting down on her knees, Kenya helped a confused London take off her track pants. Then she spread her twin's legs wide open. With no medical knowledge about pregnancy to speak of, except for what she had gleaned from watching shows on television every week for four years straight, Kenya saw that London was correct. She wasn't lying and wasn't pretending. The baby was indeed coming, and in fact, it had already started crowning.

"Where's Storm at?" London asked, tossing her head from side to side. "He said he wanted to be here to see his son being born. Is he here?"

"What?" Kenya snapped, wanting nothing more than to smack her face. "Storm said what?"

"Can you call him for me?" London was in a daze as she pushed and pushed. "Storm! Storm! Storm!"

Her constant pleas for her man made Kenya even angrier. "Shut the fuck up," Kenya ordered. Then she took a deep breath, took one of her socks off, and stuffed it in London's mouth. "Chew on this and stop calling my man. He don't want you to be the mother of his baby. That's my damn job."

Five minutes later she delivered London's baby on the living-room floor. Just as the ultrasound had shown months earlier, it was indeed a boy. Storm's newborn son had a birthmark on his lower backside, which affirmed the fact that he was a Christian, which was Storm's government last name. Kenya, amazed that she'd successfully delivered the infant, laid the crying baby on London's stomach. She stood to her feet and quickly disappeared into the kitchen. After opening the drawer near the sink, Kenya searched for and finally found a huge razor-sharp butcher knife with jagged edges. She grabbed a few clean dish towels off the rack and an old bread twist from the junk drawer, then, filled with spite, Kenya headed back to a suffering London.

Slipping in and out of consciousness from losing so much blood, London was barely aware of what was going on. Now Kenya, the same person who had deliberately taunted London less than an hour ago, dropped the dish towels next to London, then leaned down over her with the knife and the twist in her hand and lifted the newborn up. She wrapped the bread twist tightly around the blood-filled umbilical cord and deviously smiled as she thought about Storm. Then she glared vindictively at her reflection in the shiny side of the butcher knife as she cut the umbilical cord, severing all ties the baby had with London. Kenya held the baby up as she reached for the dish towels.

"Where you going with my baby?" a weak and drained London muttered as the gunshot wound on her shoulder blade continued to bleed. "Let me hold him. Let me hold my baby," she begged as she started gagging on her own blood.

"Your baby?" Kenya questioned, wrapping the crying infant in the dish towels. With no regrets, she stood up, the baby in her arms, and then sat down in Storm's favorite chair. She rocked the newborn in her arms as she watched her sister struggle to hold on to life. "You must have made a mistake. This is my baby, mine and Storm's. This is our son."

"But we're family. We're all we got. I love you, Kenya. Please don't do this. I love my son. I love him," London whispered, proclaiming her love for her sister and her baby. Seconds later, sadly, she took her last breath.

"Say you promise," Kenya replied nonchalantly as she looked down at the floor and ignored the fact that her twin sister had just died in front of her eyes because she had chosen not to get her any help.

Kenya rose from the chair and turned the music up a few more notches in an attempt to mask the sounds the frantic neighbors made as they knocked loudly on the front door. Obviously, the neighbors had realized her brother-in-law was the gunshot victim and were trying to alert the family. Kenya, who had obviously lost her mind, returned to the chair and rocked and hummed to her now deceased twin sister's newborn son while she patiently waited for his daddy, Storm, to return home so they could be one big, happy family.

"Don't worry, little one. Your real mommy's here with you," she whispered to the newborn, though she had callously allowed her twin sister, the infant's mother, to die right before her eyes on the living-room floor. Yet Kenya seemed coldly unaware of what she'd just done.

She continued to rock back and forth, with London's defenseless newborn tucked in her arms, and after some time, the knocks at the front door stopped. As the smooth sounds of jazz flowed throughout the room, Kenya cried as she stared down at her nephew, Storm's son.

Then she spoke. "Despite what anybody says, you belong to me. I deserve to have had you, not that man-stealing bitch over there." She nodded toward London, still feeling no remorse. "Storm loves me. Not her, me. Even though I can't have no babies, he loves me. And you gonna love me too." With her blood-covered fingertips, Kenya traced the tiny outline of the baby's lips. "Look at you," she said softly to the innocent and defenseless infant. "You got those big brown eyes just like my gran used to have. And look at all that wavy hair."

The last track on the CD finally played. When the music stopped, Kenya snapped out of her strange trance and squinted her eyes. When she saw her twin sister with a bullet hole in her shoulder and a messy combination of blood and afterbirth between her still open legs, reality hit her like a ton of bricks. Quickly leaping up from the chair, Kenya laid the infant, still wrapped in the dish towels, down on the couch and peeked out one of the front windows. The crowd of people was still there, and the man still lay in the driveway. *Damn. Who in the hell got hurt?* She quickly released the drapes she had nudged aside when she saw the crowd of people move out of the way so an ambulance could get through. *But who gives a sweet fuck? I got my own bullshit to deal with right about now.*

Interrupting Kenya's selfish thoughts of "me, me, me," Storm's son started to wiggle on the couch. Momentarily thinking clearly for the first time since smacking the dog shit out of London, Kenya knew she had to get the infant, whose umbilical cord was still attached, some much-needed medical attention. Leaning over London's still body, Kenya broke all the way down as she checked for a pulse. "Oh my God! What did I just fucking do? I'm sorry. I'm sorry," she sobbed as she held London's limp hand, knowing a piece of herself would forever be missing. She trembled as she spoke. Though she had just apologized in one breath, Kenya's heart turned to ice with her next breath, and she snarled, "I didn't mean it. I promise I didn't. But why did you have to keep that baby? Why? Why? You knew that shit was foul. You know he didn't rape you. You wanted that dick."

Of course, there was no movement from her twin sister. No acceptance of Kenya's erratic excuses and no begging to hold her newborn. No whining about having to abruptly drop out of school and, lastly, much to Kenya's delight, no calling out for Storm. Letting her grip on London's hand go, Kenya glanced over her shoulder at the now whimpering infant.

*You . . . you fucking little bastard!* Spitefully, with her hair practically standing on top of her head, she focused all her attention on the small bundle of joy, which was the source of all her problems and pain. *You the one that made my sister stab me in the back and Storm act a fool. A trust fund for your punk ass, a life insurance policy, for real? All that for you? After I been riding with that nigga and all his gangsta bullshit! Oh, hell naw!*

Coldly staring at the guiltless baby, blaming him for the troubles of the world he had just been born into, Kenya was back in a trance. Out of the corner of her eye, she saw the shiny, jagged edges of the blood-covered butcher knife she'd used to cut the umbilical cord. Still on the floor, she crawled around London's body, then snatched the wooden handle up and clutched the knife tightly in her hand. With the blade facing the baby, Kenya continued her insane rant, this time aloud. "Why did you have to be a boy? Why? I wanted Storm's firstborn son, and you robbed me of that," she mumbled, standing to her feet. Slowly walking toward her tiny nephew and stepson to be, Kenya once again totally zoned out. "If it wasn't for you, life would still be perfect around this bitch. But you fucked that up for me, didn't you?"

With each step she took, the once self-proclaimed Detroit Boss Bitch Diva became more and more out of touch with reality. Finally standing over the naked, wide-eyed baby, Kenya let the pointy tip of the knife, which she normally used to cut chicken and beef, press down on his birthmark, which was located exactly where Storm's was. *I should just slit your damn throat, you little troublemaker. You straight foul.* Noticing again that his brown eyes looked like her beloved gran's, Kenya felt chill bumps race down her arms. *I just wanna be happy. I want things back the way they were for me and Storm.*

Letting revenge win over family loyalty, Kenya still had no remorse in her heart for what she had just allowed to happen to London and, worse than that, for what she was about to do to London's newborn, Storm's illegitimate seed.

Before Kenya could recount any more of the gruesome tale, her friend leaped to his feet. Brother Rasul turned away, shaking his head. He had known Kenya long before she turned into the monster she obviously had become. "Kenya she was pregnant. That was your sister. Damn! Are you serious? Tell me you ain't take that baby's life too. Kenya, where is the baby now? Is he with Storm?"

Wiping the flood of tears from her face with her hands, she frowned. Then she pointed toward the front door of the house. "Naw. I already told you, 'Fuck Storm.' That little bastard is out there in the car."

Slowly turning back to face Kenya, Brother Rasul thought he might've heard her wrong. "He who . . . ? Who's in the car?"

"The baby. He's out there."

"What! You have a baby in the car out there?"

Brother Rasul wasted no time racing to Kenya's vehicle. After flinging open one of the rear car doors, he saw amid the piles of clothes a car seat holding a still sleeping, blameless newborn. He carefully removed the baby, car seat and all, and took him inside.

After sitting the car seat on his dining-room table and pulling back the blanket, Brother Rasul was overjoyed to find the wavy-haired infant alive. "All praises due to Allah." He was relieved that at least the child had been spared Kenya's still unexplained rage that had left her twin dead. "Okay, Kenya, like I said, does Storm even know what has happened or what? I know he does after all this time."

"I don't really know for sure, but fuck him. The last time his lying ass called, he was down at the hospital, seeing about his fake brother and leaving me shady messages." Her arrogance rising, Kenya started to behave like she was the victim. "He can kiss where the sun don't shine. His brother can too. He didn't like me from the jump. So yeah, he can die in his sleep."

Brother Rasul stared at the tiny baby, wondering what he was going to do, as well as what he was willing to do, to help Kenya out this time around. Besides being her confidant since day one at the strip club, he had killed a hit man to protect her, had helped arrange her man's release from a drug lord's house, and had just vouched for Storm getting credit on the strongest package in his city. Brother Rasul had done all that in the spirit of friendship. However, Kenya leaving her twin sister, her own flesh and blood, for dead and then kidnapping her twin's baby was over the top, even in the crazed street life they both led. This was some kind of awful. It haunted him and always would.

Snapping back to his present-day reality, Brother Rasul realized chills were still running down his spine. He moved away from the window. Always a strong man, physically and mentally, he suddenly felt broken. There was nothing he could do to change what his friend had endured months earlier. He knew he should have followed his first instincts. He was a born leader, taught to protect his queen. He shouldn't have encouraged Kenya to do the right thing. He himself had driven her from Detroit with that baby in tow. And now, after a bizarre chain of events, she was dead. He couldn't help but blame himself. Her death was on his hands and heart.

Dealing with the cold, hard facts, he grimaced at the memory. He'd been forced to ship two bodies home to be buried. Not only Kenya's, but her deceased twin sister, London's, as well. Deep in his faith, Brother Rasul had then done what he felt was best. Not only for himself, but for the one who, he would soon discover, was an orphan—London's infant. After receiving the devastating news that the infant's father, Storm, had also been murdered at the hands of "the family," Brother Rasul wanted to man up. It was in his nature to do so. A man of convictions, he knew the baby deserved a chance at having a normal childhood and life. Wanting to be a part of something that was good and pure, he changed his life and how he moved.

Trying his best to hide his utter devastation over Kenya's untimely demise, he sought out his ex-girlfriend, Fatima. Somehow they managed to patch up their differences. After a short time of him proving to her that she was his true soul mate, they got married. With that in place, everything would be perfect. They could give their newly adopted son, Kalif, a proper upbringing. Brother Rasul paid an enormous fee to have documents falsified to make them his legal parents.

Eerily, as the small baby grew each and every day, Brother Rasul could see something cold in the boy's eyes. It was something that sent chills down his spine. Fatima was as nurturing as any mother could be to a child, but the boy was having none of it. Kalif was only six months old when they first noticed something was different, but they tried to ignore it. However, it seemed like Brother Rasul had been here before. Ironically, the boy was the spitting image of his biological father, from his birthmark to the way his nose was shaped and the expression on his face when he was pissed. There was some sort of sinister glare in Kalif's eyes when he drank his bottle or got his diaper changed. Even his shit smelled like trouble.

The religious couple prayed five times a day and twice nightly. They hoped Kalif would grow up to be nothing like his evil, drug-dealing, "get paid by any means" father. But unfortunately, the adoptive parents knew this infant's gangster-minded bloodline ran deep. Brother Rasul, Fatima, and strange as it may seem, even little Kalif knew his ultimate fate. He was born into utter madness and would probably die that way, just like his confused mother, his evil-tempered father, and his deranged aunt. Some things happened by sheer chance, while others were dictated by circumstance. It seemed that Kalif was destined to one day grow up to be a menace to all he came in contact with on the treacherous streets of Detroit. But only time would truly tell.

And soon it did just that.

# Chapter 3

"I told you he needs to be on medication. Matter of fact, I keep telling you that, and you keep acting like I'm the one who's crazy."

"Look, Fatima. First of all, lower your voice when you speak to me, whether I'm in your face or not. And secondly, I know these days people just shove pills down their kids' throats as some sort of solution. Making them be zombies and making their systems corrupt, but—"

"*But* nothing, Ra. This boy needs help. The kind of help that not me, you, or praying can give. We've tried that for years. You see how he behaves. The things he says. The way he acts out at school. It just ain't right."

"You're acting like he's some kind of monster. That boy prays five times a day, just like me. Sometimes six. And he is Hafiz. You know how rare that is," Brother Rasul said, coming to his son's defense. Although it was no great secret that his oldest boy was getting a little out of hand, he knew medication was not the answer.

Unlike her husband, Fatima knew that Kalif was beyond standing in the corner and that threatening to whip him with a belt would do no good. While Brother Rasul often traveled, she was there and was the primary caregiver to both their sons. She was the one who usually received the frustrated calls about Kalif from the teachers. She was the one who had to deal with the cold stares of the other parents and the harsh, irate, but warranted

warnings from the school board. Fatima secretly wished
she could give back the illegally adopted menace. But
given that both his birth parents had been murdered, that
wasn't an option. At this point she was stuck.

Today Rasul was traveling, and Fatima and Hakim,
who was her and her husband's biological son, were
at home and were suffering from Kalif's unprovoked
wrath. One moment the religious-minded youth was
fine, and the next, *boom*, he was like a stick of dynamite
exploding.

As the boys sat on the couch and watched TV, Kalif
snatched the remote from his baby brother's hand. With
ill intentions, he then shoved Hakim to the floor. As he
stood towering over young Hakim, he showed no mercy.
And Kalif didn't care. Nothing and no one would dictate
how he behaved. It was as if he had a one-track mind.
Only ten years old, he felt that the world revolved around
him. The more love his parents showed him, the more he
rebelled. Strangely, the only time he showed anyone any
sort of respect was when he was praying. While Brother
Rasul tried to reason with his son, on most occasions,
Fatima was the one who drew the line in the sand.

"Hey, boy. Are you crazy or something? Don't put
your hands on my child like that," Fatima said as she
stormed over to Kalif.

"He had my remote and was messing with it. And the
other day it was my controller. I keep telling him to leave
my stuff alone." Kalif stood toe-to-toe with his mother.

She'd had enough of him acting up. Every day it was
something. Now the young king, as her husband often
called him, would pay. "Okay, Kalif. You think it's a
game to stand here and talk back to me? You can't really
think this kind of behavior is appropriate."

"Like I said, Ma, he keeps touching my stuff. And I'm not with that." Kalif's anger was starting to get the best of him. As usual, the youngster didn't care about consequences and was seconds away from swinging at his mother.

Unfortunately, backing down to her child was not high on Fatima's short list of things to do. She was on his head and didn't care about the consequences. "So you think that entitles you to just keep putting your hands on my son? You really believe all that madness is gonna keep flying? If you do, you're sadly mistaken. It stops now, Kalif. Right damn now. Don't ever touch my baby."

Kalif took a few steps back as his mother's stiff finger poked him in his chest. He didn't blink an eye. He mean mugged Fatima, as if she was a random bitch in the streets, as he started to drill her with his own questions. "So I thought *I* was your baby first. Or is that a lie? Matter of fact, I know it's a lie!"

"What you say?" Fatima was thrown off by his abrupt question.

"You heard me. Was I your baby or not? Because—"

"Because what?" she said, cutting him off while trying not to bug out. After ten years of raising him, she and Rasul knew this day would come at some point. Yet they didn't expect it to be so soon, so out of the blue.

*Why isn't Rasul home? Why does he have to be out of town? Damn!* she thought.

"Look, Kalif, I don't know what you going through or what you trying to get at, but you need to stop it. Stop acting a fool, and stop putting your hands on your little brother. Now, I'm not playing. Go sit down, before I get angry for real."

Kalif could tell he had Fatima shaken up. Seconds ago she had been all up in his face, ready to clash, but now

her stern voice was shaky. Here she stood, trying to ne-
gotiate his actions. Although his mother was willing to
avoid his controversial question, he was not. He'd overheard his father and a few of his father's friends talking
at the mosque one evening not so long ago. They had assumed all the kids were out in the parking lot, playing
ball, but Kalif was not. After coming inside to get some
water, he had sat down on the red-cushioned bench to
tie his shoe. He was sitting on that bench when he heard
what he heard. That was the evening he felt as if he was
sucker punched in the stomach. The men were commend-
ing Brother Rasul on how he and his wife had stepped up
to the plate. They reassured his father that he would receive extra blessings from Allah for adopting an orphan.

At first Kalif was confused. He wasn't sure they
meant him. Maybe his father had another family somewhere . . . a second wife, more kids. After all, that was
allowed in Islam. Remaining still on the bench, he continued to eavesdrop. Then, *bam*, just like that, the truth was
revealed. He overheard his father, or rather the one who
he had always believed was his father, speak out on the
subject. He told them that Kalif was indeed a gift from
God. He proudly proclaimed that he had done what he
did all those years ago out of love for the boy's real parents, not for extra blessings from Allah.

Kalif didn't move. He couldn't. It was as if his shoes
were cemented to the floor. It was as if everything he'd
known to be true was a lie. As the men got down on their
multicolored rugs to offer extra prayers for the evening,
Kalif remained motionless. He had to process what he'd
heard. When Brother Rasul finally emerged to greet his
child, he behaved as if nothing was wrong. And as far
as he was concerned, nothing was. However, for Kalif,

that wasn't the case. Now nothing was right, and it never would be. He vowed that everything he said and did from that point on would be an act of rebellion an and would be looked upon as exactly that. And he didn't care. He felt as if his entire life was a lie, and for that, no one would have any peace.

And Kalif rebelled now, refusing to sit down, as his mother had demanded, and to back down. "Yeah, so like I said, who am I? Can you tell me that? See, I wanna know, because you and that man you call your husband are some liars. Y'all are both hypocrites and motherfucking liars. Oh my God! No wonder you treat me like you do!" Kalif was completely enraged. Using every bit of strength, he punched the wall twice, snatched a framed picture off the nail and sent it flying across the room, then ran into the dining room and kicked over a dining-room chair.

Fatima hurried into the dining room, Hakim on her heels. With Hakim looking on in tears, Fatima was at a loss for words. The only thing she wanted to do was snatch up her small son in her arms and flee the house. Kalif, the baby she had voluntarily raised from the time he was only days old, was going berserk yet again. But this time seemed different. This time his actions seemed more deliberate. As he flung his arms about wildly, his eyes bucked. Saliva flew out of Kalif's mouth as he yelled obscenities and made threats. Threats that he soon made good on. Behaving as if his mother was no more than a stranger in the streets, the young household nuisance promised to make his mother shed every tear she had.

Knocking over the china cabinet was his next act of defiance. Numerous keepsakes and irreplaceable items were instantly destroyed. Things that the family had always been proud to display were now damaged beyond belief. Fatima's nerves were shot as the confrontation had escalated quickly. She was frazzled. She was overwhelmed, but she couldn't give up. Silently the distraught mother prayed for inner strength from Allah as she held Hakim tightly, trying to shield his ears and eyes from what was taking place. Knowing she had to at least attempt to stop her older boy from tearing up everything in the house that she and her family held dear, she lifted up Hakim and bolted into the living room. After placing her small son by the staircase, Fatima ordered him to go upstairs to his room and hide. Immediately, without a single question, Hakim did as he was told. He sensed that his troubled sibling's bout of rage was more extreme than any that had come before.

After ensuring that Hakim was well out of harm's way, Fatima turned her full attention back to Kalif and his impromptu antics. Within a mere matter of seconds, he'd shattered a wall-mounted mirror and broken two windows in the dining room, adding to his list of destruction. There were no clear signs that he would soon calm down. In fact, his voice kept growing louder. He continued belting out question after question and making one accusation followed by the next. And although he had every right to be angry that the truth had been hidden from him, this was no way to handle things. Kalif had quickly reached the mental point of no return, but it was up to his mother, birth or not, to force him back to reality. Huge shards of glass covered the dining-room floor. With only the protection of thin-soled slippers, Fatima risked cutting her feet while she attempted to avoid the shards as she made her way into the dining room.

Just a few feet away, Kalif promised to kill her if she came into his personal space. Prepared to make good on his promise, he reached over to one of the broken windows and removed a huge piece of the glass that was still in the frame. As his hand closed around the glass, his palm and fingertips started to bleed. Fatima was stunned that he didn't flinch, look at his hand, or even acknowledge the blood. He had indeed gone insane. A part of her wanted to go and grab one of the many guns Rasul had hidden away from the children, whose curiosity could put them in danger. Yet she knew the way she was feeling in that very moment, she'd shoot Kalif in cold blood. She would just have to take her chances that her son was selling wolf tickets that he had no intention to cash in and that he was just stuntin'.

A still wide-eyed Kalif stayed focused on Fatima as she got closer. He wanted her at least to deny what he already knew was true: he was adopted. He wanted her to swear on the Koran that she'd given birth to him, just as she had to Hakim. But of course she couldn't. And truth be told, she was glad she hadn't carried this monster for nine months. With each step she took in his direction, she couldn't hide the contempt that was in her heart. Kalif could see in her eyes that he didn't belong to her or to Brother Rasul. In that very moment, he knew he was alone in the world. He had no real name. He had no true family. His soul was broken. He'd be a social nomad, for he had vowed never to believe in the word of man again. The only thing he had was Allah.

As tears of resentment filled his eyes, Kalif opened his bloody hand and allowed the glass to fall to the floor. He then followed suit by dropping to his knees. Pieces of shattered glass pierced his clothing and cut his knees. He appeared to feel no physical pain. Suddenly he tilted his head back, lifted his arms upward, and cried out, "*Allahu Akbar. Allahu Akbar. Allahu Akbar.*" Then he buried his face in his bloodied hands. Seconds later, he repeated the chant once more, this time even louder than before.

Fatima stopped dead in her tracks. It was like she was in the middle of some horror movie. She didn't know what to say or do next. While the physical tirade threatening her life seemed to be over, she wasn't 100 percent sure. Kalif had drifted into some sort of a religious trance, and now he was repeatedly asking God to forgive him and save his soul. He chanted and sobbed. Sobbed and chanted. Taking a few steps back, Fatima bit the bottom corner of her lip in dismay. She was terrified of what Kalif was capable of, and at the same time, she was infuriated that he had caused such irreparable damage. Moving stealthily, so as not to set Kalif off, she made her way into the kitchen and took her cell phone off the charger. She hit the button to dial her husband, and a few rings later, thank God, he picked up.

"Rasul, you have to come home now!" Fatima belted out before he could even say hello.

Sensing the urgency in his wife's voice, the head of the household, who was devoted to his family, said with the same degree of emotion, "Baby, what's wrong? What's going on there? Where are the boys?"

"Hakim is upstairs hiding like I told him to do. But Kalif, Kalif is in the other room, going all the way through it. He tried to attack both me and Hakim."

"What!" Rasul yelled. "He did what? Why in the hell did he do all that bullshit?"

"I'm not sure. He just snapped after I told him to stop picking on Hakim. Then it was like *bam*. A light switch came on, telling him to go wild. He asked me if I was really his mother and a bunch of other things. Then he said he was going to kill me . . . waving around some broken glass. I mean, Rasul, that boy said he was going to really kill me in my own house. And he knocked over the china cabinet, kicked stuff, and broke windows." Fatima was watching Kalif like a hawk from the kitchen as she spoke to her husband.

Rasul was alarmed at what he'd just been told, especially about Kalif's parentage questions. As much as he loved Kalif, he did fear for Fatima's and Hakim's safety, and it showed in his voice. By reassuring his wife that he was on the road, was just crossing the Michigan state line, and would be home in less than sixty-five minutes, he got her to calm down slightly.

"Baby, are you sure you are okay?" he asked her. "Where is Kalif at now? Is that him I hear? It sounds like he's praying or something."

"Naw, baby. This boy ain't praying to no God we follow. He chanting to Satan." Using her hand to cover the phone, she glanced over at the stairs, then at Kalif. She didn't want to set him off any further, but she and Hakim staying in the house with him a minute more than was necessary was out of the question. Under her breath, she revealed her next move. "Yeah, so I'ma call the police. That's what I'm about to do as soon as we hang up. I'm not letting any kid threaten me and have me and my baby living in fear. This boy needs some kinda help. I keep telling you that. But you think he's more precious than gold."

"Yo, you need to pump your damn brakes and hold the fuck up. I feel that guy over there clowning, but since when do we call the motherfucking cops?" Rasul re-

plied, wasting no time in protesting the idea of Fatima
calling the law. Not because he had a slew of illegal guns
stashed around the house. And not because he had drugs
bagged and hidden in the attic rafters. He was a grown-
ass man, and if it came down to it, he would catch any
case and cop to any charge if he had to. But he was definitely not going to give the often corrupt Detroit Police
Department an open-ended invitation to come inside his
castle. "Look, I'ma call Abdul and ask him to go over
there right now. He can get Kalif back together until I
touch down. You and my little man gonna be safe, okay?"

"Okay, but—"

"Okay but nothing. I'm still the head of my household,
and what I say is law. So like I said, no damn police.
Sit tight and let me hit Abdul up. I know he's over near
Grand River Avenue and Livernois, making a few runs.
I'll tell him it's urgent. He'll be there quick."

"Rasul, that boy in there had a huge piece of glass and
was waving it at me. That lunatic you always protecting
said he was gonna kill me. Did you not hear me say
Hakim is upstairs hiding?"

"You heard what I just said. Abdul will be there. And
if you that scared of your own son, carry your ass upstairs
and hide like Hakim." Sarcasm now filled his tone.

Fatima wanted to buck and call 911. She wanted to
say so much more about what had just taken place, but
it was obvious it would fall on deaf ears. Out of options,
she reluctantly backed down on her threat. Having been
Rasul's wife for years now, she knew if she didn't back
down, the wrath she'd suffer courtesy of her husband
would be far worse than anything Kalif could think of.
Keeping her distance, she continued to watch Kalif's
unstable behavior.

# Chapter 4

Just as her husband had promised, his best friend pulled up in no time. Amir, Abdul's son, was riding shotgun, and they both got out the car quickly and headed up the walkway. Still nervous and upset, Fatima met the pair at the front door. She had tears in her eyes, and the look of worry covered her face. Speaking no words, she exhaled before pointing Abdul and Amir in the direction of the living room, where Kalif was now camping out. He had finally lowered his voice to a faint murmur, but he was still chanting. Fatima was now empowered. It was her turn to be the aggressor. She knew with a man in the house to protect her, all bets were off. The weary woman could speak her mind without fear of being attacked by the child she'd stepped in and raised as her own.

She found her voice before Abdul and Amir headed to the living room to confront Kalif. "That animal is in there. Look at my china cabinet. Look at the windows. All of this is ridiculous. I keep telling Rasul he needs to do something, but he's in denial. You know like I know he always thinks Kalif can do no wrong, just because he prays five times a day! He needs to be in a mental facility. They have one down at Children's Hospital, but your friend won't listen."

Abdul and Amir surveyed the damage in the dining room and then took a peek at Kalif. Amir was shocked by what he saw. He wanted to ask his best friend what was wrong and what had made him nut up. He wanted to know Kalif's reason for destroying his own house, and he wanted to ask Kalif if he knew he was bleeding from the knees and hand? But from past dealings in grown-up affairs, Amir felt it was best to stay in a child's place, to remain mute unless he was asked to speak. After all, he didn't want his face smacked.

Abdul quickly returned to the kitchen, where Fatima had remained, and Amir quietly followed his father. Abdul finally responded to Fatima's statement. Like Rasul, he didn't want to hear any of what Fatima had to say. They kept their families' business to their selves. The tight-knit members of the mosque they attended didn't involve others, especially the police or what Fatima was suggesting, a place for crazy people. Such attention would bring child protective services sniffing around. That type of attention, Abdul promised Fatima, she didn't want or need. He was far from blind, he told her. He could see that Kalif had some problems. There was no way in hellfire that a normal thinking person would do all the things the boy had done over the past thirty minutes and be considered sane. But judging his best friend's son was neither his place nor his burden. That task he'd leave up to Rasul and, of course, to Allah. He and his son were simply there to keep peace, so to speak.

Fatima nodded, then left the kitchen. As Kalif stayed perched in a corner of the living room, eyes shut tight, Fatima used her cell phone to take pictures of the damage he had done. She knew when her husband arrived, he would find some way to flip the script and justify what his favorite had purportedly done. The pictures would always serve as a reminder of the myriad of problems

Kalif had brought into their lives since coming as an infant to live in Detroit. Or, as matter of fact, since he was conceived and born. Fatima had never forgotten the true reason London, her college roommate and the biological mother of the thorn in her side, was dead. Storm and that damn spiteful bitch Kenya, whom her husband always put on a pedestal, were the cause of London's demise. And Kalif was a product of the devil's work.

Thank God Rasul was a few minutes away from home now. Normally, he'd swing by Somerset Collection, an upscale mall, and pick up a designer purse or two for his devoted wife. As of late, he'd been on the road more than most women would understand. And she never gave him any fever. So she definitely deserved to be blessed. Receiving her panicked call had thrown him off his game plan. The most important thing to him now was making it home to sort things out. Kalif had been showing some signs of mild hostility and withdrawal, but Fatima's description of the boy's behavior was the last thing Rasul had expected to hear upon answering her call. And her telling him that Kalif knew they were not his birth parents had been the icing on a cake of bullshit.

When he turned onto the block, he took notice of Abdul's vehicle, which was parked in front of his house. After pulling in the driveway, Rasul turned off the engine. He knew whatever had taken place inside the house was bad. Amir had texted him that although Fatima was justifiably upset, she wasn't being overly dramatic about the mayhem. Making his way to the porch, he saw Amir sitting on the top stair. Hakim was right by his side, looking bewildered. Rasul picked up his son and held him tightly in his arms before putting him down. Placing his hand on his Amir's shoulder, Rasul reassured him that everything was going to be okay. Then he went in his pocket, pulled out a few dollars, gave them to Amir, and instructed him to walk Hakim to the corner store to get a juice and some candy. He usually frowned upon sugary snacks, but all things considered, a child's sugar overload was the least of his problems.

Rasul was not inside the dwelling for even five seconds before the situation became painfully clear. Kalif was out of control. No matter what the reason was, what he'd done was unacceptable. Rasul finally could bear witness to what Fatima, as well as Abdul, had stated. His home—well, at least the dining room—looked like a wrecking ball had swung through it. But sadly, it hadn't. The truth was his beloved son was to blame. After thanking Abdul for stopping by, he informed him that Amir had taken Hakim to the store. He then asked Abdul if it was at all possible for his youngest son, Hakim, to stay the night with them. Wanting to be of assistance, his best friend readily agreed.

After Abdul left with Amir and Hakim, and Rasul and Fatima were alone in the house with their eldest son, Rasul hugged his wife tightly. Fatima broke down in tears and was close to collapsing. She didn't know what was going to happen next, but she prayed her husband would take charge. Kalif still hadn't moved from the spot he had been in for well over a hour now, and he was still bleeding.

"Look, baby, go upstairs and let me deal with this," Rasul told Fatima. "I need to speak to my son man-to-man."

Glad to oblige, Fatima excused herself, but not before whispering in Rasul's ear, "I don't know exactly how he found out. I don't know who told him, but the bottom line is he knows."

After watching his wife go up the stairs, Rasul waited for her to close their bedroom door. *Allah, please give me strength.* Readying himself for what seemed like a day of reckoning, he approached Kalif, who was still zoned out.

"Son, look at me. Look at me. It's your father. Do you hear me talking to you?"

Kalif failed to move. After a few minutes of eerie silence, his lips parted slightly, as if he was going to respond to Rasul. Instead, the young boy started reciting different surahs from the Koran. Rasul put both of his hands on Kalif's shoulders and shook his son. Two, three, four good times, but Kalif was still out of it. Realizing it would take a stronger effort, the large man brought his hand down across Kalif's face. He did not intend to bring harm to him, so Rasul was careful not to use all his strength. Feeling the sting on his face, just like that, Kalif was jolted back to reality. Rasul hugged his son. Kalif was hesitant to accept the genuine emotion Rasul was exhibiting, because of what he knew to be true. After he had held it in for these past few months, it was finally time for confessions.

"Who am I?" Kalif stood up, wide eyed, waiting for a response.

"What do you mean, Who are you? You're Kalif Akbar, that's who you are. My son, your mother's son."

Kalif gave his supposed father a cold stare. Although he was considered a child, he refused to be lied to. He would have no more of the secrets and the deception. "I know I don't belong to either of you. I know my real parents just must've thrown me away like I was garbage or something. Or am I an orphan, like y'all said I was? It doesn't matter one way or the other. Either way, I'm not your son, and I don't belong to you. I'm nothing. Oh yeah, maybe an extra blessing you and your wife can get from Allah."

Even though Fatima had warned him about what Kalif claimed to know, Rasul hadn't expected this torrent of words, questions, and accusations. Rasul was not ready for this day to come, even though it was destined to be. "Okay, look, son."

"I'm not your son, so please stop saying that," Kalif protested, with fever in his tone.

"Whoa. You gonna stop with all that bullshit right damn now! So okay, I know you confused. And I seriously get that you hurt behind what you think you know. But there ain't no way you gonna disrespect me or your mother any longer. And make no mistake, we are your parents, period. And if you ever in you fucking life even whisper or daydream about bringing harm to my wife and Hakim, I'ma forget the love I have for you and act accordingly. We a family, all four of us, and that's how we gonna stay."

Kalif was definitely deep in his feelings, but he was far from being stupid. He knew he never would have displayed such anger, issued murderous threats, and torn up the house if Rasul had been there. And now that he was here, Kalif knew he was pressing his luck if he tried to go toe-to-toe with him. Indeed, he wanted answers, but getting them with a black eye, a busted mouth, or Rasul's foot dead up his ass would not be the way. Kalif calmed all the way down and waited for the truth to be revealed.

Rasul headed down into the basement, and Kalif followed him and sat down on the couch. Rasul sat on a chair. He then explained to Kalif everything he needed, wanted, and deserved to hear. Not wanting ever to go over the story again, Rasul left nothing out. He began with the very day he met Kenya at a strip club. He explained that she was Kalif's maternal aunt and the twin sister of his birth mother, London. He told Kalif that London was roommates and best friends with Fatima, and that they cofounded an anti-drug organization up at Michigan State University back in the day.

Rasul then connected the dots about the wild club night when Kalif's uncle was killed in a shoot-out, one that left Rasul with scars. Rasul lifted his shirt to give young Kalif a visual of the everlasting street souvenirs. Wanting to let his boy know he was holding nothing back, Rasul told him the he and his deceased uncle were on rival squads.

"I didn't know it was him was at the time. He and his boys stormed the place I was working at and murdered the owner in cold blood. Everything from that point on was chaos. But when it was all said and done, me and your aunt Kenya, who, by the way, was a dancer there, remained tight. It was because of her that I met your biological mother, her identical twin, London. Her spirit was beautiful. And then, of course, I met your mother . . . upstairs. Who, by the way, loves you very much, just like I do."

It was a lot to take in, and he was shocked, yet Kalif stayed focused. Despite a lump in his throat, he found the courage to speak. "Well, what about my real father? Did you know him too?"

"Yeah, I did. His name was Tony Christian, but the streets called him Storm. I can tell you that judging by the small bit of interaction I had with him, dawg was a true soldier. A real stand-up guy."

"So if Storm was so stand up and London's spirit was so beautiful, why they give me away? Why they didn't wanna raise me?"

Rasul knew this was going to be the hard part of the conversation. Even though years had gone by, he hated every time he had to revisit in his mind the tragic events of those days. He was strong in his faith and had taught Kalif to be that way as well. He had had such love for Kenya, and the part he had played in driving her back to what would ultimately be her death was a constant source of guilt. He just couldn't shake it. Fatima was far from being a fool. She had quickly noticed that every year, on the anniversary of Kenya's death, her husband would go into a dark place and become so depressed. He would deny it, but she could see through his yearning for and mourning of another woman.

"So listen, Kalif. I know you're hurt right now. And I know that you are confused, but let me tell you one thing. You were loved, and you were wanted. Both of them cared about you. Both of them wanted you. Some things jumped off that shouldn't have, and it caused sort of like a family feud. But in the middle of all that, you were definitely a ray of hope to your birth parents."

"What kind of stuff? And what happened to them? Were they together? Do you have any pictures of them?" Kalif was full of questions and rightly so.

Feeling it would be best not to go too deeply into the fact that his aunt had killed his mother and his father had been gunned down by a drug organization in his own front yard, Rasul sugarcoated the facts. He knew how the truth tormented him, and he didn't want to pass that type of everlasting burden to Kalif. "You know the type of life I live from time to time. Well, Storm was deep off into the game. So deep he couldn't get out. And truth be told, he had no desire to. He was making plenty of money and took care of home the way a grown man is supposed to do. He and your mother were just caught up in that bullshit, and unfortunately, their lives were not spared. This game is served cold, like ice cream."

Kalif lowered his head. Knowing how Rasul got down, he could easily imagine his birth parents had been warriors as well. That gave him a small bit of comfort. It was easier to digest that they were dead and thus couldn't raise him than it was that they didn't want him. But he still felt as if he was no more than a lost soul drifting in the darkness. "Well, how did you get me?"

Rasul knew he had to bend the truth once more. Before answering, he silently prayed for Allah to forgive him. "Well, your father's brother was also killed, and they had no other people. So one of Storm's homeboys got at me. I flew out there and got you. You were only a few weeks old. I brought you back here, and me and your mother been loving you ever since. So, you see, even though Allah didn't bless us to share the same blood, he blessed us to share the same deep, committed love. Do you understand?"

Kalif said that he did, even though a part of him knew there was more to the story. But for now, he decided it was wise for him to leave it alone. He'd heard enough. Done enough. And after suffering for days, he felt his mission was complete. Rasul had confessed his and Fatima's awful truth. He agreed to talk out any issues he had moving forward, instead of acting out.

Rasul exhaled. He had dodged the bullet of the real story of Kalif's conception, birth, and adoption. At least for the time being. He prayed things would go back to normal.

# Chapter 5

A few years went by, and the place Kalif called home was still in turmoil. And most of the time, the young menace was at fault. He was into any and everything that his parents frowned upon: getting suspended from school, ignoring the teachers, berating his peers that taunted him, and refusing to do what his mother had asked him to do. The only person he halfway listened to was Rasul. And that was because his father had no problem whatsoever with chin checking him strong arm style. Kalif never bucked when Rasul handed him his ass on a platter, but that physical pain was short lived and swiftly forgotten about. The mentally exhausted parents placed him on a PAL football team in their neighborhood, but even playing for the Westside Cubs didn't help him. In fact, the daily endurance training only gave him more strength to fuel his always brewing fury. Kalif was physically fit and mentally unhinged, which was a dire combination to have when you lived in Detroit.

The last few times Kalif had been summoned to the school's office, the administrators had demanded his parents get him some additional professional help, and that included having him put on a medication. Rasul had stood strong for years and had refused to alter his stance on the subject of mind-altering chemicals, but he finally had to concede that Kalif needed medication. He was not home enough to discipline his teenage son, and he knew Fatima and Hakim needed all the extra protection and assistance they could have to shield them from Kalif's impromptu bouts of fury. The medication he was put on slowed him down some. The three small tan-colored pills he took daily seemed to have the troubled teen thinking more clearly, or so they said. To keep the peace and ensure that his parents didn't feel bad, Kalif made sure he followed the dosage schedule. At least when he saw fit.

Monday through Friday, during school hours, Kalif spent time on his prayer rug, which he carried to school and stored in his locker. It didn't matter to him that the other students teased him about this. His spirit was immune to their constant ridicule. Allah was the only judge he had and the only thing that he feared. No human walking the earth on two legs or otherwise could alter his actions.

At 12:20 p.m. on this day, Kalif was doing his normal routine, while the other out-of-control teenagers at Central High School were busy acting up in the lunchroom. He'd just finished wudu, which was cleaning himself in preparation for prayer. After grabbing his rug out of his locker, Kalif placed it down in the far corner of the lunchroom. He, along with a few other students that were Muslim, started their midday Dhuhr. Kalif acted as the imam and led the prayer. As the sacred words were spoken in unison, a small group of bullies gathered in the lunchroom. They'd made it their mission to cause as much trouble as possible. Like Kalif, each had been called to the office on more than several occasions. Just as Kalif and his friends were ending their prayers, the bullies made their way across the loud lunchroom. When they were a few feet away, the most vocal member of the group spoke loudly to Kalif, interrupting the sacred ritual.

"Hey, you ho-ass nigga. Why you always down on your knees like some little bitch?"

Kalif ignored him at first and urged the others to do the same. *Allah, grant me strength*, he thought. Unfortunately, his peace of mind and patience for bullshit was tested once more.

"I know y'all hear me talking. I know y'all little black face terrorist ain't deaf." The loudmouth put his size nine Jordan on the edge of Kalif's prayer rug.

Kalif knew the boy was jealous of him. This had been proven on more than one occasion. Apparently, the girl he liked had some sort of crush on Kalif. However, the devout Muslim could care less about that female or any other. If it wasn't about a scheme to get money or about his God, it didn't matter to Kalif. Once more he asked for strength and patience in dealing with this nonbeliever. Kalif knew that the devil sometimes would try to test God's chosen, so he held it together the best he possibly could.

"Look, we don't want any problems," he said as he stood. "And trust me, neither do you. So for *real* for real, why don't you go on back where you came from? I ain't in the mood or habit of asking the next man to do some shit he should be doing anyhow."

"Y'all hear this pussy-acting gangster and shit? Bitch nigga, don't tell me what the fuck to do. You might tell these other Ali Baba ducks what to do, how to do it, and when to do it. But I'm built different. I'ma beast. I'ma a vulture." He squared up with Kalif and stood toe-to-toe. "So now that you up on your feet, trying to be all VIP, what you gonna do? How you 'bout to carry it?"

The altercation had caught the attention of a girl named Jada, who was sitting nearby with a group of friends. She had been trying her best not to get involved, but she was tired of seeing Kalif get bullied daily. It was like this mob of unruly guys had nothing else better to do. She'd heard through the school grapevine that the entire thing was about a girl. Nonetheless, the way those guys kept treating Kalif was awful. She had to speak up.

"Damn, so y'all gonna just keep running up on them like this?" she called from her seat. "Why don't you leave them the fuck alone? They ain't doing shit to you."

"Listen, bitch. Stay up outta this, before your fat, twice-over ugly ass gets dealt with. 'Cause trust me, that shit can pop off quick, fast, and in a hurry," the disgruntled teen snarled.

Not the least bit worried about the tables turning, Jada laughed, then stood up and walked closer to the altercation. She wasn't the smallest female at the school, and no way did she have the cutest face. But that didn't matter. She was confident, direct, and she was not scared of most things, including a fight. The youngest of five siblings and the only girl among them, Jada was good with her hands. She had to be to hold her own among her brothers.

Kalif had been fighting not to overreact to the situation, but now he was seconds away from snapping. He had a splitting headache, and his mind was racing. *Fight in the cause of Allah those who fight you, but do not transgress limits, for Allah loveth not transgressors. And slay them wherever ye catch them, and turn them out from where they have turned you out, for tumult and oppression are worse than slaughter. But fight them not at the sacred mosque, unless they first fight you there. But if they fight you, slay them. Such is the reward of those who suppress faith.* As hard as he had fought to remain calm, he'd allowed the guy to get all up in his head.

This loudmouth had embarrassed him and had called him out in front of the huge group of gawkers that had gathered, so there was no turning back for Kalif. All the previous times when Kalif had been the focal point of ridicule at school for being different, no girl had ever come to his defense. But now Jada was taking up for him. However, it didn't look good to have a female fighting his battles. And it didn't set well with his soul. In Islam, it was a man's job to be a protector of women. Definitely not the other way around.

Kalif glared at the loudmouth. "Time and time again, I've warned you. I done gave you a pass, and you think you bigger than the game," he growled. "You pissed 'cause ole girl like me? Well, dummy, I ain't thinking about her, but if I was, you wouldn't be able to do shit about it but fall back and hope to get my sloppy seconds when I'm done with her."

"Nigga, say what? You think I care about some ho?" The guy felt small because the gawkers were laughing at what Kalif had just said.

"You heard me, pussy. You wanted a reaction to that shit you was talking, well, you about to get it. So what's good?"

"Yeah, whatever, terrorist ass. Fuck you, your god, and that fake-ass prophet Muhammad, or whatever his name is!"

It was one thing for this guy to come at him. Kalif could let that shit go. But now the youth with the reckless mouth had insulted Allah and Prophet Muhammad, peace be upon his soul. Now Kalif was going to war. Holding nothing back, Kalif socked his nemesis dead in the mouth. The crowd was in awe of Kalif's strength, but they were not expecting what came next. Kalif followed up that bloody blow with several more, then easily body slammed the other boy. The boy fell to the floor, and Kalif leapt on top of him and went to work. Loudly chanting verses from the Koran, he zoned out, much as he'd done with his mother years ago. Yet this time no familial bond held him back, and he had no desire to slow down.

For years, he'd put up with working on his firecracker temper, just as the psychiatrist he saw once a week had suggested. But Kalif's tolerance for abuse and his self-restraint had expired. Making sure this battle would be forever etched in his opponent's memory, Kalif slowed down his powerful punches. Not missing a beat, he leaned in close to the guy's swiftly swelling face. "Today you die. Today you will know to respect me and all that I believe in. Today belongs to you," Kalif whispered into his ear before sinking his teeth down into the teen's flesh.

Hearing the wannabe thug scream out in pain like a little girl gave Kalif pure satisfaction. He wasn't done inflicting injuries. He was handing out a life lesson to all that had gathered to see the brawl. With his teeth, Kalif ripped the boy's ear damn near off his head, and then he spit the detached bloody lobe on the floor. Ignoring the gasps from random females, Kalif went on to bite a plug out of his aggressor's jaw.

When they saw their once fearless leader was leaking from the mouth and missing part of his earlobe and jaw, the bullies realized the time for action was slipping away. With their leader sprawled on the lunchroom floor, they jumped into action. Yanking Kalif by his shoulder, one of the six wannabe junior goons made his presence known. A struggle between them ensued, and the other five goons quickly jumped in. Though it was now six to one, Kalif took each blow like a champ. There was no way that he was going to go down like this. Arms swinging, jaws cracking, eyes taking direct hits, Kalif's friends wasted no time showed their allegiance by joining the brawl.

Not wanting to be left out, Jada threw a punch at one of the bullies before some cheering onlookers shoved her back into the crowd. But she would not be deterred. Now was her time to strike. She managed to get in a few random licks and kicks of her own, including when the heel of her shoe came crashing down on the forehead of the loudmouthed leader, who was still lying on the lunchrooms floor. She grinned with satisfaction when the skin over his left eyebrow split wide open.

Seconds later security guards swarmed the lunchroom. They surrounded the pile of brawling kids and snatched the ones off the top first. Kalif was near the bottom of the pile, and he managed to squirm away from the security guards. His adrenaline was at an all-time high. While all the others in both "camps" were ready to call in a day, Kalif's thirst for blood and revenge did not waver, and he continue to throw punches at whoever was within arm's reach. With each blow he landed, he gave a yell in Arabic, and his voice seemed to echo throughout the lunchroom, rendering the mostly African American student body speechless. He managed to knock one guard unconscious, but that didn't stop him. Unbeknownst to his parents, Kalif had deliberated omitted taking his prescribed meds for three days straight, despite having recently been diagnosed with paranoid schizophrenia in addition to his ADHD. Although he had maintained his composure, for the most part, when the bullies started taunting him, Kalif was now in a full-blown rage. It was if he had the strength of several heavyweight cage fighters.

As the crowd scrambled to get away from Kalif and his wild wrath, Jada didn't move. In fact, she continued to attack the bigmouthed leader, who was now cowering in a fetal position, begging for mercy. The hands and feet she was putting on him had more to do with her own personal experience than with just taking up for a fellow classmate. She, too, had been bullied by the fake thug and his homeboys for being overweight and having a severe case of acne. She had never once confided in her older brothers about the bullying, and up until this point, she'd held the pain and humiliation she felt deep inside. She'd often been depressed in the past, but on this day, she had an awakening. She wasn't going to take it anymore.

Unfortunately, before she could celebrate her newfound freedom, one of the young thugs swung on her right before he got body slammed by a security guard. The thug's fist connected directly with her temple. Just like the loudmouthed bully who had started the brawl, she was now leaking. However, although she was dazed, she never lost her balance and stood strong on her feet. Seeing that she was a bit stupefied, one of the security guards took advantage of the situation and grabbed hold of her arm. Then backup security personnel handcuffed both her and a still defiant Kalif and led them out of the lunchroom through separate exits.

As Kalif and Jada left the lunchroom, the two of them locked eyes. Having no remorse for what she'd done,

Jada smiled at Kalif. He nodded at her, acknowledging that she was a true soldier and would someday make someone a good wife. Regrettably, this brawl, although not Kalif's fault, was not his first, and he had yet another go-round in the disciplinary office. His and Jada's punishment was simple and swift. Both of them got expelled from school.

Fatima hung up the phone, having just received the latest rundown of Kalif's antics from the principal. She turned to her husband, who was standing by the kitchen doorway. "He needs to be put away after what they just told me. He needs the type of help we can't give him. Rasul. Why won't you listen to me? We've tried everything. Considering the way he was even brought into this world, he is cursed. He was born a nuisance." She took a deep breath. "I would say his father's crazed bloodline runs through that boy. But it's easy to see in him the personality and demonic spirit of his auntie, who was fucked up in the head. I still pray for my best friend, who had to live with that monster of a sister all that time."

As Rasul listened to his wife not only urge him to have Kalif caged up like some wild animal, but also drag his once secretly beloved Kenya through the mud, he wanted to object. The father of two boys wanted to tell her to leave Kalif to him and tend to their biological son, Hakim, who was visibly her favorite. He wanted to say that if she loved her deceased best friend as much as she claimed, she should be able to embrace her son. As he began pacing the floor, he wanted to tell her to stop criticizing Kenya. She was deceased, and there was no need to point fingers or blame her. But Rasul knew it was best to hold his peace, because his wife would never get over, forget, or forgive him for his constant devotion to another female, dead or alive.

He decided then that he'd just go sit on the front porch and wait for Kalif to return home. In the back of his mind, he knew Fatima was right. They were raising a savage. Working hard on being a new person himself, Rasul knew that the old him would have beaten Kalif senseless with his bare hands until he bled out of both eyes for all the trouble he continued to cause. As he sat down on a chair on the porch, he silently prayed for patience.

# Chapter 6

After getting kicked out of Central, Kalif was moved to an alternative high school and was thrown into a mix of the worst young hoodlums and thugs in training Detroit had to offer. Blackening more than a few eyes and never backing down in any altercation, during his senior year he quickly rose to be one of the most notorious soon-to-be alumni the faculty had ever been elated to get rid of.

Under normal circumstances, a teenager's senior year was filled with excitement, both for the child and the parents. A pinning ceremony. Cap and gown pictures. Homecoming dances. And, of course, the prom. But Kalif's final year of high school was mentally draining for his family. It was a year not of celebration but of disappointment. Despite the fact that the grades he received at the worst alternative high school in the city were decent, Kalif was a known menace to the staff and, as of late, to the local police. Kalif was far from interested in what his family thought of him or in being a role model for his younger brother. It was his parents' job to raise Hakim, not his.

Kalif banded together with a group of weak-minded troublemakers who were out to instill just as much fear in others as he was. Before they found Kalif, the only thing Li'l James, Pit Boy, and Keys had needed was a leader with some sort of a brain. And in between his respectful prayers to Allah five times a day, Kalif offered them that. Although he would tell his cohorts about the benefits of Islam, he didn't discriminate against his boys because of their faith or lack of it. If the next man wanted to eat his breakfast, lunch, and dinner with the devil or wanted to marry his ugly daughter, it was not Kalif's concern. As long as that guy was putting in work for the good of the team, he was good to go.

Repeatedly, the twisted teen ringleader came up with scams and schemes to get revenue and pull them out of poverty. They had their hands in everything, petty or not, and wreaked havoc right and left. Hitting local car lots was simple. So was stealing car radios, catalytic converters, tires, and air bags. As time passed, the crew's need for money grew, and so did its size. Their rapid growth led them to attempt bigger jobs. They began stealing entire vehicles in Metro Detroit and taking them to a chop shop in the North End. Some jobs worked out perfectly. They hit licks and came up with their pockets on full. However, other jobs went terribly wrong, resulting in stays in juvenile or near death at the hands of the hardworking residents and Middle Eastern shop owners that had the fortune to catch them red-handed in the act of stealing. With their smash-and-grabs at the liquor stores that graced every neighborhood corner, they never had a shortage of bottles, scratch-offs, or Newports.

Kalif had his mob running into the Korean-owned beauty supply stores and snatching expensive bundles of weaves, clippers, and anything else of value. They were in and out before anyone could even think about calling the police. Knowing that the response time of Detroit's Finest was one of the worst in the nation, Kalif recognized that this type of crime would be simple to pull off. With Michigan being an open-carry state, just about everyone and their mother carried a gun, so business owners were scared of being shot. And most foreign business owners would rather fight with the insurance company to get a check for their loss than stand before a judge and answer for shooting a possibly unarmed black teenager, not to mention that they might face certain deportation.

When one crime got to risky, Kalif, a mastermind, would come up with another and would swiftly move on. Misguided in his faith, he claimed that Allah spoke to him in his sleep, telling him how to survive in this wicked, coldhearted world. Most of his homeboys were skeptical of that, but they never openly questioned Kalif, for fear of being cut out of the financial windfall they constantly enjoyed. Either way, the self-ordained Linwood 4Lyfe Posse, as they were referred to in the streets, were wilding out. However, they were stupidly documenting some of their crimes on video.

"Okay, we almost there. Get ready to pull over so we can get this bread." Kalif watched the numbers on the houses increase.

When they reached the Grosse Pointe home listed on the small piece of paper he held, Kalif ordered the driver to stop the vehicle. Having prepped his boys on how things needed to go down, Kalif and the other occupants piled out of the car. In an attempt not to draw unwanted or unneeded attention to themselves, no words were exchanged. All of them were dressed in off-white paint pants and shirts so that no one stood out from the rest. Kalif took the lead and made his way to the back of the house. Raising his hand, he signaled that the rear double-glass door was still unlocked.

He'd been at the house in the earlier part of the week, doing a landscaping job with one of the Arabs from the mosque. That guy had told him that the home owner was almost three times older than his wife and made major money working as an exclusive legal consultant for one of the local auto factory, either Chrysler or Ford. *I swear, this is gonna be the only day I do this bullshit. I ain't cut out for being no do boy*, Kalif had thought as he planted flowers on the back patio that day. With the curtains open, he had easily seen that these people were living like a king and queen. He was from a two-parent household, and he and his little brother hadn't grown up struggling by any means. And His father still kept his hand in the game, so the family had stayed good. But that was his father's money and his hustle. Kalif was all about becoming a man, standing on his own two feet, by hook or by crook.

Kalif had ear hustled as the elderly home owner's much younger, uppity wife complained on the phone to one of her friends. She bragged about all the money her husband constantly spent on her, the plastic surgeries that she'd had, and the many fur coats he'd blessed her with. When she laughed about the fact that the old man's dick wouldn't stay hard even with the little blue pill and then gloated about leaving him soon, Kalif shook his head. Taking her husband for everything that he was worth all because his dick didn't get hard anymore was wild. Then he heard her mention that there was a burglar-alarm system in the house, but that it had not been worked properly for over a year. Hearing that was a godsend, for he knew that information would come in handy sooner rather than later.

The master plotter started to scheme. Maybe doing this petty landscaping job for his father's friend would pay off, after all. When the wife noticed Kalif's strength as he dug a small trench in the backyard, she invited him in. She had him bring a designer trunk down from her attic and then casually mentioned that her husband was out of the country, on business. Even though it had a padlock on it, the trunk was extremely light. Using his cell phone, Kalif had inconspicuously snapped pictures of the visible valuables inside the house when she went to get her purse in order to pay him a few dollars. Wanting nothing more than to snatch those valuables up while he was there, Kalif knew he'd be the number one suspect once the crime was discovered and would undoubtedly be locked up before nightfall. Instead, he left the back door unlocked on his way out and hoped her high-class ass would be too lazy to double-check.

Now, with his crew behind him, Kalif opened the back door. Thanks to the hustle gods, everything was just where Kalif had seen it during his first visit. Armed with huge Home Depot garbage bags, the crew all put on thin latex gloves and went to work. It was on, as they wasted no time on admiring the over-the-top furnishings. There would be time for that later, when they were back at their spot. They went from room to room, from floor to floor, ransacking the place. Jewelry, rare coins, laptops, and even what appeared to be expensive camera equipment were the first to be loaded up. The wife's collection of furs was then quickly stuffed into the bags, followed by countless designer purses.

Kalif smiled as he thought about the braggadocious white Barbie doll on the phone sometime tomorrow, crying to one of her friends about the loss she had incurred. But he knew that she would add that her old, "no dick getting hard" husband would easily replace her treasured items. She would have to leave him another day. So this was the perfect come up on what had been a slow week of thievery for Kalif.

In a low but strong whisper, Kalif ordered his team to speed up and get the last items they could into the bags. Aware of not wanting to get caught up, he checked the time on his cell. They were on a mission, and time was not on their side. Kalif had staked out the wife's comings and goings for a few days straight. He knew they had a little over fourteen minutes to be in and out before she returned from the gym. As his boys snatched up everything of value and filed out of the house, they knew they were going to eat good and celebrate tonight.

Kalif lingered after his team left. In the far corner of the living room, he spotted the trunk the woman had him bring down from the attic. The lock he had seen on it that day was no longer there. He crossed the room, and when he opened trunk, Kalif felt as if he'd won the hood lottery. Titling his head to the side, he rubbed his chin with his gloved hand. Sometime after he'd brought the lightweight trunk down, it'd been filled. If he and his homeboys didn't get anything else out of this suburban household, they had to have this. This was the mother lode. Momentarily, Kalif stood motionless, admiring the ridicule number of firearms. He didn't know why the old man and his wife had so much firepower or why she'd placed everything in the trunk. Kalif could only speculate that she had gathered them all to take with her when she broke out, but he could really careless. Those guns belonged to him now.

Before the hooligan made another move, his cell rang. Normally, he would not stop to see who was calling him in the middle of a job, but his mind told him otherwise.

Upon seeing that the caller was one of his boys out in the waiting vehicle, he paused. *Why in the fuck this nigga calling me?* Of course, he then answered. "Yeah? What up, doe? Speak on it."

"Dawg, I think that bitch is home! She back. Dude, she back," a panicked voice belted out.

"What? Why you say that? She shouldn't be here for at least ten more good minutes." No longer calm, Kalif held his cell back some from his face so he could check the time.

"Yo, dawg, I hear what you saying. But I'm telling you some white bitch just pulled up in the driveway. She in a dark blue BMW, a two-door."

Kalif didn't waste any more time arguing over whether the home owner's wife was indeed outside. He had none to spare. His main and only concern was A, how he was going to get out of Dodge and not get caught. And B, how he was going to carry this big trunk filled with guns, get out of Dodge, and not get caught. *Fuck! shit! White people always on time, Damn!* He knew she would be coming through the door in mere minutes. Not knowing if it would be the front door or the rear door, the one he and his team had entered through, Kalif pushed the open trunk back alongside the wall. He could just chill midway between the doors and wait to see which one she chose, then quickly exit through the other.

Sure, he would be able to get away and would be happy with what they had already safely removed from the house and loaded in the truck. But then he would have to leave the surprise treasure he'd just discovered. Kalif promptly weighted his options as his palms began to sweat. Risk getting knocked and catching a case by being greedy. Or tiptoe in retreat, knowing full well he would not be able to sleep later, after seeing what he had seen. The thought of leaving those guns was too much. There were no ifs, ands, or buts. He had to have them. So the bottom line was no matter what way it went down, he and white-body Barbie would have to bump heads.

With his impromptu plan to secure the firearms ready to execute, Kalif remained motionless in the middle of the long hallway. Whichever way she entered the house, the obvious would rapidly become apparent. She'd immediately take notice that her once perfect home was in utter disarray. That could result in her maybe bolting back out the door, screaming bloody murder, or possibly pulling a gun on him. Considering what was in the trunk, someone in that household had a taste for weapons, high-powered ones. in fact. Praying to Allah to keep him out of harm's way, he cracked his knuckles.

Seconds later, Kalif heard the wife on the front porch, ending a cell phone conversation. *This dirty bitch stay on the phone, talking shit.* Like a lion on the prowl, he rushed toward the front door. After tucking himself near the hinges, he took a deep breath, then quietly exhaled. If Kalif was having any second thoughts, all they could be was thoughts. That "leave while there was no risk of harm" train had already pulled out of the station.

Ready for what was going to happen after what came next, Kalif imagined himself already at the spot, with all the weapons laid out in a display. Staring down, he heard her keys rattling. Then he heard a key being inserted into a lock. After watching the top cylinder turn from one side to the other, he then focused on the doorknob. As it twisted, his eyes widened while his heart raced. He had to do this just right. There was no need for things to get out of control. It was not his intention to turn a simple B and E into a heinous murder. Up until now, young Kalif had never taken another human life. But today could easily be the day he did that for the first time if it meant that he would get that trunk and its contents. The stakes were high.

*All right. Here the fuck we go. This is it.* When the door cracked open, his soon-to-be prey placed one foot inside. From where he stood, he could see she had an armful of bags. She struggled to come all the way inside the house, and then the heels of her sandals clacked across the floor. She still had yet to turn around, mumbling something about the central air. Finally, she dropped the bags on the floor.

*I can't let this lady see me, 'cause if she do, I gotta kill her ass.*

Off his meds for days now, Kalif emerged from his hiding place. After pushing the open door, he made his move before it shut completely. He rushed up behind her, and the next moments unspooled like a late-night movie. Latex gloves still on, he covered her mouth so she couldn't scream. Part of him felt as if it was Christmas and attacking her was his present. As he pulled her in close, he felt her hot breath and trembling lips on his right hand. She tried to break free. Yet the more she squirmed, the tighter Kalif's grip became. He had no more time to waste. Even though he knew her husband was out of town, there was no need to procrastinate. He could not be seen. Being identified was not an option. The consequences would be dire. Raising his left arm, Kalif clenched his fist, and then he brought it crashing down on the back of her skull. Half her attacker's height and weight, she was done. Allowing her limp, plastic surgery–enhanced body fall to the floor next to her many packages, he thanked Allah for granting him the strength.

As she lay unconscious on the foyer floor, Kalif towered over her. Licking his lips, he bent down on one knee. *Yeah, you don't need this right here. You and old boy can just add this to the list for the fat insurance check y'all gonna get.* He removed each diamond ring from her fingers and a tennis bracelet from her wrist, then gathered the surrounding shopping bags, which had designer names on them. After tossing them into the trunk with the firearms, Kalif walked back over to his victim. He picked up her converted cell phone, then went to her text messages. When he came to the name Hubby, he grinned. He wrote the words "Divorcing your limp-dick ass" and then pushed **send** with satisfaction. With malice, Kalif then slammed the phone against the marble floor. Wanting to make sure it was good and broken, he stomped on it twice for good measure.

"Well, looks like my job here is done. Good luck, you rich, insulated bitch," he mumbled, then headed back to the trunk he had to have so badly. After closing it up, he bent down and then used his legs to lift it up. Using both handles, Kalif carried the trunk out the same door they'd come in through, with a huge smile on his face and mischief on his mind. Much to his homeboys' surprise, he came over to the vehicle like he lived on the block. He had the driver open the rear hatch, and then he stuffed the trunk inside the already crowded rear of the vehicle.

"Yo, let's roll. We good this way!" he said after he closed the rear hatch.

Before long they hit East Warren and headed toward downtown, on their way back west. Popping bottles would definitely be next on the agenda.

# Chapter 7

It was unseasonably warm. Yet the air-conditioning system had yet to be turned on at the semi-crowded mall. Without a care in the world, the infamous crew made their way through the glass doors, Kalif leading the way, as usual. They were doing what they always did after hitting a lick: going shopping, hitting the park with a few bottles, and putting something up in the air. They were ready to live extra large, as each man's cut was higher than normal. Kalif's play at that mini mansion would have them all the way off scraps for some time to come. After pawning what they could, they had sold the rest of the stolen goods on the streets. Except for the guns, which Kalif had rightfully claimed as his own. Thirty-nine hundred dollars a piece was the final tally. That illegally earned income was burning a hole in the young guys' pockets. So some gathered around the Sprint kiosk and inspected the new iPhone, while the others locked eyes with a few females passing by. In true Detroit fashion, they got on the random females.

"Yeah, what up, doe?" Li'l James called out as the flock of girls slid by.

Checking out the loudmouthed guy, the leader of the pack could easily see he and his boys had money. After all, he was dressed from head to toe in designer wear, and so her spidey senses flared up. This was going to be the lick the females needed. In the game of getting money by hook or by crook, their luck had hit a dry spell. They needed a come up, and these guys could be just that. After all of them crewed up from the other side of the kiosk, she raised her eyebrow, then answered Li'l James. "We good this way. Just out here chilling," she cooed back, messing with her braids.

"So why don't y'all slow down? Pump y'all's brakes and chill with us," Pit Boy said, trying to coax the situation to jump off. Placing his hand on Li'l James's shoulder, he went into straight stunt mode. "Me and my homeboys about to get off into some serious spending and whatnot."

"Oh yeah?" a girl named Jewels replied, looking him up and down as her cousin stood over to the side, still twirling her braids.

"Yeah, we is. And we need some females' opinions on what looks good. So you got us or what?" Pit Boy waited eagerly for a response, although he knew what the answer would be.

Now the group of eight—what Fairlane Town Center security would consider a small mob ready to take over the free world—made their way first into Foot Locker. With the ratio of three females to five guys, two of the guys would be left ass out. Kalif, who was not into tricking off his money on some "just because" bullshit, was good. While the others had the salespeople running back and forth, bringing out this and that, Kalif kept his face in his phone's screen. It was obvious he was plotting their next move, so Amir made sure the others gave his best friend space. He, Li'l James, and Pit Boy would be the lucky ones with the girls.

Keys was good with not jacking off his cash on some rats on the prowl. Some rats that hadn't even given up the pussy. He opted to stay close to his boy's side. He stood well over a foot taller than the others and had grown a full beard by the age of sixteen. More serious minded than the rest, Keys had learned early on that most females didn't find him attractive. Amir, Li'l James, Pit Boy, and even Kalif, when he wanted to be bothered, were first, and Keys was last on the totem pole. With arms folded, he watched and shook his head as the other guys tricked their funds away.

With no clear picture of who was with whom, they all gathered all their bags and happily headed to another store, one that sold Gators exclusively. Twenty minutes later, they were footwear ready for flossing at the park and being VIP at the club. It was like Christmas in July or income-tax time all rolled into one. Heads held high, the entourage marched through the mall as if they were hood royalty. And to most other random shoppers, they appeared to be. Next stop Macy's. They created head-to-toe havoc in that place, as well, and the three females, Jewels, TayTay, and Jada, were glad they'd slowed down and linked up. When the fellas blessed themselves, they showboated by showering the girls with gifts. Judging by the way they were dressed, the girls were no strangers to the finer things in life, so being treated like queens was what they wanted and expected from any men they dealt with. The leader of the trio of females made sure she kept her eye on Kalif. She hoped he took notice of her, but he didn't. To him, they were just some sack chasers that were in the right place at the right time.

Next, they headed to Lids and Jimmy Jazz, and it was as if the fellas' funds could not be tapped out, which kept the girls entertained. After checking the time, Kalif instructed his crew and their female companions to follow him to the upper level of the mall. Still very much deep in thought, he had yet to buy a single item. But he was not in the mood to spend money. His focus was on making more. It had to be that way. That was the difference between being a good leader and a great one. The group received a few cold, hard stares from the security guards, but it was hard for those guards to approach the young black adults and perform their regular bullshit routine of fucking with people. That was because all of them, except Kalif, had numerous shopping bags in their possession. With no legitimate reason to harass them and order them to vacate the premises for loitering, all the weak rent-a-cops could do was fall back and hate from afar.

By now TayTay had latched on to Li'l James's arm. Jewels and Pit Boy were making googly eyes at each other, both eager to take their newfound friendship to the next level. Amir was trying his best to get close to the third girl, Jada, but she seemed to be more focused on Kalif than on him. After buying her items in the first couple of stores, he had fallen back from spending on her.

After finally making his first purchase of the day, Kalif left GNC with several bottles of vitamins and a detox cleanse. Making sure he stayed in great physical shape was important to him. Although he didn't mind using a firearm if need be, a man should always be good with his hands and ready to throw them if need be. His father had taught him that years ago, and Kalif still swore by the lesson. Two doors down from the vitamin shop was another hip-hop fashion store, and Kalif led them all there. This store was owned and operated by someone he knew. Ibn Abood attended the same mosque as Kalif and his family. Though Ibn was least fourteen years older than Kalif and of Arabic descent, he treated Kalif as an equal. After the small gang of Kalif's followers filed into the clothing store, they immediately went from rack to rack, picking out this and that. Kalif shook his head, knowing they would all be broke, their pockets back on craps, before the next daybreak. Nodding his head, he greeted his friend Ibn, who'd stepped out from behind the showcase.

"*As-salamu alaykum*, my young friend," Ibn said happily, extending his hand.

"*Wa alaykumu as-salam*," Kalif replied, taking his hand.

After speaking to the employees who were hurrying to assist Kalif's boisterous crew, Ibn said, "Everything is good with you?"

"Yes, Ibn, everything is everything."

"I see, I see. Your friends have plenty of bags in their hands. Making money, pretty girls. You are all out here living your best life, as you young people say." He smiled, and Kalif did the same. Not beating around the bush, Ibn cut straight to the chase. "So, yeah, I haven't seen you around lately. Where you been? I've seen your father, but not you or, as a matter of fact, Hakim, either."

"Well, I can't speak for my little brother, but I've been somewhere else, praying. I ain't missed a beat. Real talk." Kalif glanced down at his cell, hoping to change the subject. "That's why I stopped what I was doing and came through. It's time to pray, and I know you got a place for me."

Ibn obliged by showing his young Muslim brother to the rear storeroom. After taking not one, but two prayer rugs down off the shelf, he laid them down. They cleansed themselves, and the elder, Ibn, then made the call to prayer. As soon as they were finished, Ibn took up right where he'd left off, asking questions. There had been quiet whispers among the brothers of faith at the mosque about a crime possibly involving Rasul's oldest son. And some had even made loud accusations of certain guilt. Kalif's abrupt absence from the mosque made his innocence seem questionable, to say the least. Not wanting to disrespect Rasul at all, Ibn chose his next words carefully. He knew it might be hard for the wayward youth to open up and confess his wrongdoings to his father, so Ibn was giving him a pathway to repentance.

"So, look, I'm not trying to be in your business."

Kalif remained silent, sensing what was coming next. Then seeking to shut down the conversation, he said, "Good. Then don't."

"Okay, okay, Kalif. Relax. Don't get all upset. I was just trying to help you out, my young brother." Ibn placed both his hands up, trying not to come off as aggressive. "You are a smart guy. You always have been since just a kid. And I see all your people out there look up to you." Ibn nodded his head toward the front area of the store. "You are getting money and making big moves. But you gotta know the streets are talking."

"The streets are talking, huh?" Kalif said sarcastically. "And just what are these streets saying?"

"Kalif, look, outta respect for your father, I want to offer you advice. I don't want you out here getting into big trouble for small things."

Digging into his pocket, Kalif pulled out two medium-size knots. One with all hundred-dollar bills. And the other with twenties mixed with a few fifties. Feeling like he was some sort of John Gotti, he held each wad of bills in his hands. "Yo, Ibn, nigga. Do this look like some sort of small thing right here? Do this look like I'm out here playing around?"

Ibn watched Kalif perform. He allowed him to go through all his theatrics to try to show how smart he was and how he was on the come up. Finally, Ibn spoke, but not before placing his hand in his own pocket. Opening his wallet, ready to teach life lessons, Ibn snarled, "Okay, so you think you're a big man, huh? You think because you betray your Muslim brother who trusted you with a job, embarrass your father, and bring shame to his name, that makes you a man?"

"Say what!" Kalif wasn't used to being spoken to like this. He wanted to lash out, but he had to control himself.

"Yeah, you think everyone is stupid. You think robbing a house and hitting a woman in the head makes you a boss? That is bullshit. Do you really think we all don't know it was you? And then you have the nerve to be out here spending that dirty money so quick. All that you have in your hands and all that money your friends have spent today means nothing in the great scheme of things. It all doesn't add up to the limit on this here." After slamming a black credit card down on a box, Ibn took a step back and laughed. "Yeah, you see that right there. That plastic can get me more cash in five minutes than you can get by doing all the petty stuff you been doing.

That's a Centurion Card, a Black Card! It cost five K plus to even have one."

Kalif wanted to deny the accusations. He wanted to call Ibn an outright liar. But he'd just finished praying side by side with his Muslim brother, and he couldn't do it. Allah wouldn't allow it. Instead, he heard him out. Kalif was more than intrigued. Whereas he normally felt like he was on top of the world with all the money he was making, now he felt out of his league. He might have not liked being knocked down a few pegs, but he definitely had to respect it. Ibn was schooling him up on that real white-collar gangster game.

"Five K. Are you serious?"

Ibn now knew he had his attention. It was now time for him to hold class. "Yeah, I'm dead-ass serious. And you can be just like me. But you have to move smart and smooth. You can't be reckless in everything you do. You have to do wrong as right as possible, and hitting a woman and robbing her blind is not where it's at."

Kalif had a minimum amount of shame, and he neither denied nor confirmed what was obvious. Instead, he decided to zero in on Ibn's knowledge. "You mean fly under the radar as much as possible. But tell me more about this card and how I can cop one."

Ibn smiled as he picked the card up off the box and placed it back in his wallet. "It's not that easy. It comes with time and hard work. Allah blessed me, and He can bless you too. What you know about flipping houses? It's a serious business to get off into if you trying to gateway off into something else major."

"I don't know much," Kalif replied, rubbing his chin. "But if it's making money involved, I'm down."

"Okay. Well, look, we gonna link up later this week. Put my number in your cell and hit me up. Google this website and check out some houses. And for now, let's keep this between me and you. Your father doesn't have to know."

After the group of small-time outlaws finished making their purchases, Ibn watched them leave the store, knowing he was about to have another warrior on his strong hustle-and-grind team.

# Chapter 8

It was nearing six in the evening. The sun was still beating down. The Far West Side park was packed, and the smells drifting off the grills filled the air. After the State of Michigan took over Belle Isle, everyone went to either Chandler Park or River Rouge to kick back and have a good time. Dressed in the outfits they'd bought during the earlier part of the day, the girls hooked back up with the guys.

As promised, they brought a few more friends to even the odds. Keys now had someone on his line to keep him company. She had missed out on the shopping spree, but TayTay had reassured that this crew's money was long. It was apparent that they were far from stingy. Amir was happy to see two more girls as well. Maybe he'd have more luck with one of them than he'd had with the standoffish beauty that had her eye on Kalif, who could care less.

"So damn, dude, what got you so caught up?" Amir said as he leaned on the car, next to Kalif.

"It's something ole boy at the store trying to put me up on. A new hustle."

"Oh yeah?"

"Yeah. Dawg say it's, like, zero risk factor in the bull-shit. Just straight revenue."

Amir watched the girls post up over by the monkey bars rolling up. He urged Kalif to make sure he figured out Ibn's true angle before getting them all off into something they couldn't easily get out of. Then he slowly strolled toward the fresh, funky smell that was calling his name. Kalif lowered his head and went back to searching the website Ibn had recommended. Seemingly minutes later, he was interrupted yet again. This time by one of the females. Taking Amir's place, she, too, leaned back on the vehicle. Kalif barely glanced up to acknowledge her presence.

"So, hey, Kalif. I see you over here, focused," she said.

"Yeah, I am," he grunted, not wanting to be bothered. "And before you get started trying to run game, I ain't into all that tricking like my peoples. I'm married to the game and to Allah, so . . ."

"You was always into your books or something and praying."

"Huh?" Kalif raised his head, puzzled by her statement.

"I'm saying you were smart even when you were getting in trouble. That's all."

Kalif put his cell in his pocket. The mystery female who had been eye fucking him all day at the mall had him intrigued now. She was talking to him as if they were old friends. But he knew that couldn't be the case. She looked like no one he knew or had known. Folding his arms, he suspiciously looked her up and down. "Okay, you got me over here bugging out. What you know about me and what I used to do? And how I used to be? Am I supposed to know you or something?"

Despite hours of being around each other, she knew he hadn't recognized her. She'd told her friends when they first approached him and his boys at the mall that his name was Kalif. But after he'd failed to even look her way, her cousin Jewels and TayTay had assumed she was lying about knowing him.

Finally, she came clean. "Yes, I know you, Kalif Akbar. You changed my life forever."

"Say what?" Kalif was now hanging on her every word.

"Yeah, well, kinda, sorta. Thanks to me having a major crush on you, I got this." Flashing her perfectly manicured nails, she pulled her long braids back from her face. As she turned her face to the side ever so slightly, Kalif could see a scar. He was still confused. Allowing her braids to fall back in place, she smiled and shook her head. "Damn, boy. How many girls you done had out here who have fought alongside of you, getting they shit split wide open? The last time I saw you, I was leaking, and they was dragging me out of the lunchroom."

"What in the hell?" Kalif couldn't believe what she was claiming. As he thought back on that day years ago, he remembered that that girl had been almost three times the size of this girl.

"Yeah, I know. I lost a lot of weight. That dude we got the best of that day got his sisters to jump me a few weeks later. They broke my jaw, and I had to get it wired shut. And *bam*." She twirled around, showing off her well-stacked assets. "This is the result. I'm an all-new person, with, of course, the exception of this ugly scar."

Kalif was floored. He remembered that day as if it had just happened. He smiled as he had a flashback of her jumping right onto the pile of twisted bodies and swinging her fist. She was from Zone 8 and had a bunch of brothers, or so he was told after the fact. He had wondered from time to time about what had happened to that big-breasted soldier. And here she was. "Damn. This shit is wild as hell. I guess it is you. Wow!"

"I know, right? I was gonna tell you who I was earlier, but just like when we was younger, you stayed concentrating on something or other."

For the first time in well over a year, a female had his total attention. And after the way she had had his back when he didn't have jack shit to offer, she was truly deserving of it. There was only one problem. He didn't know or couldn't remember her name. She remembered so much about him, he was kind of embarrassed to ask her name, but he had to.

"So, look, my mind was all over the place back then. What is your name again?"

"It's Jada. Jada White." She blushed, not knowing what to do with her hands. "Jewels is my cousin, and the others are my, let's say, workers."

"Workers, huh? Okay. Well, Jada . . . Ms. Jada White, I owe you at least dinner or something. A guy still ain't tricking like them thirsty fools over there." He laughed at them all getting high as a kite. "But I gotta eat, and so do you. I mean, damn, you little as hell now. You do eat, don't you?"

The unexpected reunion was going better than Jada had hoped for. She and Kalif spent the rest of the evening walking around the perimeter of the park. With the numerous fights, a few random gunshots, and half-naked hoes running from car to car, trying to get some attention, it was just a regular night at Rouge. Kalif had her mesmerized. He put her up on a few irons he had in the fire that were sure to pay off big-time. In return, she enlightened him about the schemes she and her crew of female bandits were into. It was a perfect match made in hellfire as they jointly plotted. There was no way Allah would bless this union of shear madness on the horizon, but to Kalif's warped way of thinking, this was fate. Jada wasn't Muslim, but he wasn't trying to fall in love. He was simply trying to fall into some real money. She, on the other hand, wished for more.

Whatever their motives, the next month would prove to be legendary crime-wise in the city of Detroit.

# Chapter 9

While sharing the same bloodline might have bridged the gap between Kalif and Hakim, being raised in the same household did nothing to close that gap. Like night and day, Hakim was the exact opposite of his older sibling. Hakim was equally smart academic-wise, and he was not ashamed to let others see him in a positive light. He made the honor roll every year and was the recipient of numerous academic accolades. And with his high test scores and excellent grades in middle school, Hakim gained entrance to Cass Tech, a magnet high school. His excellence flummoxed his parents. Sure, they had raised him to believe in himself. And, above all, to be nothing like Kalif. However, Hakim had far exceeded his parents' expectations. Even Fatima, who loved him more than life itself, hadn't been capable of imagining that her youngest son would do so well.

Hakim was one of Cass Tech's most gifted students. Instead of playing sports or being involved in some sort of crazed wrongdoing, he attended Cranbrook on the weekends and over the summer. The school accepted only the cream of the crop from all the schools in the Metro Detroit area, and Hakim excelled there as well.

Fatima gave her son everything he could possibly want or need. If it was new clothes he wished for, then she'd shower him with them. A just released video game?

It was his. When he dreamed about a new car on his sixteenth birthday, she made that happen. It was more than apparent that Hakim was her favorite child. Hakim knew it. Rasul saw it. And Kalif felt it—and felt hurt. Hakim refused to condone any of the illegal activities his older brother engaged in or was suspected of engaging in, and he strayed away from any type of sibling relationship with Kalif, which further cemented his older brother's reputation as the black sheep of the family. The two brothers barely saw one another, which was fine by them both. Hakim had his mother to depend on, and he knew she had his back. Their bond was unbreakable. Kalif had Islam, the often coldhearted streets, and his Linwood 4Lyfe family.

Rasul was torn. Back in his heyday, he had been a force to be reckoned with. It would not have been possible back then for any son of his, blood or not, to behave as Kalif had been over the past few years. Once deep in the game, Rasul had had a body count in double digits. Men had feared him far and wide. They had respected his judgment, and his word had been final in most situations. Yet as of late, his close friends and the men at the mosque were questioning his thought process. Word had gotten back that Kalif and his crew were suspects in a robbery at a home that one of the mosque members had taken him to do a job at. Rasul could do nothing but lower his head as the accusations were leveled at his eldest.

Rasul was on the road a lot, making sure the corrupt heroin pipeline set up years ago was always running properly. He wanted to take Kalif with him. But Kalif bucked at the idea of being trapped inside of a car for hours at a time. Since he was still doing wrong himself, it was hard for the towering man to condemn his boy for his transgressions. Prayer beads in hand, Rasul asked Allah to give him guidance and show him the way to soften Kalif's heart. When Kalif would show up to Jum'ah, he would receive the cold shoulder from most of the elders. "Let the boy be until he self-destructs" was the basic sentiment of all. Kalif felt their eyes burning holes in him, so he finally stopped going to the mosque altogether. Instead, he would pray solo. Brother Rasul hated that his son had that stigma attached to him in their close-knit community, but the menace had earned his stripes.

Rasul gave little to no attention to Hakim. Since the boy was a 100 percent his, meaning his biological seed, this didn't seem possible. But it was. Like his wife, Rasul would show up at all Hakim's awards ceremonies and show love when need be. But it was easy to see sometimes that Rasul's fatherly support was forced.

After months of attending Cass Tech, Hakim met a girl. Much to the delight of Fatima, who was now pregnant with twins, the girl was everything a mother would wish for, for a son. Whenever Hakim would bring her around, Stacy was kind, smart, pretty, and respectful. She had one small fault, something that Fatima knew was going to be a problem where her husband was concerned. Stacy was a devout Christian, a Baptist no less. And she was dedicated to attending church services every Sunday, for hours on end. And so the Muslim father protested his son's attachment to this girl. Hakim had his father's middle name and had been raised in the Islamic faith since birth. As far as Rasul was concerned, no son of his was going to do what Hakim had been doing "for the sake of a girl."

This was no ordinary Thursday evening at the Boston-Edison home. Rasul was not on the road. A pregnant

Fatima was feeling well enough to cook a huge dinner. Hakim was not at some after-school program, up in his room studying, or at his girlfriend's house. Though he was rarely around as of late, Kalif was at the place he called home as well. With the table set, the entire family sat down. Everything had been prepared Halal, just as Rasul always requested. After asking Allah's continued blessings, the members of the family filled their plates. No more than five minutes of calm silence filled the air before Rasul spoke.

"So, Hakim, how is school coming along?" Rasul asked.

Looking up from his plate, the younger son knew his father didn't care about how he was doing in school. Hakim knew this was the warm-up. He knew this question was just the prologue to the real play. But out of respect, he played along. "It's going great, Dad. I can't complain. My test scores have been pretty good, so I'm definitely in good shape."

"Yes, baby, you certainly are." Fatima smiled at her son, then redirected her attention to her husband. "He has received several college scholarship offers already. So that's a blessing."

Rasul could not help but to agree. Hakim earning a free ride to college was more than he could hope for. Allah had indeed answered his prayers where that was concerned. But now he had to speak about what he felt was the real issue at hand. "That's good to hear. A man that can learn can always teach. And that's what Allah wants us to do. Obey, learn, and guide. And, of course, attend the mosque."

Kalif had yet to say a single, solitary word. Instead, he had opted to continue devouring his dinner. It wasn't often he got to enjoy his mother's home cooking, so wasting time speaking about his little brother's academic achievements was not on the menu.

*Here we go,* Hakim thought. He knew it would only be a matter of time before his father got on his case. He pushed his chair back from the table, as he'd just lost his appetite. Before waiting another second for his father to attack, he beat him to the punch. "Look, Dad, if you are going to start in about me not going to the mosque, please don't. I have a lot of schoolwork to do. And besides, Kalif doesn't go anymore, either. Yeah, my friends tell me stuff."

"What?" Rasul replied, his voice deeper now.

Kalif lifted his head and frowned. "Hey, don't drag me into your little bullshit argument. I pray five times a day, no matter where I'm at. Me and my God solid."

"Please, you guys, calm down. And, Kalif, watch your language," Fatima begged. She had been hoping that for once they could have a nice family meal without any drama, but she now knew that would not be the case. As she placed her fork down on the table, she slowly rubbed her hand over her stomach. The twins had been quiet all day, but now they were moving around as if they sensed the bullshit in the air.

Rasul shook his head. "Naw, Fatima. This boy needs to get back right. He done lost all his damn mind! He's so smart, he dumb. He doesn't have time to attend the mosque or volunteer, but he has time to go to church damn near every Sunday! What's that all about?"

"What? Hakim? You going to church now? Where the hell I been at? I'm with Pop. What the fuck that's about? You bugging now for real!" Kalif exclaimed.

"Watch your mouth, Kalif! You not out in them streets you run around in all day and half the night, doing God knows what," Fatima said loudly, demanding respect. Her husband nodded, since he agreed that the boys should refrain from using foul language in their parents' presence.

"Okay. So what? I'm going to church. What's the big deal about that? I can make my own choices. It's my life." Hakim was not backing down. As far as he was concerned, it was each to his own, and he was not about to change his mentality. Furthermore, it was not like he was some little kid that had to be told what to do. And today he would prove that.

"Please leave this alone," Fatima pleaded, feeling the twins move more and more.

"Naw, Fatima. He wanna know what the big deal is," Rasul replied. "The big deal is you been Muslim your entire life."

"And . . . ?" Hakim retorted. His overconfidence was growing with each moment he stood his ground.

"And now, Negro, you hook up with some hot-in-the-ass little tramp, and she got you forgetting about everything we instilled in you just like that!" Rasul was now on his feet, yelling.

As the veins started to bulge by each of his temples, his wife tried once more to defuse the situation before it became any worse. "Please calm down, everyone—"

"Dad, she's not a tramp, so please don't call her that!" Hakim interrupted. "How would you like it if someone called Mom that?" Defiant, Hakim then stood to his feet, as well, on the other side of the table.

"Little punk, I know you ain't comparing that girl in the same breath to your mother," Rasul shouted. He was a few meager seconds away from knocking his son back down in the chair for daring to try to stand toe-to-toe with him in his own house. And then Hakim had had the nerve to raise his voice, as if he wanted something more than words to pop off.

As much as Kalif enjoyed his golden-boy brother being the center of madness, the fact that Hakim was denouncing Islam did not escape him. "Whoa, whoa. So let me get this straight. Not only are you getting some ass, but she also got you going all the way against the grain? You not praying and just being a pagan! So dang, Ma, how you like your favorite son now? He showing out, ain't he?"

"Man, whatever." Hakim waved his hand, dismissing Kalif's crude comments.

Hakim ignored his brother now, as he had most of the time while he was growing up, but he was not going to run and hide. Since the beginning of time, he had been taught to remove himself from any explosive situation involving his older sibling. He'd done his fair share of hiding under the bed or in the closet or calling his father and asking him to come home and get Kalif under control. That was Hakim's norm. But today no more. That behavior was out the window and off the table as an option. He knew that Kalif was half crazy if he was on his meds and that he was all the way gone if he was off them. But now, at this moment in time, Hakim was feeling just as crazy and was willing to go all out for his girl.

Fatima saw where this was headed. All she had wanted to do was have an innocent family dinner like they used to. Her heart was in the right place, but it was painfully clear that the devil had other plans. She sobbed while begging her husband and sons to stop yelling and

making matters worse. She had come to expect this behavior from Kalif, but not from Hakim. "Come on, y'all.
Please . . . This is getting out of control."

Rasul refused to go further in on his younger son.
"Getting out of control? It already has, but I'm about to
end this bullshit once and for all. Look, Hakim, as long
as you're under my roof, you're gonna do as I say, not as
you may. Are we clear?"

"You mean like Kalif, who you love so much and who
can do no wrong, even though he's running wild, robbing
people, selling drugs, like you and him both do? Is that
what I should be clear on?"

Rasul had to hold himself back from taking a swing
at his child. Fatima saw the fury in her spouse's eyes
and stepped in between the two of them. There had been
arguments in their household before, but none as bad as
this and they usually involved Kalif. She wanted Rasul
just to give Hakim a pass, but things had gone beyond the
point of that happening. Knowing she'd have no chance
with Rasul, she then turned to her baby boy. With tears
flowing, she pleaded with him to just be quiet and go to
his room. Unfortunately, her baby boy was now wanting
to become a man. Fatima trembled with worry, knowing
what being a so-called grown man who went against her
husband entailed. Before she could say or do anything
else, Rasul let all the way loose and laid down how things
were going to go. And in their household, he had the final
word, and his word was law.

"Look, little smart-mouthed nigga begging for my foot
to go up your ass, the bottom line is you going back to
the mosque and stopping all this church mess—flat out
point-blank, period. You gonna stop seeing that bad-in-
fluence female and get yourself back on track before you
burn in hellfire!"

"Yeah, that sounds about right to me," Kalif said gladly, agreeing with his father for once. "Hakim, man, fuck that church, and fuck that nonbelieving bitch you running with, and for real, fuck burning in hellfire," he joked. "I heard it told that shit hot as a motherfucker!"

Hakim was furious. They had been warned. He had enough of them disrespecting the girl he loved. "Dawg, ain't nothing funny. And I'm not gonna tell your crazy ass no more times to stop calling her out her name! Go somewhere and take your meds, or better yet, go kill yourself!"

Kalif was now on his feet, as well, caught deep in his emotions. "Wow. Dig that. So li'l bro trying to flex up on me, huh? I'm amused you finally got some balls. But let's see how big them motherfuckers is. Now, like I just said, Hakim, fuck that stankin' pussy bitch you been running with. Fuck her church, and double fuck that con man preacher that be stealing all the money!"

Hakim was heated. He was here for it and definitely had time. Fed up with the verbal abuse he was suffering at the hands of his father and his brother, he fired back, ready for the consequences that were sure to follow. "Naw, you thieving piece of shit! Fuck you! Fuck Islam and fuck Prophet Muhammad too!"

Those words were it. Those words were the deal breaker that led to full-blown pandemonium. Fatima sobbed, still trying to keep her baby boy out of harm's way. Rasul headed around to the other side of the table to snatch his youngest son up. Kalif immediately had a flashback of the day he handed the last guy his ass for insulting the prophet. That day was all too fresh in his mind. Ignoring the fact that his pregnant mother was acting as a shield for Hakim, Kalif reached over her shoulder and socked his little brother in the jaw. After his fist made contact, he shoved Fatima to the floor and swung once more. He was blinded by rage. Even though he had broken almost every principle that Islam was based upon, Kalif was still a strong believer and demanded respect for his religions. After pouncing on top of Hakim, he went straight to work. He started pounding his younger brother's face as if he was no more than a stranger in the streets. Both of his brother's eyes were swollen in a mere matter of seconds. His lip was busted, and he was bleeding out of his left nostril.

Seeing his wife now on the floor, holding her stomach, Rasul stopped himself from punching Hakim, as well, for being overly disrespectful. As Fatima screamed out in agony and asked Allah to help her, Kalif was finally brought out of his wrath. After standing up, he looked over at his brother, who was lying in one corner of the room and was balled up in the fetal position, and then at his mother, who was lying in another corner and was hysterical. Rasul was trying his best to comfort Fatima. He ordered a semi-dazed Kalif to call an ambulance. Kalif did not react. Either he didn't hear his father, or he didn't care. Instead, as if nothing was going on, he reached over the table, took a half-eaten piece of baked chicken off one of the plates, and took a bite. Without saying a word, he then walked out the front door and left it wide open.

Having passed by Henry Ford Hospital, the ambulance pulled into Harper University Hospital. That was where Fatima's doctors were and where she felt the most comfortable going. After they rushed her into the emergency room, she was swiftly taken to the high-risk pregnancy unit. After being examined by several physicians, including her own, she was put on bed rest for the remaining months she had left before delivery. She was told she could go home and be in her own bed. However, if she experienced one more scare like the one she had just endured, her doctors would have to admit her or possibly induce labor. As she lay there, trying to regain her composure after all the drama she'd just gone through, she looked over at her husband. He had tears in his eyes for her, but anger at their son still filled his heart. This was obvious to Fatima, who had been by Rasul's side for years, through the good and the bad.

"So after all this, can you just leave it alone? Can you just let Hakim figure it out on his own? You do know it's against the teachings of Islam to force your beliefs upon someone else, don't you?" she said quietly.

Sympathetic to his wife's wishes, Rasul begrudgingly agreed to let the matter rest. However, he made it perfectly clear that Hakim was going to have to apologize for speaking to him as he had if he wanted to remain underneath his roof. "There's no way in hell that boy ain't gonna bow down."

Fatima had once felt the same way their youngest son was feeling now. Taking a small sip of water from the white Styrofoam cup on her bedside table, she braced herself for a conversation that was a long time coming but way overdue. "Rasul, I love you with all my heart, and I always have. But just as you treated me and my feelings as if they didn't matter years ago, you doing the same to our son now. Even though I agreed to get back with you, I was far from being naïve. If that no-good Kenya you worshiped so much had lived, you would have been raising Kalif with her, not me. See, my love for you was one of purity. Yours for me was one of necessity and convenience. Am I wrong?"

Rasul wanted to protest but couldn't. The truth was exactly what it was, the truth. He had basically chosen another woman over Fatima back in the day. But that was the past. And just as Fatima was still holding on to the past and harboring animosity, he, too, was holding on to it. He knew that was why he favored Kalif over Hakim. That boy was the last link he had to his old life, which included Kenya James, the boy's maternal aunt. Even though it had been over two decades since he saw Kenya for the last time, his mind often wondered, *What if?*

Fatima was not blind. Whenever she caught her husband drifting off into deep thought, she knew Kenya's ghost was present. And she felt that this ghost would forever haunt her and their relationship. She had realized early on that she could never be number one in Rasul's life, and neither could their own biological child. So instead, she and Hakim just existed for him. Consequently, they had formed their own bond, just as Rasul and Kalif had done. And so they were all living in a house divided. And that house of division came tumbling down earlier today, and they would probably never be able to rebuild it. The foundation had not been strong from the jump.

"Bae, I'm sorry if you've felt like that. I swear it was never my intention to treat you or our son like that."

"Well, if you want to make things right for me, Hakim, and these girls"—she made a circular motion as she rubbed her stomach—"Kalif has to go once and for all. You saw how he beat my baby all in his face. And you saw how he just pushed me down like I mean nothing to him. That monster wouldn't even call for help! Mix all that with the mess he out in them streets doing, and it's just shameful. Now he has to go, or me, Hakim, and the girls all will. It's that simple."

Always in control of his family, Rasul wanted to argue the fact. Yet he knew his wife was right. Not about one or two things, but about them all. Kalif was hardly at home as if was, so telling his oldest boy he was no longer allowed back inside the house he had grown up in was seemingly effortless. But then again, where Kalif was concerned, nothing was ever easy.

# Chapter 10

It was the dawning of a new day. Kalif had finally linked back up with Ibn. They met at a restaurant in Dearborn, and there the game plan was laid out. Ibn explained how he would go down to the city-county building on Woodward, where they had listings of homes for sale. Also, he let Kalif know that he had a person tracking all the court actions and foreclosures in Metro Detroit. If people were losing their home or were even close to it, Ibn knew. He was a real estate piranha with a hidden agenda in tow. After a few meetings of the mind, Ibn put young Kalif in a position that could only bring him money. Normally, Ibn and his family kept their business dealings tight, close to the vest. But Ibn was a renegade. He always went against the grain. He saw that same mentality in Kalif, and he wanted to benefit from that quality. He knew that since Kalif was African American and his credit was fresh and untapped, he could use him to make certain moves the Arabic community was being blackballed for.

Kalif had enough of his own money to purchase two single-family dwellings at auction, and Ibn fronted him the funds for a third. Kalif was off and running. Since the prior week, when his father informed him that he was no longer welcome at the house, he'd been staying in a ho-tel room. That had been eating up some of his cash on hand, but now the young warrior felt things were about to change. Always plotting the next caper, he and his boys had hit several more suburban homes, thanks to Jada and her girls.

Jada and Kalif had been spending more and more time together. Some nights she even stayed with him in the hotel room. Even though they slept in the same bed, Kalif never tried anything. Although most men would consider Jada a dime, Kalif was more interested in her mind and her moneymaking skills than in getting some pussy. Jada, of course, still yearned for there to be more, and she prayed that her time to be Kalif's wifey and number one would soon come. Until that time, she continued to prove to him her loyalty.

Jada and her overly flirtatious crew had recently met a few white businessmen out at a strip club by the airport. After a few drinks, the men had loosened up and bragged about their fabulous homes, their high-maintenance, pain-in-the-ass wives, and their expensive vacations. After getting even more intoxicated, the black meat–thirsty businessmen let their guard all the way down and joined the scheming females in a hot tub at a nearby hotel. While all the girls but one kept them entertained by doing this and that, that one girl went through the men's pockets and took pictures of their IDs. Jada had then put Kalif up on game, and the rest of this crime had been on him and his boys. In the end, everyone had got a cut, and all had been good.

Jada, Kalif's ride-or-die, always opted to reinvest her cash in helping Kalif's vision and dreams materialize. The scar-faced beauty knew that what was good for him now would one day most likely be good for her. Jada had recognized Kalif's greatness years ago, even before he had realized it.

Before buying those houses, Kalif had stacked enough extra money to kick things into full gear once he had them, and he had made a list the length of his arm of the materials he'd need to get his house-flipping business all the way off the ground. After the auctions, he headed to the Home Depot on Seven Mile and Meyers Road, and right outside the store, he found all the skilled labor he needed to renovate those houses. The workers were posted up in their own trucks, their tools ready, and they worked fast and for cheap wages.

Whenever Kalif needed a clean-out crew, he knew where to go. There were plenty of willing men down in the Cass Corridor, near the homeless shelters. If Kalif got a few guys from down there, he'd always make sure they were well fed, besides getting paid. If some needed shoes or coats, Kalif made sure to provide those as well. Ibn had provided the blueprint for Kalif's charitable deeds, and that was what Kalif followed. He believed that if he did things correctly, soon he'd have one of those Black Cards Ibn had boasted about.

In no time at all, one of his dilapidated homes was transformed into a respectable house. No sooner had he got windows installed and the doors put up than Kalif heavily insured the property for as much as possible. And since the house was not located in the best of neighborhoods, Kalif had one of his homeboys' uncles post up at the place. Kalif was no fool. He knew that as soon as he put in fixtures and a hot water tank, let alone a furnace, the thieves and crackheads would be ready to relieve him of them.

Kalif was used to being in his own world, but he missed his pops. He wanted to get in touch with him and show him how he was coming up in the world with this house thing. It had been a little over a month since they'd last spoken. Kalif knew the harsh eviction notice he had received was not his father's doing. He knew Fatima had been the driving force behind it. He knew she had had something against him ever since he was a small child. And after finding out the extra details related to his adoption by Rasul and Fatima, he could easily understand why the only mother he knew would be bitter and full of animosity. Several times he had picked up his cell to call Rasul, but he hadn't placed the call. One day they'd link back up, but now was not the time.

Instead, Kalif would pray to Allah to guide his hand and steady his often troubled mind. Sometimes the medication he took from time to time worked, and other times it didn't. He fought through any mental blocks he would suffer, knowing that getting these houses completed was the most important milestone on the road to becoming a real boss.

# Chapter 11

Jada and her girls had been getting over for months. They had all been bringing something to the table quality-wise. They were on a roll. They felt unstoppable. If there was a scamming scheme going on in Detroit, there was no doubt those femmes fatales had their manicured hands in it somehow. Seductive, they were always on the prowl. Jewels was not only Jada's cousin, but she was basically the enforcer of the tight-knit group. Even though they all rocked out together, bitches being bitches, there was always the possibility of bullshit. Who had the best weave, whose eyelashes were on fleek, and who had the most men on their line. Jewels kept everyone in check.

It had been a long day. Jada, Jewels, TayTay, and two other girls, Nia and Euri, had been out handling business. The day before they had driven out to Birch Run premium Outlets, and today they had gone to Great Lakes Crossing Outlets. The trunks and the rear seats of both vehicles they had taken were packed. Any and every garment, purse, and accessory the five-woman team had shoplifted was stuffed inside. TayTay and Euri were good at swiping, so they had really stepped up and added to the piles of illegally gotten goods. Nia hadn't wanted to be outdone, so she had written a few bad checks.

On the road heading back home, a semi had jackknifed on I-75, causing a major backup. Instead of crying about the wait, they had exited at Oakland Mall and had made it do what it do. Bags in hand, they'd then gone back to their cars, knowing the traffic was clear by then. Before long, they had finally made it back to Nia's house. Now they were slowly sorting through everything while smoking a few blunts and finishing off a bottle of pink moscato.

With two of the girls on the Far West Side, working Michigan Avenue, and the other three holding Eight Mile down, they had multiple strip clubs on lock both east and west. With duffel bags filled to the top with every designer you could think of, and with countless packs of expensive hair stolen from out-of-town beauty supply shops with low-budget security practices, they were making money hand over fist. When things would slow down, they had other work to do, as Jada always had the girls lined up to step off into some real gangster white-collar-type shit. They knew it was dangerous, but they also knew the payoff was exceptional. It was a spin-off of the bullshit they used to do out by the airports. But this was a few steps up in the "oh hell, naw" department.

A bad experience was what had led Jada to consider white-collar work. It had all started when she called a meeting with the girls to discuss a new business venture. "Okay, so I have everyone's accounts set up. For the most part, most of the information is false. The only thing authentic is our pictures. And as soon as the shit goes down, I'll make sure our pages go dark and are deactivated immediately." Jada had smirked, knowing this was going to bring them even more money to jack off. They had been planning a trip to Dubai in a few months, and they would need all the cash they could get in order to spend freely.

After downloading both Backpage and Tinder, each girl had logged in and started to troll for possible victims. Unfortunately, it didn't take long for a gang of "definitely married but lying about it" middle-aged men to make contact. The game plan was easy. The girls seductively teased the men online. After their soon-to-be victims were good and on the hook, phase two came into play. They arranged to meet up in person. Most times in public. Yet in an extremely out-of-the way place. None of the girls were concerned with the men seeing them, then getting turned off. As polished as they were from head to toe, they were banking on it being the complete opposite. The married men would lust after them all the more. When they met up with the men, the girls took pictures of their initial meeting on the sly and secretly recorded their conversations. The rest was like child's play. As soon as the men pulled up their pants, the extortion would begin.

After five or six times of getting a decent payoff, the mischief-minded females ran into a problem. They were blindsided and definitely didn't see it coming. It all started when a white executive at one of the top three businesses in the area hit up TayTay. He wrote that she was one of the most desirable women he'd seen in a long time. His thirst for her was almost comical. He was sloppy with the things he revealed in her message box. It was not hard to figure out this was his first go-around at the social media pussy-and-dick swap meet. Not only did he provide her with his real phone number, not a fake one or a Google number, but his honest to God personal phone number, but he Cash-Apped her repeatedly when he felt she was ignoring him.

Plotting with her girls, TayTay decided he was going to be the big fish they need to land to ensure their trip out the country was truly memorable. It was time for him to find out what cheating on his wife could cost him. The clever clique had no remorse whatsoever for what they were about to do. After all, the men they duped were married, not them.

Brad called TayTay and told her he wanted to take her out to dinner and then go shopping at Somerset Collection. She was in need of a new purse and maybe an ankle bracelet. He promised her that and more. After she pulled up to valet parking at the restaurant and then went inside, she found him at a table, nursing a drink. When she approached the table, he stood and pulled out her chair for her. TayTay almost forgot this was business and not pleasure. After she ordered king crab legs and lobster tail, Brad insisted she get another portion to take home. TayTay happily obliged as she downed two strong Long Island iced teas.

When it came time to pay the bill, he took out his credit card and paid, never once bothering to see how much the damage was. While he had his wallet out, he tempted his new companion with six crisp hundred-dollar bills. He promised her that if they could just get a room for an hour or so, they could still go shopping. TayTay knew better than to go against the blueprint Jada had drawn up. But the money, the dinner, him pulling out her chair and hanging on every word she said had her gone. She'd given it up for far less to grimmer men. Once she was back in her car, she followed him to a hotel. When they both stepped inside the lobby, TayTay was so tipsy, she didn't even notice that Brad didn't bother to check in. They walked straight to the elevator and to room 217.

After he slid the key card in the slot, the green light flashed, signaling that the door was unlocked. As TayTay walked inside that room, she never imagined what was coming next. Thank God she blacked out when Brad's wife snatched her up by her long weave and dragged her over to the bed. TayTay's perfect gentleman stood back, looking amused, and watched his better half duct-tape the black girl's wrists together. Using a razor blade, she then sliced TayTay's clothes off, exposing her naked body. Brad and his wife then took turns violating her. The predator had become the prey. When they were done having their fun, Brad did as he always did after his and his wife's little parties. He deactivated his Backpage and Tinder accounts and lay low until another girl came along and tried to get something for nothing.

As for TayTay, she finally came to in that hotel room. She had a headache and could hardly remember what had taken place. The only thing she knew for sure was that she was naked and every hole on her body hurt. After crawling over to the phone, she dialed Jada. On that day, the crew knew they had to get out of the streets and find a better way to make money.

# Chapter 12

Kalif had just ended his conversation with a hysterical Jada. He was hotter than fish grease after she told him what had gone down. He had always known what the girls were doing was risky, but the way all of them, his boys included, were living made prison or death a possibility at any time. Jada had always had his back no matter what, and she had yet to get the dick. She was loyal and looked up to him, as did both crews. His own boys were out committing random crimes and just trying to stay afloat while Kalif focused on real estate. Kalif had been putting every penny he had and Jada blessed him with into getting at least one house ready to flip.

Needing a quick cash come up, he thought about doing an insurance job on the house, but that would defeat his purpose, which was to get his hands on extra money to finish that first house. With the weight of the world on his young shoulders, he had to think quickly if he was going to save face with everyone that depended on him. When he remembered the stories his pops used to tell him, an idea came to him. The entire lower level of the house was complete, as was the basement. Jada and her crew had sworn off tricking niggas out of their bread, but they were still smooth as ever with getting that gear.

After praying, Kalif could think more clearly. He and Pit Boy jumped in his truck and hit up Detroit Store

Fixture. After purchasing multiple racks and a few tables, they brought them back to his house. While he had Pit Boy and Keys bring everything inside, Kalif called Jada and told her to meet him over there. When she arrived, Jewels was riding shotgun, as she always did. The two cousins were more like sisters.

With everyone standing around the living room, Kalif explained that they were taking it back old school. Instead of the ladies going out in the streets and hustling hard to sell their stolen goods, they would use his house as a booster trap. The basement and the first level would be set up like a store, and the workmen would continue to remodel the top floor. The ladies would invest in a pound of good weed and would sell that as well. With this plan, most of Kalif's problems where Jada and her girls was concerned were solved . . . well, at least temporarily. Now he had to get his own team financially straight and on the come up. And he knew it took money to make money.

"I'm surprised to hear from you so soon. What's going on with the houses? You still good over there?" Ibn said when he answered the phone.

"Yeah, Ibn, the first house is coming along," Kalif told him. "I can't complain. But I need to holler at you about something else. Are you at the store?"

Ibn informed his young protégé that he was at his cousins' gas station on Joy Road and that he could just come through.

In less than twenty minutes, Kalif was pulling up at the gas station. After he, Ibn, and Ibn's cousins all greeted one another, Kalif was allowed behind the thick

Plexiglas. Ibn and his cousins were smoking a hookah, but Kalif wasn't interested. His time was limited, so he wanted to get down to the business at hand.

"So, yeah, look, I know I owe you for that other house, but I need to get some more money moving my way . . . some major shit," he told Ibn. "My girl ran into some trouble, so I had to look out for her and come through in a big way."

Ibn was silent, still smoking the cherry blend. Finally, he said, "Well, what kinda dough you talking about?"

"At least eight or nine racks real quick should hold me over . . . maybe an even ten."

Ibn liked Kalif and his hustle. He knew one day he would need Kalif for something else. And now all his mentoring had the potential to pay off. However, one thing or person was standing in the way of that. And that person was Rasul. Somehow word had gotten back to him that Ibn was helping his kid out. Rasul didn't like it one bit. He didn't want to see his son fail, but he knew what Ibn and his family were involved in, and he wanted Kalif to have no parts of it. The father of two and the longtime respected member of the mosque had seen Ibn and company lure young black kids into doing their dirty work.

Since Kalif was not your average youngster, Ibn knew he first had to invest in Kalif in order to gain his trust. Everyone knew Kalif was a certified nutcase, and the only thing he loved more than money was Allah. So when Kalif had come into his store on the humble that day, it was as if God had aligned them so that they could do business together. But now Rasul was on his head and threatened all-out war if Ibn kept inserting himself into Kalif's life.

"Look, Kalif, it's like this. I'd love to help you out. You know me. I trust you. You trust me. But your father . . ."

"My father?"

"Yes. Rasul stepped to me Friday after Jum'ah and warned me to stay away from you. He thinks I'm trying to bring you harm instead of helping you. I tried to explain, but you know your father better than me. It was zero tolerance."

"What in the fuck!"

"Yeah, so I respect Rasul, and so does my family. I don't want any trouble."

Kalif was infuriated. It was bad enough his father had allowed his moms to ban him from the house he had once called home, but now he was out here trying to block his hustle. That shit had to be addressed and quick. "All right, dawg. Let me handle my pops. I'm all day long, all day strong. I'ma get back up with you sometime tomorrow."

Kalif hopped back in his car and drove to the hotel room he had been staying at. After taking out his Koran, he read out loud from it. Then he prayed. He asked Allah to grant him patience, fortitude, and a sensible, strong mind in what he was about to do. He was no longer living under his father's roof, so the way they would soon communicate and interact would be something different altogether. For years he had purposely stayed out of his father's business dealings, even when asked to ride along. Kalif was content to make a name for himself without the aid of his pops. As far as he was concern, Rasul had his life and a circle that he dominated, and Kalif was trying to do the very same thing.

# Chapter 13

Jada came into the hotel room that she and Kalif had been sharing. Seeing her beloved on the prayer rug, in deep thought, she knew something was going on. Anytime Kalif would stay on his knees and chant in Arabic, his mind was troubled. Trying her best to make some sort of emotional connection, Jada eased over in his general direction. Not wanting to startle him, softly she spoke his name. After she called out to Kalif four or five good times, he finally answered. When he turned his head to look at Jada, it was easy for her to see that he was off his meds. She'd been dealing with him long enough to spot the outward signs. Kalif looked tired. His eyes were bloodshot, as if he'd been drinking or smoking weed. He rubbed his hands together, as if he was plotting how to take over the world.

Trying her best not to alarm him, Jada made insignificant conversation as Kalif stood up and began pacing the room. As he went from the bed to the window, from the window to the bathroom, then back to the bed, his footsteps grew heavy with each motion. Jada fell back. She knew from past experience, Kalif had to work the shit out in his mind before attempting to return to his normal self. After forty-five minutes, he started to slow his steps down. Clutching his ears, Kalif titled his head backward and asked Allah to help him. Then the chanting started once more.

Jada was deeply in love with Kalif. He could do no wrong in her eyes. Far from being naïve, she knew he didn't share her feelings. He often expressed that he had love for her but was not in love with her. Jada had a choice to except that truth or not. She considered herself a rider and stayed around, toughing it out. There was nothing that she wouldn't do for him if he asked. And some things she stepped up and did without him having to ask. Jada knew he liked that quality about her. Sometimes he'd even speak about her being a male version of himself, but not Muslim. And since she knew Kalif thought highly of himself, she took that statement as a compliment.

He knew she was down in the trenches with him when shit wasn't always pretty. Kalif often praised her for that. With desire and lust in her soul, Jada felt if she stayed posted by his side long enough, things would soon be in her favor. They had to. She would grow on him, just like in the movies. The fact that Kalif cared enough to help get her and her girls off the streets and to a safe location spoke volumes in her book.

While Kalif continued to pace, though more slowly now, Jada updated her Instagram page, adding a few new items they'd easily stolen from a boutique on Livernois. When she looked up, she smiled, as it appeared that Kalif was finally coming back to himself.

"Hey, what up, doe? What's good with you?" he said.

"Nothing much. Just chilling. Working on a few irons I got in the fire," Jada responded, as if Kalif had not been in the loon zone ever since she'd arrived at the room. "We have a gang of new stuff, and if I wanna really make this house hustle happen, I gotta put in the legwork."

"You know what, girl? That's what I really like about you. You never stop on that paper hunt."

Kalif went into the bathroom. He turned on the hot water and then reached for a washcloth as a warm mist started to rise from the sink. Lifting both arms, he took off his T-shirt. Jada tried to play it off that she wasn't all in, but Kalif saw her checking him out in the mirror. Not wanting to lead her on, he quickly allowed the water to saturate the washcloth. He then covered his face with the washcloth and scrubbed harder than a normal person would. It was as if he was trying to rid himself of the sins of the world. Once he was done, he left the bathroom and searched through his large-size duffel bag. He removed a winter-white wifebeater, then slipped it on over his chiseled frame. Taking a seat on the edge of the bed, he was now ready to clue his homegirl Jada in on what was going down.

"Yeah, so apparently, my old man is trying to block me from coming up. I got that word not too long ago."

"Say what now?" Jada raised an eyebrow, wanting to get some understanding.

"Yeah, I went to go holler at my boy about some business."

"And?"

Kalif's voice took on more of an evil tone when he said, "And he told me, my pops found out me and him was getting that paper together, and my pops wanted that shit to cease immediately. I swear, that bullshit got me on ten in this bitch! I'm out here trying to just do me. I don't know, Jada. Why wouldn't a man wanna see his son succeed? I'm not trying to walk in his damn shadow. I wanna be self-made. I wanna grind out for mines, so when I get on top, that shit will really mean something."

Jada walked over to him. Given the mood he was still in, her maternal spirit kicked into overdrive. Gently, she placed her hand on his shoulder to comfort him, but Kalif abruptly stood, shutting that down. He didn't want her to get any ideas. When they were in the bed at night, she was on her side, and he was on his. Even though he obviously needed consoling, he was not interested in it coming from her. Or from any woman, for that matter. Time and time again he had reminded her that until he got all the way right with his pockets and with Allah, he wasn't gonna fornicate again. At one point, she had pondered if he was gay because he didn't want the pussy, but then she had heard tales from around the way about how Kalif used to knock the hoes all the way down when he was coming up. Accepting his rejection now as just another ordinary day, she quizzed him on how he was going to handle the situation.

"First, I'm about to just sleep on it and get my mind right. I ain't really kicked it with my father since he let my moms put me out. So I already know this conversation could go all the way left as soon as I hear his voice or he hears mine."

"Yeah, I understand. Just try to stay calm when y'all kick it. After all, he is your father. Try to think before you speak, because some things you can't take back, just like actions. Remember, you taught me that."

Kalif looked at Jada's face finally and cracked a smile. "Come on now, dead ass. I know you ain't talking about family, is you? Your ass done denounced your peoples years ago, let you tell it."

Jada didn't return his smile, nor did she intend to. Matter of fact, she rolled her eyes, sucked her teeth, and wanted to throw up in her mouth all at the same time. "Yeah, sure did, with their abusive asses. I told my mother, and she act like I was lying. So yeah, fuck all of them. Jewels don't fuck with them, either. She knows how they are. Trust me, Kalif, the entire bloodline's tainted. Nothing spawned from my grandmother is decent, not me, or Jewels, either, when it comes down to it, sad to say."

"So I guess you bat-shit crazy, too, just like me," Kalif teased while turning on the television. *The Family Business* was coming on in a few, and he damn sure didn't want to miss that wild-plot shit. He stretched out on the bed and locked his fingers behind his head. A little later he fell asleep while watching the bright screen like a hawk, thinking about what the next day would hold.

It was a little after seven o'clock. Kalif had completed all his morning prayers. He had slept well and was ready to speak to his father with a clean heart. The once obedient son didn't want to argue, but he was definitely not going to let this slide. Rasul had put him out in the black-hearted streets of Detroit to man up and provide for himself, so why he would try to block his hustle was beyond him. As Jada stepped out of the shower, Kalif turned his back on her so that he did not see her body clad only in a towel.

He reached over to the nightstand and removed his cell from the charger. He went through his contacts and then pushed his dad's tag. Kalif had his father listed as Big Poppa. His heart raced some after he pushed the green icon. A few rings later, Rasul's voicemail came on. Kalif felt his stomach drop, but he didn't leave a message. After waiting five or ten minutes, he hit redial. This time the call went straight to voice. When Kalif slammed his cell down on the carpeted floor, Jada knew he had to have at least cracked his screen.

"What happened?" she asked, already knowing the answer but still hoping he would confide in her.

"He ain't pick up, that's what happen. That shit was ringing at first. Now it's going straight to his damn voicemail. He probably ducking me. He probably know I'ma go nuts on his ass, and he brushing it off. He ain't ready."

Jada had finished getting dressed. Wanting Kalif to stay as optimistic as possible, she urged him to call again, saying his father may have been in the shower or something. Kalif snatched up his cell from the middle of the floor. He took a deep breath before dialing Rasul once more. And just as he had figured, the same thing happened. Voicemail.

"Man, fuck all this. I'ma go by the crib this evening. That's what a nigga gonna do. Me and my old man gonna get all this shit straight once and for all. He can't avoid me when I'm standing right in his face. Not him or my mother! If they wanna make me out to be the bad guy so bad, then, shit, I'ma be just that."

Jada's ears perked all the way up. Loyal, dedicated, and trustworthy beyond measure, she had been hanging tough with Kalif for months, and he had barely spoken about his family since getting banished. This was her time. Her mind was all over the place. She wanted finally to meet his parents and show them she could potentially make their son a good wife one day. Maybe if they gave her their seal of approval and their endorsement, she'd have a solid chance with Kalif. Carefully choosing her words, she eased her way on in.

"So, Kalif, maybe I should ride with you. I mean, I know how angry you be getting, and I don't want you to get pulled over by the police for speeding, or some stupid shit like that, if shit don't go your way. Plus, for real, you know the insurance ain't right and your L's suspended."

Thinking nothing of it, Kalif agreed. It hadn't taken much convincing on Jada's part. He told Jada they would probably go over there about four thirty, so she should meet him back at the room right before then. Jada was ecstatic. She tried to contain her excitement before he noticed and changed his mind.

It was early enough that she could get herself all the way together to meet her future in-laws. The first thing she did was swing by the house they were slanging clothes at. After picking out what she believed to be the perfect outfit, she took two packs of the most expensive weave they were selling. TayTay watched her girl hurry through the house as if it were New Year's Eve and the clock were about to strike twelve. Since the dramatic incident at the hotel room with Brad, TayTay hadn't gone outside much. Instead, she had posted up, drinking wine, smoking weed, and oftentimes doing too much of both. TayTay's world was in the house, and in that house only.

With everything she needed in hand, Jada roared out of the driveway and headed up to Greenfield Plaza. The twins who did her hair and nails were both on the fourth floor, so she could get her hair done by one and then her nails by the other without having to wait. After that, all she had to do was get her makeup and lashes done and get dressed. By her calculations, she'd be putting on her last wedge wraparound sandal when Kalif arrived at the hotel room.

Kalif was a little late getting back to the room. Instead of coming in, he blew the horn twice. Like a dog hearing a whistle, Jada came running. She climbed in the truck and shut the door. After fastening her seat belt, she waited. And waited. And then waited some more. She'd gone out of her way to look top notch, and he had yet to notice. It was as if he didn't care enough about her feelings to even acknowledge the drastic change she'd undergone since this morning. This was a further blow to her bruised ego. With a lump in her throat, Jada sucked it up, as she always did where Kalif was concerned. She chalked it up to him being preoccupied and distracted about possibly chin checking his father for the first time ever in his life.

A few blocks away from his house, Kalif pulled over, reached into the middle console, and grabbed his cell phone. With one hand on the steering wheel and his cell in the other, he tried his father's number yet again. He was hoping for the best but expecting the worst, and his call went right to voicemail.

"I should just text him and have him meet up with me at the Coney Island or some shit. I mean, it's obvious he's avoiding my calls," he muttered.

Conniving was Jada's middle name. She had been waiting for the opportunity to meet the famous Rasul and Fatima from day one. Even when they were back in school, she had wondered what sort of home life Kalif had to make him behave the way he did. Now it was finally time to have at least some of her curiosity curbed, and Kalif was trying to shut it down. There was no way she could allow that to happen. Besides, she had put a lot of work into looking as good as she did. She'd even taken a few selfies in an effort to build up her confidence with Kalif. She was going to meet his people if she had to drag him over there kicking and screaming.

"Look, I know it must be hard to stand toe-to-toe with your father, but you do need the extra income that ole boy can offer, correct?" she said.

"Yeah, you right." Kalif didn't hesitate to agree.

Jada kept at his mental, knowing he was off his game and caught up in his emotions. "Well, if you don't step to and straighten this out quick, the opportunity may be off the table. Then what?"

Once again, she had no trouble getting Kalif to see eye to eye with her. A few minutes later, they were turning off Linwood, then parking in front of a nice-size house with an emerald-green awning. The lawn was cut and lined perfectly. And the porch had two gigantic flowerpots on both sides, filled with all the pretty flowers Jada used to see down at the Eastern Market with her granny back in the day, when her home life was normal. Once out of the truck, Jada tugged on her tight-fitting sundress, pulling it down. Then she leaned over and checked her face in the side mirror.

Momentarily, Kalif stood on the sidewalk, as if his legs had ceased to work. Jada stood by his side, with a dumb smirk on her face. Seeing a small bit of smoke coming down the driveway, Kalif finally spoke. "Dang. They must be in the backyard, barbecuing. Maybe that's why my old man ain't answer the phone. The reception is fucked up back there."

At this point, Jada could care less what the reason was that his father had not picked up. They were only feet away from her destiny, and she was feeling herself. She hadn't cleaned up for nothing. With a brave face, Kalif led the way, and Jada trailed behind him like a puppy dog begging for a treat. She could tell from his step, he had not come to play games. He had an agenda, and so did she. When they passed the open side door, Jada tried to sneak a peek inside the house but couldn't manage to do so. The couple was moving much too fast. Maybe she would ask to use the bathroom to wash her hands after Kalif's parents invited them to stay for dinner. The food on the grill smelled delicious. Jada quickly decided she was going to say how good her own food was, even if it wasn't. She would then beg her soon-to-be mother-in-law to give her secret family recipes.

Once they reached the backyard, all the anticipation and fanfare evaporated. Kalif didn't find his father, mother, or little brother. Instead, he saw some strange female hovering over the grill, fork in hand.

Not wanting to alarm her, Kalif asked where his family members were at. "Hey, what up, doe? Where my peoples at? And who are you?"

"Yeah, who are you?" Jada asked, joining in on the questioning as if she had a right to.

The young girl giggled as she closed the lid on the grill. "Oh, hello. My name is Stacy. I'm friends with Hakim. And I know from the pictures I've seen on the mantel inside, you're Kalif."

"Yeah, this is Kalif," Jada replied. She had become suddenly territorial, and she tried to grab ahold of Kalif's arm.

Instinctively moving his arm away, Kalif got closer to Stacy. "So yeah. Okay. You're Hakim's girlfriend I've heard so much about, huh?"

Stacy blushed, showing Kalif every inch of the silver braces in her mouth. "Yeah, I guess so. At least I hope so." Dressed in a light pink polo-style shirt and black jeans, she was prepped out. What appeared to be her own natural long hair was pulled back in a ponytail. With her bubbly personality, Kalif could easily see why his little brother liked her so much. She reminded him of their mother.

"That's cool." Kalif had enough problems with his father that he had to work out. So dealing with the fact that Stacy was the one behind dragging his brother to church every Sunday would have to wait. "Where is everybody at? Why they have you out here slaving, cooking some . . ."

"It's lamb chops and grilled mixed vegetables. Hakim's favorite. He had to run to the store to grab Mama Fatima some fresh asparagus to throw on here as well. She's upstairs with the twins. You want me to go get her?"

"Maybe in a few." Kalif grinned while checking his brother's girl out.

Jada rolled her eyes. She didn't know what it was about Stacy that had instantly rubbed her the wrong way, but it was something. Maybe the fact that the young girl appeared outwardly to be everything that Jada wasn't. Or that she had referred to Kalif's mother as Mama Fatima, a title Jada should be using as well. Whatever it was, she'd been around Kalif long enough to tell when he liked someone or didn't. And from where Jada stood, she felt her man was being a little too chatty and friendly with the female that had ultimately broken his family up. Feeling vindictive, Jada thought she'd bring that fact up and throw salt in the little Miss Innocence game Stacy was running on Kalif. "So do you go to one of those megachurches or not?"

Stacy did not falter. She proudly announced the name of her church home. Not knowing she was doing anything wrong, she invited Jada to attend service sometime. She mentioned they had no real dress code policy; it was come as you were. Of course, Jada took that as a low-key dis of what she had on. Jada wanted to read Stacy the riot act and tell her exactly how much everything cost that she had on from head to toe. Before Jada could fix her mouth, a car pulled up in the driveway. Once the guy behind the wheel was outside of the vehicle and marching toward the backyard, she assumed this could only be Kalif's baby brother.

"Hey. I'm Jada," she said as she jumped in front of him, slowing down his stride.

Not saying a word, Hakim stepped around the skimpily dressed female with the painted face.

"What you doing here, Kalif?" Hakim placed his arm around Stacy as if she needed protection. "Mom called me on my cell and said you was out here in the backyard with some girl."

Without hesitation, Kalif turned and looked up at his parents' bedroom window. He saw Fatima standing there, arms folded, peering downward. He didn't motion to her, and she didn't wave to her son. That was their normal relationship, and it had been this way for some time, even before they had the big fight and he got thrown out. So he wasn't fazed by the coldness. It was second nature. Jada, however, was still trying to be in the mix and was desperate to be recognized, so she waved up at Kalif's mother. Fatima snarled momentarily, looking at Jada as if she was nothing more than filth. Then she promptly closed the curtain, leaving Jada speechless.

This was the first time Kalif had laid eyes on his younger sibling since he had left him bloodied on the dining-room floor. It was easy to see that Hakim had a few souvenir scars from that evening under his left eye. Whereas part of Kalif wanted to reach out and apologize for what he had done, he still believed that anyone that insulted the prophet—peace be upon his soul—needed to get dealt with one way or another. So it was what it was.

"Look, dawg, don't be so hostile. I'm not here to see you, anyway, so you can fall back on that tough-guy act with me. You already know how I get down, so if I was on anything else, you'd know that shit by now. But, dig, I'm here on another mission. Where is Pops at? I've been calling him and ain't get no answer."

Still posted at Stacy's side, Hakim had animosity and pure hatred in his tone when he said, "He's not here. He went up to Muskegon to visit Unc and make sure everything is everything with him."

Jada was beyond nosy. She couldn't help it. She inserted herself in the brothers' conversation. "Unc? Who is that? I've never heard of him. Is that y'all real uncle or something?"

Kalif and Hakim both ignored her question, but Stacy jumped right in. "No, that's Pops's homeboy, S. P. Black, from off Mt. Elliott, he used to get money with. They're like brothers, and they behave like brothers are supposed to act. Isn't that right, Hakim?"

Kalif and Hakim both knew what Stacy was trying to say, but they ignored her, just as they did Jada. Their issues went back farther than the physical altercation of a few months ago. The two brothers had been feuding since Hakim came out of the womb, and no wise, slick comments were going to make all that was wrong with them right. It was what it was. Stacy had tried, and that was all she could do.

Standing off to the side, Jada was infuriated, and it showed. She had shifted her weight to one side and had twisted her lips. She had put in real work trying to be everything to Kalif, and he continued to box her out. Here Stacy was, standing by her man, calling his parents Mama and Pops, looking at framed pictures on mantels, and cooking as if this was her house. And apparently, she knew the long family history. Sucking her teeth from anger, Jada pouted. She couldn't even get a simple wave in return from someone standing at a window. She was used to getting shit on by her own family; now Kalif's family had joined in on the disrespectful behavior. Fed up, Jada turned and headed slowly back down the driveway toward the truck.

"So yeah, I'll just try to get back up with Pops later." Kalif reached in his pocket and pulled out a small-size knot. After peeling off a few hundred-dollar bills, he tried to hand them to his brother. "Here. Give this to Mom so she can buy something for the twins for me. Regardless of how y'all moving right now, I'm still family. And one day I want to finally meet my baby sisters when Mom stops bugging."

"Don't hold your breath. Besides, no one wants that dirty money you always have," Hakim said.

Since he refused to take it, Kalif placed it on a lawn chair. "Come on now, you Uncle Tom nigga with an attitude. We was raised on dirty money, so stop fronting for your little girlfriend. Truth be told, that shit should be running hot in your veins more than mine."

"Ain't shit in them filthy veins of yours but evildoing and ice water! Or maybe you the spawn of Satan for real."

"Okay now. Keep running off at the mouth and you not gonna be this girl's hero no more," Kalif barked with certainty. With his chest sticking out, head held high, he left the backyard and headed to the truck. He passed Jada on the way. When he had almost reached the truck, Stacy came running down the driveway.

Jada twisted her expression, wondering what this Goody Two-shoes bitch wanted to rub in her face next. But Stacy ran right past Jada and straight to Kalif.

"Listen, Kalif, just have faith," Stacy said. She smiled and touched his arm reassuringly. "Things are going to get better. It's just gonna take some time. I heard you pray all the time, so you know how powerful God is. And just so you know, your father speaks very highly of you, no matter what you may think or what Hakim says."

"Girl, bye with all that extra," Jada muttered. She waved her hand quickly as if dismissing the girl who was years younger than her.

Kalif gave Jada an "old-school grandmother" death stare. Then he nodded at Stacy, acknowledging he heard her and was taking in all that she had said. Kalif was appreciative of the words. He always put on a brave front where his people were concerned, but he was human just like the next person. He needed that affirmation.

Kalif and Jada climbed in the truck without uttering a word. As Kalif put the truck in drive and drove off, Jada looked back over her shoulder at Stacy, who was waving. Jada silently vowed to one day slap the young bitch dead across her face.

# Chapter 14

Jada was all in her feelings, and rightfully so. It felt as if she'd been sucker punched in the face. The pit of her stomach ached from sorrow, not hunger. Kalif had just dropped her off at her car and hadn't said a single word about what had just taken place. They had ridden in silence. Here she was, in the most expensive outfit they had stolen. Hair slayed. Nails on fleek. Face flawless. It was like the prom, the homecoming dance, and her wedding day all rolled into one. Jada had gone all out in anticipation of meeting Kalif's parents. And for what?

When he was off his meds and being unpredictable, Jada was there. When he would wake up sad, she was sad with him. And even when he would wake up in the oddest state of mind, Jada never left his side. When he would pray for days on end some weeks, she made sure Kalif at least took a break to eat something or have a cup of hot tea. The dedicated female felt that after all she'd dealt with while hanging out with their complicated son, she had earned the right to sit at the table with Kalif's parents. Jada felt that she deserved at least a "Thank you for helping to look after this insensitive savage we raised."

Kalif's father had not been at home to take part of the awkward situation. And Hakim, whom she had heard so much about and had even felt sorry for, had acted as if she was not there, either. And most hurtful of all, Fatima had given her the ultimate cold shoulder. Kalif's mother had made it perfectly clear by closing the curtain on Jada's face that there would be no invitations to the family reunion anytime soon, if ever. There was no other way to take what she had done. Jada had fought back the tears. She'd been devastated. Her hands had trembled, but she had tried to remain brave and keep her front up. She hadn't even got an opportunity to step foot inside the dwelling Kalif grew up in. All her plans had been shut down. Fatima, the mother of two grown boys and two baby girls, had room in her life for only one daughter-in-law. And from the looks of things, that uppity bitch Stacy had already filled that esteemed position. Jada had to come to terms with the fact that even though she thought highly of herself, others didn't.

Now, as she weaved in and out of the heavy rush-hour traffic on the Lodge, Jada turned the volume on the radio all the way down, then turned the radio all the way off. Her head was pounding, and the only thing she wanted to hear was dead silence. Her spirits were low, and she needed to have a drink and to smoke a blunt. The only thing that gave her a small bit of relief was the fact that it was raining. At first it was light, but now the rain was pouring down. *At least their little fucked-up barbecue is getting rained on. With they fake bitch asses.* Lost in her train of thought, Jada accidentally drove by her exit.

The rain got heavier, and it was difficult to see, and the windshield wipers didn't help much. Still bothered by being shunned, Jada took her eyes off the road for only a few seconds. Those few moments in time were all it took for her to almost lose total control of the car. At the very moment her vehicle roared through a huge puddle of water that had quickly accumulated, she hit a curve in the road. Since she was not holding the steering wheel tight enough, the car hydroplaned. When the four tires came back down to meet the pavement, she was just a few feet away from slamming into the concrete and steel barrier next to an embankment. God was on her side, as she barely got the Nissan back under control.

*Oh my God! This is too much. I can't take much more of this bullshit with Kalif or this street life.*

Jada had to calm her nerves before she ended up killing herself and anyone that had the misfortune of being in her path. The next thing she knew, she was parked on the top level of MotorCity Casino and was considering driving right off the edge. Like Kalif always claimed to be, she was a nomad, too, in life. The only thing that had been keeping her sane all this time was her love for and devotion to a man who apparently didn't feel the same about her. Using the palm of her hand, she banged her forehead, angry she had been such a fool. All the signs had been there all along, but dumbly, she had chosen to ignore them. She had been blinded by love, but no more. From this point on, when Kalif needed her, she wouldn't be around. Maybe he could find some Suzy Homemaker– looking ho like the one Hakim had hanging on his arm. Maybe a female like that was more Kalif's speed, especially since he wasn't giving up the dick.

As it grew dark, Jada continued to sit there, feeling sorry for herself. Staring at the illuminated green top of the Fisher Building in the distance, she let the tears flow. Eyes puffy and nursing a migraine, Jada allowed her self-inflicted pity party to go on for what seemed like forever. Her once perfect makeup was ruined, and she'd bitten off two of her gel nail tips. Ignoring constant calls from her homegirls, even from her cousin Jewels, Jada knew she had to get her mind back right. Not one of all those missed calls was from her schizophrenic hustle partner. He had made no attempt to check up on her. It was so crystal clear what had to go down next. She had to go back to the time in her life when she was team her, not team him. She had to show her girls she was still the same female boss and go-getter she'd been for all those years before she saw Kalif and his crew at the mall.

Starting the engine, Jada took a few deep breaths and shook the last of her "playing victim" demons out of her system. With a new attitude and a new perspective on life, she slowly backed out of the spot where she had just considered taking her own life. Her game plan was to swing by the hotel room she'd been sharing with Kalif, pack her belongings, and temporarily post up over at the booster trap. Jumping down on the freeway, Jada felt reborn, rededicated to her hustle and, most importantly, emotionally detached from a man who could care less. Bottom line was that if it was "Fuck her," then it was "Fuck him," and most definitely, it was "Fuck his family." Stacy included.


With the sudden downpour, Hakim and Stacy rushed to get the meat and vegetables off the grill. After donning oven mitts, they ran outside and placed everything on the grill into pans. Then they ran back inside and put the smoking hot pans on the stove. Fatima was in the kitchen, helping them to get organized. As the three of them scurried about, ensuring that dinner would be saved, there was an obvious elephant in the room. As a matter of fact, there were several. Each of the trio was deep in thought about Kalif's impromptu visit.

Renegade to his soul, Kalif had been banned from the house for months now. And just like that. out of the blue, he had popped up, and with some common hood rat in tow. Fatima was more than angry that the child she raised had shoved her to the floor and had savagely beaten her baby boy, and then he had the nerve to show his face here. In her book, he should have been ashamed to see her or anyone else, unless he had come to make amends. But there had been no apologies offered today or before. No phone calls. No letters. No cards or smoke signals, not even to Rasul. Kalif had done what he always did when he did wrong; he'd acted as if nothing out of the ordinary had occurred. And worse than that, he'd been mad at the other person for having the nerve to be mad at him.

Although Kalif prayed five times a day, sometimes six, and could recite the Koran front to back, that didn't make him a good Muslim. Daily, he broke every rule of Islam and made excuses for doing so. Long fed up, Fatima was at ease with him out of the house, a house he'd made so unbearable to be in. Up until today, when she saw his face, Fatima had been content. She had derived the joy from the infant twins, Hakim, and of course her husband, whenever he was at home, and had felt at peace.

"Why did he even come by here? What did he want?" Fatima bent down and placed one of the pans in the oven. "He has some nerve. I can't wait until your father gets back from visiting S. P. Black in Muskegon. He's gonna have to do something about Kalif once and for all."

"Ma, I don't know why he was here. I didn't really give him a chance to say. After he asked where Dad was at and why he wasn't answering his calls, that was it. When he found out, he was back being on that gangster talk tip he does."

"Well, I hope he has at least been taking his medicine. And I hope he leaves us alone," Fatima said before she opened a cabinet and took out plates and a few medium-size bowls. "He has got to be crazy, just showing up, with that face-painted whore prancing around my backyard as if she belongs here, acting as if he's done no wrong." Hearing that Rasul had not been answering the troubled boy's calls did give her a small bit of comfort. It meant that maybe for once he was on her side and not Kalif's.

Stacy wanted to remain quiet. Hakim had already read her the riot act for speaking to both Kalif and the girl he was with. When she'd returned to the backyard after running behind his older brother, Hakim had wanted to ask her to go home, but he'd chosen to just suck it up and move on. But he had firmly informed Stacy that this was family business that didn't concern her. As she stood over on the far side of the kitchen now, she listened to her boyfriend and his mother go on and on. She couldn't believe half the things they were saying. She was not naïve in terms of what Kalif had done as far as jumping on Hakim and even knocking his own mother on the floor, but this was still their son and brother. And no matter how much of a sinister human being they made him out to be, she thought that he had seemed as if he just wanted to belong. Stacy felt she had seen something in Kalif that she had never seen in Hakim. The prodigal son seemed to have a hungry drive and a strong confidence. She had heard it in his speech. Had seen it in his demeanor as he moved. And most certainly had noticed it in his eyes.

After they all sat down at the table and started to eat, Fatima had to excuse herself, as she had heard one of the babies crying.

Not wanting to cause a further rift between herself and Hakim, Stacy vowed to hold her peace. Yet she could not do so. "Hakim, I swear, I'm not trying to overstep my position. Especially after you asked—or should I say, ordered—me not to."

"Okay. And?" A disapproving expression on his face, Hakim looked up from his plate. Moving his fingertips around his fork, he felt his anger build. Though he was generally even tempered, he had had about all he was willing to take where his older brother was concerned. Far from being a fool, he, like Jada, had easily noticed the strange vibe that seemed to develop between Kalif and his girl. Despite the fact that he had held on to Stacy tightly, he hadn't been able to stop her from squirming free and going to Kalif's side to ease his so-called pain.

"I mean, at some point, don't you and Kalif have to forgive each other? You can be the bigger person," Stacy urged, wanting a reconciliation between the brothers and an end to their beef.

Hakim put his fork down. After moving the chair away from the table, he stood. Shaking his head, he decided to divulge to Stacy the underlying reason why Kalif had been exiled from the family. "Okay, guess what? Since I see you so much on his trail and think he's the victim here, check this out. You the real reason he can't come around here no more."

"What?" Stacy's curiosity had been piqued.

"Yeah, see, when I stopped going to the mosque all the time and started hanging out with you at church, what did you think was going to happen? What did you think my people were going to say? How did you think they were going to take that? I mean, I was raised with Islamic beliefs, and just like that, they think I turned my back on everyone. My mother was disappointed, but she felt I was old enough to make my own choices. My father was disappointed and pissed. He still is."

Stacy looked stunned. If Hakim's family harbored those feelings toward her, they had done a good job of masking them. "I know your mom is always super nice to me. But is that why your dad seems so standoffish?"

Hakim shrugged his shoulders and grinned. "Come on, Stacy. Why do you think that every time you come over here, he conveniently finds something else to do? Or somewhere to go? He doesn't like you. He doesn't even like seeing your face."

"I never noticed it, I guess. But wow. That's not cool at all."

"Well, pay attention next time. You'll see."

"Dang. Okay, I guess I will. But you didn't say what Kalif not being welcome has to do with me. I'm lost." Stacy was caught up in a whirlwind of truths exposed.

Hakim had been hiding the harsh reality of what had happened that night from Stacy. He truly cared for her and didn't ever want to do anything to hurt her feelings or break her heart. She was a nice girl and didn't deserve to suffer because of his family's hang-ups. However, she wouldn't stop pressing him. She wouldn't stop low key jocking Kalif, so she needed a dose of get right. "Because just like my father, Kalif doesn't like that I have stopped going to the mosque and hanging out with my Muslim friends. And for that, he blames you. They both do. So that day, like all the others, they ganged up on me."

"What?" Stacy's eyes bucked. "Are you serious right now or just playing around?"

"Naw, I'm dead-ass serious. As serious as this scar on my face. Kalif and my pops are thick as thieves. They always have been. Truth be told, the only reason he got kicked out was that my mother finally put her foot down and threatened to take the girls and bounce."

"Oh my God!"

Hakim continued with Stacy's strong double dose of reality, knowing it would break her spirit down. "So yeah, my father and Kalif was tag teaming, calling you a bitch and a ho. They would not stop. I kept asking them to stop. And my mother was begging them to leave me alone. But they wouldn't. Especially Kalif. He was calling you every single ugly name he could think of, saying you made me turn my back on Islam. When I finally had enough and stepped to him, it was on. We got to bucking."

Stacy was speechless. Maybe now that the peacemaker knew the truth, she would fall back on all that Kalif worshiping she'd been hell-bent on doing. After a strange silence, Stacy burst out crying. With her face buried in her hands, Hakim felt a small bit of remorse, but she needed to hear the real and get off his brother's nut sack. Wiping her tears, she announced that she was ready to go home and that she didn't know if she ever wanted to return. Without trying to persuade her to stay, Hakim obliged. Like her, he was too emotionally drained to argue.

As he drove Stacy home, Hakim made up in his mind that one day, somehow, his big brother would pay for all the pain, humiliation, and now heartache he'd caused in his life. Rasul and Fatima may have allowed Kalif to get away with treating people like they were no more than a piece of shit. They had sheltered Kalif from the consequences of most of his horrid actions. They'd blamed Kalif's violent outbursts on the fact that he was on meds or he was adopted, and they'd used that as an excuse not to mete out punishment. But to Hakim, that special treatment would one day cease. He'd make sure of that.

"I'll call you later," he stated as he pulled up to Stacy's house. It was more of a question than a statement.

"Yeah, we still have to talk about prom." She gave him a faint smile, indicating that although her feelings were hurt now, she'd get over it. She was optimistic. "And trust, one day your dad and brother will both like me."

"Neither one of them matters to me, Stacy. Believe that!"

When he pulled away from her house, Hakim thought about all the scholarship offers he had received and about his future.

By the time Fatima returned downstairs after calming down not one, but both the girls, the house was empty. The only thing she could do was shake her head, for she knew that somehow Kalif and his bad karma had ruined yet another family function.

# Chapter 15

*I swear, I don't know who my father thinks he is. I mean, what in the entire fuck? First, a nigga kicks me straight outta the crib like I really was sleeping there anyhow. Then, when I'm out here in these Detroit streets, doing my thing, putting in work, he hating. How in the hell he trying to block my hustle? I'm out here living my best life, and he letting my mother dictate his. I don't know what happened to the man my pops used to be. Maybe old age done crept up on him or some shit like that. Whatever the case is, ain't nobody or nothing gonna stop me or slow down my flow. I'ma get this bread until I take my last breath and Allah calls me home, accepting me into paradise. For now I'ma make this move and deal with the self-righteous "Do as I say, not as you may" Rasul Akbar.*

Not about to give it any more thought, Kalif put his game face on. After pulling up at the West Side gas station, he parked his truck over toward the end of the building, away from the pumps. He killed the engine, then sat back and gathered his thoughts, devising what exactly he was going to say. He'd been trying to get at Ibn ever since that awkward reunion with his baby brother, but he had not received an answer. Just as Rasul's cell was doing, Ibn's was going straight to voicemail. After texting once or twice, Kalif quickly figured out what must be going on.

*Ain't this about nothing. Pops probably got that dude so spooked, he really ain't gonna put me up on that next level of play a brother needs. But one way or another, I'ma make it do what it do.*

Kalif leaned over to the glove compartment and opened it. After grabbing a small stack of assorted bills he had inside the glove compartment, he counted out close to fifty-eight hundred. When he added what he had in his pocket, he ended up with eight racks in total. In the middle console, he kept rubber bands. Since he'd started hustling, he'd picked the trait up from his father, of all people. After double wrapping his funds with a royal-blue rubber band, he stuffed the money in his front pocket.

*Allahu Akbar.*

Kalif jumped out of the truck, then swag-strolled across the lot. Before he could make it a few yards, a man asked him if he could spare a few dollars. He shook his head no and kept walking. Then two teenagers promised him that they had the strongest weed in the city. Turning both of them down didn't deter their hustle. They went right on to the next person that pulled up. After entering the small building through the side-by-side glass doors, the seasoned thug headed toward the front counter. Seeing the same faces he'd seen when he met Ibn, Kalif felt at ease when they all greeted him as if he belonged. When they signaled for him to come behind the counter, as he'd done before, Kalif grinned.

Once back there, Kalif got right to it. He asked the older looking of the three guys back there, the one with the carved wooden cane, if he had heard from Ibn.

"No, I have not spoken to him since sometime yesterday. I thought he was having you meet him again up here.

But I guess that's not the case." The guy gave Kalif the eye as the other two made sure their pistols were handy.

Kalif saw the potential deadly play that was about to go down, and swiftly squelched any reservations the men may have developed. "Hold tight, fellas. I come in peace. I've been calling him, and he ain't hitting me back. I'm trying to do this business with him, and he bullshitting."

The older-looking guy, whose name was Nieem, nodded for his people to stand down as he rubbed at his long gray beard. The older man saw this as a possible opportunity, not a threat. He hadn't been ear hustling when Ibn and Kalif spoke at the gas station, but it had been hard not to overhear Kalif complaining about his father's blatant interference. "Look, I will try to call him for you. My cousin is crazy sometimes. He gets caught up in dressing fancy, messing with females, and does not take care of business that is important to family."

Kalif didn't say a word as Nieem placed the call. Instead, he made himself at home, taking a cold juice out of the rear of the cooler. After twisting off the top, he downed the apple-flavored juice in almost one gulp. By the time he was finished, he could tell that Ibn had answered for his cousin. By the sound of Nieem's tone and the look on the others' faces, it was not hard to realize the conversation was not going well. With each foreign word spoken, Kalif saw the chances of him getting some extra bread to really come up dwindling. He put both hands in his front pockets and felt the money he'd brought in with him. Even though whatever Ibn had in mind could help elevate him to the next level financially, Kalif was not in the habit of begging. He wasn't going to beg his mother to stay at the house. Beg his father to allow him to make money. And, lastly, beg Ibn's sand nigga with an attitude pussy ass to put him on.

After Nieem ended the call, he faced Kalif. "Okay, Kalif. It's like this. Ibn said your name got some sort of red flag by it. You must have caused another person some sort of grief. Or is it about his affiliation with your father? Tell me something, so I know how to proceed with you. Or I, like my foolish little cousin, will have to part ways with you. But don't worry. That juice is on me."

Nieem was used to dealing with regular hood fools that came into the gas station, asking for a handout, or stayed out there in the lot, begging. But this wasn't that. And never would be. If he was expecting a straightforward answer, Nieem did not receive that. He'd never met Kalif before yesterday. He did not know how the young man thought or operated. He didn't know that standing there, waiting for Kalif to plead his case, was a futile act. Whether he knew it or not, he was looking at a Detroit thoroughbred. Someone cut from a different cloth. A man whose pedigree would not allow him to grovel.

With great pride, and with his chest stuck out, Kalif stood his ground. He could care less where he was at. Or that he was at a disadvantage, given the number of potential foes in the room. He'd never let the next man hoe him, eight to eighty. As far as Kalif was concerned, he had learned the flipping-houses game and would make that do what it did. He was a hustler. Born to be in the streets and never go legit. So this denial of a favor was only a temporary minor setback.

Li'l James, Pit Boy, and Keys were hungry to put in work just because. Each of them was ready to get back to work. Although their pockets weren't particularly hurting, they definitely could use a bump. Amir wasn't hurting for cash any way it went. No matter what kind of dirt he did, he made sure that at 9:00 a.m. he was in class.

He was now in the second year of his pursuit of a bachelor's degree, and his parents made sure he was straight. Kalif was just as smart as Amir and Hakim, but he had decided long ago that the regular, straitlaced nine-to-five lifestyle was not for him.

"Old man, you funny as fuck with that mouth of yours. But dig this fly shit right here. I don't give two hot shit fucks if your peoples over there got guns on they hips or not. Unless they gonna produce them bitches and put in work, then they best fall back, 'cause I ain't scared to die. But I bet I skull drag all three y'all sand niggas around this bitch by them long beards first. Trust that."

"You talk big," Nieem managed to slip as Kalif ranted.

"Old man, I live big too. You better ask about me. And of course I don't know what you and Ibn was saying in that old, secret squirrel language and shit, but I ain't no dummy. Far from it. So if he don't wanna do any more business with me, I'm good with that. Not half-assed good with that. All the fuck way good. Tell that fuck boy I said I'm gonna eat regardless. The struggle ain't never that real for me to bow down to no man. I only lower my head to Allah."

Kalif dug his hand in his pocket. After removing the stack with the royal-blue rubber band, he peeled off a ten, since it was the smallest bill he had. "And after you just came on me about that weak-ass processed juice you around here selling to my people, here you go. And your petty, crippled ass, you can keep my change. Just consider it my li'l contribution to that Taliban you probably funding. Stay up and don't get deported."

Kalif turned to leave with confidence. He was heated that the old man and Ibn thought that they could treat him as if he was a chump. He had never once tried to portray that he was the richest man in any situation, but he was in the game. And the game he played dictated that if there was a way to make money, a real man would make it happen.

After he walked out the door, he encountered the same set of people posted up on the revenue prowl. By the expression on Kalif's face, the man wanting some spare change knew better than to try to push up on him for a contribution. That was a dead end and a no go for him. Yet, in true Detroit fashion, the guys trying to sell weed were relentless. No sooner had Kalif stepped foot out the door than they were on their hustle like flies on shit.

"Yo, we got that fire. Shit Kush," one said, hyped.

"Naw. I already done told y'all I'm straight."

Still, the other guy was persistent, hell-bent on not taking no for an answer. Cocky, he took his shot, cutting into Kalif. "Come on, dawg. Spend some of that bread I know you holding on to, to playboy with us. The play is good."

Kalif slowed down. Then he stopped altogether. His mind clicked. Sometimes he would put up with some random bullshit; other times he wouldn't. And the fact that these dudes had been on his head so hard and then had the nerve to call themselves sizing him . . . Well, he had a problem. Normally, he didn't get headaches; he gave them. But after that round he had just had inside with the old man, who had also tried to insult his gangster, it was go time. He felt one coming on.

"What the fuck you just say to me? Do y'all know me or something?" Kalif growled.

Not expecting that reaction, both guys kinda fell back. By the way Kalif was dressed and by the whip he was pushing, they knew chances were good that he was strapped.

"It's all good, my nigga. We was just trying to put you on, that's all. We good, though," said the second guy.

"So you slimeball bitches was trying to put me on? Imagine that. Where in the fuck they do that at? Y'all got me twisted."

"We said our bad, damn playboy. You bugging." The first guy threw up his hand as if he was dismissing Kalif.

Instantly enraged by their blatant disrespect, he ran up on one of them. With a clenched fist, he fired up on the guy. His fist slammed into the man's jaw several good times, and blood started to leak from his victim's mouth. Kalif could easily see that the dude was dazed from the attack. Allowing him to fall onto the black tar pavement, he set his sights on his homeboy, who seemed to be frozen in his tracks. When the two locked eyes, the guy snapped out of his trance and tried to get in motion. Sadly, it was too late. Kalif snatched him up by the back of his collar. After slapping him twice, he body slammed him. With both weed salesmen now lying side by side on the pavement, Kalif warned them about fucking with people who didn't wanna be fucked with. To add insult to injury, he then vindictively stomped on both their faces, rearranging their dental. Seeing even more blood spilled made his dick get rock hard.

Not fearing retaliation, Kalif turned his back. Slowly, he continued to walk toward his truck, praying that either of the men had the courage to want some more smoke with him. Kalif lived for days like this. If they had time for it, so did he. Before Kalif pulled off, he separated his money once more. After returning the original amount to the glove compartment, he was ready to roll. The cowards were still on the ground, nursing their wounds. *Fake-ass pussies*. He turned on the engine, and then he popped one of his Islamic speeches into the CD player. He wanted to get his mind right and centered as he drove. He'd tried to go another route with flipping the houses, but now it would be back to business as usual.

After pulling out into traffic, he weaved in and out as he drove down Joy Road. When he got to Greenfield Road, he made a left, then hit 96. He was headed back out to the room he was staying at. Once there, he would devise a plan and put a few irons in the fire and set a couple of traps. He would eat, and the streets would feed him, period.


Nieem went to the front area of the gas station, holding the ten-dollar overpayment for the juice. He peered out the door as Kalif, head held high, walked to his truck. He watched Kalif suddenly stop when he was interrupted by the pests that were relentlessly posted around his gas station. Nieem waited to see if he would purchase their product before he would pass judgment on Ibn's associate. The three men appeared to be having some sort of verbal exchange. Then, seemingly out of nowhere, Kalif lunged at one of the guys. Nieem witnessed Kalif putting his hands on the guy and then manhandling his partner. Holding on to his cane as his legs grew weak, Nieem got excited. It was like watching a prizefighter go to work. Nieem, a proud man dressed in Muslim garb and a fake good citizen was glad that the green light he had installed had been not working properly for months. Therefore, there was no video footage of the attack streaming to the police department, and the cops had nothing to post on

Facebook or other social media outlets if they decided to pursue this lawbreaker.

Watching the slick-talking, brutal beast finally drive away, the elderly man smiled as he rubbed his beard, the very same one Kalif had just threatened to skull-drag him by in the storeroom. He was not angered by the way that beast had just spoken to him; he was actually elated. Kalif had all the makings of a true warrior. Nieem could see in his eyes that he had integrity and would not fold for any man, no matter what the circumstances or the situation was. He knew that this Rasul, whom Ibn respected and feared so much, had indeed raised his son properly, old school style. Something deep inside of Nieem was saying that he and some of his colleagues' prayers had just been answered. After kicking the people begging off his premises, he headed back to the storeroom, then to his office. Once behind his desk, he pulled a small bag out of a hidden drawer. Fumbling with the contents of the bag through the plastic, he reached over for his cell. In his homeland language, Nieem spoke by phone to three different people, two of whom were overseas.

"*As-salamu alaykum*," Nieem greeted colleague after colleague, in great spirits and with blessed hope for the near future.

"*Wa alaykumu as-salam*," each colleague replied, elated to speak to Nieem.

In each conversation, after asking about their family's health and overall well-being and attending to other formalities, Nieem got to the reason for his call. "Yes, *aetaqid 'anana darabna aldhahab*. We have struck gold. *Laqad altaqayat lltw bijandiin*. Moments ago, I met a soldier. *Hu fi alwaqie mutawahish*. Yes, yes, he is indeed a savage."

   Nieem explained what he wanted to do, and all the
men were in agreement. They trusted Nieem's opinion
and knew he would not steer them or their consortium in
the wrong direction. The stage was set. After placing the
calls, Nieem sat back in his chair. Locking his fingers, he
rested his hands on his large stomach. After closing his
eyes, he replayed the encounter that had just taken place
in the storeroom. A slight smirk graced his face. Allahu
Akbar. *We will soon meet again, young Kalif. Very, very
soon.*

# Chapter 16

After retrieving his personal items from the locker in the prison's waiting room, Rasul headed to his vehicle. Blessed that he had not been forced to see the inside of a prison cell in over twenty years, he looked up to the heavens and thanked Allah for His saving grace. His homeboy was not as fortunate: he had just come from Baraga Max up north and was now being housed at Ernest C. Brooks Correctional Facility in Muskegon. S. P. Black was doing his third tour of duty. The first was for capital murder, and this go-around was for felon in possession of a firearm. Which to Rasul and many others was straight-up bullshit. How could any man that lived in the black-hearted city of Detroit not be expected to be armed at all times? It didn't matter what time of day or night it was, Motown had it jumping where crime was involved.

With real business on the floor to handle, Rasul knew he needed a face-to-face with his peoples. Besides hello and goodbye, there wasn't much of anything he chose to say over the phone or in letters. Fuck GTL's good recording asses and double fuck JPay's handwritten statements. Conducting anything on either one was an indictment waiting to happen. So when need be, a road trip to the Feds' joints take up north, down below, or even across state lines was nothing to take. Having gotten a clear understanding of matters with his fam, Rasul was now ready to head back to the city. Before pulling away from the prison, he grabbed his cell phone from under the seat, where he had it stashed. He hit the side button, and the phone's screen was illuminated. Rasul saw he had eleven missed calls, as well as five text messages and a few voicemails.

*Damn! What in the hell is going on with all this? Fatima, Hakim, and Kalif? Let me make these calls.*

He called Fatima first. No more than two complete rings sound before his irate wife answered.

"Hey, Fatima. What's wrong? What's going on?"

"You didn't listen to the voicemails I left you?"

"Naw. I just saw you called, and I called you right back. I didn't even read these text messages I got. But what's the deal? Tell me now."

"The deal is that horrid monster came by here earlier."

"What monster? What in the hell you talking about?"

"I'm talking about Kalif. He just showed up here out the clear blue sky."

"Okay and . . ."

"What you mean, okay and? Okay, and didn't you tell him he was no longer welcome over here?"

"Yeah, I did tell him you felt that way."

"Oh, so after all he did, you telling me you don't feel that way too? You just threw me under the bus? Wow!"

"Wow, nothing. What about forgiveness, Fatima? It's been months. I mean, after all, he is your son."

Fatima was silent for a moment as she chose her words. She knew her husband wasn't going to like her response. "No, Rasul, he is *not* my son. He never really was. No matter how much I tried to accept him as being so, he never was. Kalif is *your* son. Truth be told, he is the love child you and that rotten bitch Kenya wished y'all had had. Well, at least you wished. Now tell me I'm lying. You think I forgot how you played me over her back in the day? Remember?"

Rasul was silent as he recalled the conversation.

*"Look, Fatima, I already told you, there's no way in hell you gonna talk to me the way you did, let alone tell me what to do."*

*"You act like that's your woman, not me," Fatima cried out through his cell, which was on speaker.*

*Rasul continued to fumble with the bassinet he'd just purchased for the newborn baby boy, not really caring about what she was saying. "Where is this conversation going? You gave me my keys back, so that's what it is."*

*"So okay, Rasul, you choosing her over me? Are you kidding me?"*

*After a few seconds of dead silence, Fatima regretfully got her answer. "Yeah, I guess so." He lustfully thought about Kenya, who was upstairs, in his shower. "So go do you. I'm straight."*

*"You act like you wanna fuck that dirty bitch!"*

*"Maybe I do. So, like I said, do you!"*

The sound of Fatima's voice brought him back to the present. "Yeah, Rasul, my supposed loving and forever devoted husband, remember that conversation we had? Yeah, of course you do!"

Fatima went on, refusing to give him a moment to speak. It took him nearly five minutes to take control of the conversation, and when he did, his words were powerful. Rasul was aggravated. Fatima would not let go of the past, and he was sick and tired of begging her to do so. "I'ma tell you what. I'm done hearing you complain and whine. I'm over all your throwing up the past in my face, and I'm damn straight tired of you dragging that boy every chance you get. You never liked him from the jump, and it showed. I don't know what I was thinking about in the first place even marrying you. So guess what? You don't need to threaten me anymore about taking the girls and leaving. I'ma do you one better. I'm gone. I'll be by later to get some of my things. Shortly after that, you can expect that I will divorce you and move on. I will take care of my daughters, but I will move on. So yes, my dear, you are free."

After that exchange, Rasul didn't give his wife a chance to respond. Instead, he hung up on her so she could absorb what he'd just said. If she stepped to him in the correct manner, maybe he'd rescind what he'd said, or maybe he wouldn't. But one thing was for sure. The way she was treating Kalif was ending now, today, this second. She knew the deal when she said "I do" years ago. She knew that he and Kalif were a package deal.

Not giving Fatima any more thought, he left the prison premises and parked at a nearby McDonald's. There he read his text messages, which were all filled with empty threats from his wife. *Delete. Delete. Delete. And delete a few more times.* Then he proceeded to listen to his voicemails. Two of the most important ones, he replayed. They were from Kalif. He said he wanted to speak to him. He said it was very important. *Damn. See? Mystery solved. He didn't just pop up out of the clear blue sky. Kalif had called a few times, trying to get at me, and couldn't. So yeah, he came by the house. Big fucking deal. My son came home. Fatima be doing the most overreacting.*

After grabbing a coffee and filling up his tank, Rasul jumped on the highway. The next call he would make would be to his youngest son, Hakim. After hearing

Fatima's version of what happened, Rasul did not find it hard to guess what Hakim would have to say. After taking a nice-size gulp of the hot adrenaline booster, he dialed Hakim's number. His son picked up right away.

"Hey, son. It's me. What's going on? How you feel?"

"Not much, Dad. I'm just heated. Have you spoken to Mom yet?"

"Yes, son. We just spoke briefly. But what's going on that has you so up in arms?"

"Mom didn't tell you Kalif came over here, looking for you?" Hakim's tone was sarcastic, and his father sensed it right away.

"Matter of fact, she did. But why would that have you heated? Did he put his hands on you or something?"

"Well, no, but he was trying to show out in front of Stacy like he was some kinda big shot or something. Telling me to watch how I was speaking to him, like he was a boss."

"So he showed out in front of that girl you insist on running with, huh?" Rasul slowed his speed down when he saw a state boy lurking. "Yeah, okay, but once again I asked you, Did he lay hands on you or bring any harm to you, your mother, or the girls?"

Hakim had been down this road before. He knew it was no more than a dead end. His father would never change when it came to Kalif. And just as he was done with his brother, he would now add his father to that short list. "Never mind. I'm good. My bad for even bringing my issues with that bloodthirsty lunatic to you anyhow."

"Look, Hakim, you need to man up. You need to be responsible for you and how you carry your own self as a young man. Stop focusing on your brother and his faults, before I shine the light on yours. You do know you're human, don't you? We all are."

"Yeah, I know we all human," Hakim said begrudgingly.

"Okay, and just so you'll know, nine outta ten times moving forward, you probably won't have to worry about Kalif stopping by there, looking for me. So that's one less thing on your plate to worry about. Now you can have free time to read your Bible."

Hakim was done talking, as was Rasul. They ended the conversation before it got more out of hand. It had definitely been headed in that direction. Hakim's resentment of both Rasul and Kalif had only gotten worse. As it stood now, he wished them both to hell fire. As for Rasul, he next prepared himself to get back in touch with his oldest boy, who he always felt needed him the most. He'd heard from some of his Muslim brothers that Kalif was heading toward a lengthy prison sentence or down what could end up being a deadly trail. Rasul dialed Kalif's number, but after four or five rings, he met with a voicemail that wasn't set up yet. He'd try again later.

# Chapter 17

After he returned to the room he was sharing with Jada, it didn't take long for Kalif to notice something was different. The nightstand on her side of the bed had been cleared off. There was none of her nail polish, her lotion, or those crazy hair bonnets she wore. When he glanced over at the side of the bed, he realized that the huge bootleg Gucci duffel bag into which she stuffed most of her personal items was gone as well. The final sign that Jada was gone, possibly for good, was that all her Chinese beauty supply human-hair wigs, which she worshiped like gold, were missing from the dresser drawer.

Kalif fell back onto the center of the king-size bed. He kicked off his Tims, then pulled off his socks. Stretching out, he realized he would lose no sleep from Jada being gone. Sure, he liked her company from time to time, and she was mad loyal and helpful, but he wasn't into keeping no bitch that didn't want to be kept. Whatever reason Jada had for jetting was hers and hers alone. There would be no calls to inquire about her whereabouts. That wasn't how he operated. With his eyes closed, Kalif thought not about Jada being gone, but about how that old man had tried to play him like some common sucker back at the gas station. *If they think me and mines ain't gonna go for ours, they got the game messed up.* That was his last thought before he drifted off.

Nearing thirty minutes later, Kalif was awakened by his cell ringing. *Damn. What now?* He needed the rest physically and mentally, so he was annoyed he was being disturbed. He picked up his cell and looked at the screen. An unfamiliar number had popped up. He was not ducking or dodging anyone, so Kalif answered, but with an uneven, dry tone. To his astonishment, it was Nieem. *Oh hell naw. What this rude, ancient sand nigga want?* Wiping the sleep out of the corners of his eyes, he sat all the way up on the edge of the bed.

Not wasting time with any small talk, Nieem apologized for their "misunderstanding" earlier in the day. Then he invited Kalif to share a late meal at a restaurant in Dearborn, where they would discuss a business venture. Nieem mentioned that an associate of his had just been blessed with his eighth son and would be celebrating by feasting on fresh lamb, grill spiced chicken, brown rice, and Kalif's favorite, hummus. Kalif was all about business and all about good food. And since the old man came to him correctly and humbly, he asked no questions before swiftly accepting the dinner invitation. Nieem texted him the address of the restaurant. Ironically, it was the same one on where he'd met Ibn. And since it was located on Michigan Avenue, it wasn't too far out of the way. Seeing how it was a celebration in a city that was populated mostly by Middle Eastern people, Kalif would dress appropriately.

After the call, Kalif placed his cell on the charger, then turned the television on to watch the news, both local and national. After getting undressed, he took a dump, followed by a long hot shower. While he was in the shower, his cell rang once more. Later on, Kalif would find out he'd missed his father's call. But after linking up with Nieem later, would speaking to Rasul even matter? That depended on whether he wanted to order dessert or not. Either way it went, Kalif would start a fast come daybreak.

Jada was devastated. She felt hurt. She felt betrayed. She felt used and most of all bitter. Truth be told, although Kalif had never made her any promises, Jada had still thought deep down inside that even if he wasn't in love with her, he did have love for her. At least that was what he had claimed anytime she'd tried to bring up the subject of commitment.

Surrounded by her cousin and TayTay now, she tried to get herself together. Unfortunately, as brave as Jada attempted to be, the tears kept falling. Her heart was broken. The ride-or-die, down-for-whatever female had rolled the dice with a street nigga and had lost. Kalif had shattered her soul, and it seemed that he hadn't even noticed or didn't care. It had been hours since she'd taken all her belongings and abruptly left the hotel room. And still the love of her young life had not called to check on her or even to ask why. Jada knew for sure he'd been heading back to the hotel, because Jewels had been with Pit Boy when he and Kalif spoke. Her cousin had said she plainly heard Kalif say over the phone that he was going to the room to chill out and would be on the block later.

As she helped Jada get her things put up, TayTay stayed close, while Jewels went on the block to see if she could low key get some information about what was up with Kalif. She even thought if she hung around long enough, Kalif might show up himself. And if he did, she'd surely cut off into him about why he had fucked over her cousin. TayTay listened to Jada blame her untimely breakup with Kalif on some girl named Stacy. Jada said that if it wasn't for that "stick up the ass" whore trying to push up on Kalif, he'd probably be over here now, begging her forgiveness. Jada let it be known that just as the flirty female had checked Kalif out, he had disrespectfully done the same, as if Jada had not even been standing there. Jada wanted to scream. She wanted to punch a hole in the wall. And more than anything, she wanted to punish Stacy for the fact that Kalif wanted her.

TayTay, still depressed about the brutal rape she had suffered, continued to console Jada. And Jewels was on a mission to, more than likely, get her face damn near smacked off if she tried to check Kalif on her cousin's behalf. However, one truth had not been told. Kalif had never, not once, insinuated or hinted that he wanted Jada to leave the room they shared. This play was of her own doing, and it stemmed from her own jealous imagination. Jada started to second-guess her decision, but it was too late. She'd gone much too far to turn around, but she had not moved enough to go forward. For now, Jada was disoriented and full of regrets. But one thing was certain: she'd lost Kalif, probably forever.

# Chapter 18

When Kalif arrived at restaurant, he saw nothing but foreign vehicles parked in the lot. After going inside the restaurant, he was greeted by the hostess. Apparently, she'd been given a description of Kalif, because she didn't even ask him his name. Nor did she inquire about whom he was meeting with. He was instantly led to the rear area of the restaurant. As soon as Kalif bent the corner, he saw not only Nieem, who was seated at the head of the long table, but Ibn as well. There was also a few faces that were not familiar to him. Everyone happily greeted Kalif, and he was asked to have a seat near Nieem.

"Ah, I see you are dressed for the occasion. Nice, very nice." Nieem leaned over to get a closer look. "May I?"

"No problem. Of course." Kalif lifted his arm so that the old man could easily touch his sleeve. His outfit was one that had been custom made for him, so Kalif appreciated the compliment and the nods of approval from the others as well. With the exception of Ibn, they were all dressed in the same fashion as he was.

"I'm pleased and extremely impressed. You have my admiration, young man," Nieem said, giving Kalif his blessing, before turning his attention to his cousin. "See, Ibn? This is the way you need to dress. Not that trash you wear that makes you strut around town, being Hiram. You can learn a thing or two from this man here."

Ibn was mute. He had not opened his mouth even once yet, even to greet Kalif. Up until a few days ago, when Ibn ceased returning Kalif's calls, the two of them had been close, exchanging money and business ideas. Now there was dead silence between the two men, as if they'd never met before. Kalif found that strange, but he didn't force the issue. He was there to listen, observe, and see in what way Nieem could assist him in his effort to get a few of those sought-after Black Cards that Ibn had always bragged about.

"Thank you. All praises due to Allah," Kalif said as he opened both hands, palms turned upward.

As more men gathered at the table, Nieem requested that Ibn and Kalif switch seats. Each did as asked. Ibn still had yet to speak to Kalif or even look him in the eye, for that matter. Now that Kalif was seated at Nieem's right, the old man asked him a boatload of questions. Some were simple; some were deserving of a more detailed explanation.

"Young man, it's been brought to my attention that you are special," Nieem said.

"I'm no more special than the next man, in Allah's eyes, if he prays and follows most . . . well, some of the word revealed to Prophet Muhammad. May peace be upon his soul."

Once more Nieem was impressed with Kalif. He was envisioning even more what the future might hold if Kalif and his "family" struck an alliance. "But I heard that you are Hafiz. A most prominent and prestigious thing to be. Is this true?" All the Middle Eastern men gathered around the table seemed to put their conversations on hold as they awaited the young black man's response.

Kalif was never one to brag about the gift Allah had so graciously bestowed upon him. He had never understood how a person who followed Islam could not have the sacred book memorized. "Yes, it's true. Allah gave me that blessing when I was ten, almost eleven."

"Amazing, simply amazing. Well, of course I will not try to test you or challenge your word. I will ask only that you give us a few hours of your time this evening," Nieem responded.

"Hours?" Kalif was puzzled. He knew these types of celebrations could go on a long time, and he certainly intended on staying to the end, but he had had no idea he would be there for hours.

"Yes, and if you check the time, you will understand why we will all adjourn to the other room before the first course is served." Nieem rose from his seat. He needed assistance walking as his cane was not enough.

Kalif checked his cell. It was indeed time for prayer. He followed the other men, and they entered what could only be described as a makeshift mosque. After preparing themselves properly, the barefooted men stood behind their rugs. Nieem asked his young guest if he would do the honors. Kalif obliged and called them all to prayer. The men, especially Nieem, were once again stunned and impressed with Kalif when he pronounced each word perfectly, better than some of the men born in the old country.

When the time for prayer was over, the meal was served, and the celebration began. In keeping with Islamic tradition, no women were allowed in the room unless they were serving food. Each man had his fill of the Halal prepared dishes, and then Nieem and Kalif went together to a secluded location in the restaurant. Now away from the others, they could get down to the business of business. Which was what a patient Kalif had been waiting for. Pit Boy had texted him during dinner, saying it was not important but to get at him when he was free, so that was the only other thing Kalif had to handle. And of course, he had to return his father's call from earlier. But both of those calls could wait.

"First of all, let me offer my apologies yet again for our little misunderstanding. It is never my intention to speak out of turn to one of my business associates." Nieem tipped his head, showing remorse.

"Business associate? Is that right? How so?"

Nieem was a man of action. He had always felt that mere words were not enough. "Yes, Kalif. Unlike Ibn, I see you and me doing great business together. Great business beneficial to us both. You like making huge sums of money, don't you? I mean, we all can stand to have more of it in our possession."

Kalif was indeed intrigued. He sat back in the chair and folded his arms, waiting for the plan to make all these huge sums of money to be revealed. "Of course I do. I'm listening with both ears open. So please fill me in."

Nieem then signaled for the man who'd help him walk to come over. He emerged from the shadows in a corner of the room. When Nieem extended his hand, the man placed a small plastic bag in it, then dismissed himself. "This is how, Kalif. These right here will make us all millions very quickly, if done right."

Kalif looked disappointed, and it showed. He'd taken time out of what was a long day to get dressed and break bread with a bunch of men twice his age, and for what? To be shown a bag of small white pills, with the promise that he'd be a millionaire with the quickness. "With all due respect, Nieem. You can't be serious. You think that's something so new? Everybody and they mama and mama's mama got Percs. That hillbilly heroin ain't shit special."

Nieem looked over at his manz and shook his head. "See, that's the problem right there with not only you but other seasoned moneymakers as well. You all don't see the bigger picture. The international picture. See, these are not the regular Percocet, oxycodone, or even tramadol you have flooding the streets right now." Nieem opened the small plastic bag and emptied the contents onto the table. After picking up one of the light beige pills, he held it up and then suggested that Kalif do the same. With a smile on his face, Nieem went on to explain the importance of what they were holding and how they could change the drug climate in Detroit and the surrounding areas with these pills. "Son, this is called Captagon. Have you ever heard of that?"

Nieem had Kalif's interest now. He told the old man that no, he had not heard of this, and he urged him to continue.

"Well, it's like a combination of all the pills that I mentioned. Those are the ones that's flooding the streets now, correct? And also they are dipped in a low grade of heroin. It's like a two-for-one high. My people have nicknamed it Captagon Dip, or CD for short."

"Yeah, like I said, everyone slinging them bitches." Kalif shook his head, thinking about how the game had changed since even he had started out. He'd overheard his father and his boys complaining about the same thing. Too much accessibility to everyone. No exclusive come up.

Nieem laughed at Kalif's choice of words, his "nigga slang," as he and his people commonly referred to it in their own language. "Well, trust when I tell you everyone doesn't have these bitches. These are shipped straight from Saudi Arabia and Syria. Uncut, highly addictive, and sometimes lethal if misused. If you make the proper moves, like I said, we both can be rich." He paused. "Or, in my case, richer," he joked.

"I've never heard of it. I mean, what's it make a person do? Is it an upper or a downer? Is it gonna have people out here like crackhead zombies or like them nodding dope fiends?"

"I know you are young, but have you ever heard of mixed jive? Some of everything was added to the heroin. It made the people nuts. Well, this is kinda like that, in the way that it will have the user being bigger than life and begging for more."

"Are you serious?"

"Yes, Kalif, extremely serious. Matter of fact, you have one of those smartphones. Google it, as you young people say, and check it out for yourself."

Kalif did just that. Instantly, the pill he'd known nothing about until now popped up in the search engine. Amazed, he started to read to himself.

*Abuse of fenethylline, with the brand name Captagon, is most common in Arab countries. Counterfeit versions of the drug continue to be available, despite its illegality. Captagon is the most popular narcotic on the Arabian Peninsula. Many counterfeit "Captagon" tablets actually contain other amphetamine derivatives that are easier to produce, and they are pressed and stamped to look like Captagon pills. Some counterfeit Captagon pills that have been analyzed do contain fenethylline, however, indicating that the illicit production of this drug continues to take place.*

*This drug used by militant groups in Syria. It is man-ufactured locally by a cheap and simple process, and it sells for between five and twenty dollars per pill. Militant groups also export the drug in exchange for weapons and cash. Though Islamic law forbids the consumption of alcohol and drugs, many users there see Captagon as a medicinal substance. Soldiers on the front lines of the Middle East's deadly wars consume the pills daily. The pills give them a complete sense of fearlessness. The weak become strong. The strong become even stronger, and those facing death are not scared to die.*

Kalif had read enough. Being on prescription medi-cation, he'd never, not once, dipped in heroin, let alone heard of Captagon. Speechless, he lifted his head. Nieem was staring him in the face and grinning.

"Okay, so what do you think? Can you do something with these or not?" the old man asked. "I have access to millions of these little moneymakers. The reason me and my people have not tried a heavy push on them before in the United States was your people."

"My people? What's that supposed to mean?"

"No offense, but your people are creatures of habit. They get their minds on one way of doing things and stick to that way even if they fail to see progress. Think about this. Cocaine was just cocaine until someone came up with the idea of transforming it into crack. Let's be honest, besides the beauty supply game and those damn Church's Chicken restaurants, my people just about have Metro Detroit on lock. They have the gas stations, the liquor stores, grocery markets, and now real estate. Are you going to just be another person on the sidelines, or are you ready to get into the game?"

Kalif could not argue with the old man's reasoning or logic. Nieem went on to explained how he saw their new venture turning into an unbelievable amount of revenue for young Kalif, enough to catapult him to near kingpin status.

"Why me?" Kalif questioned, pushing back from the table. "It's plenty of dudes out here that been getting money in the dope game that wanna come up. This ain't really my thang."

"Why not you? You are Muslim like us. We are a family because of that bond. Those others have been doing what they do for years and have grown stagnant, for the most part. You, Kalif, are hungry and yet still loyal. You can move among your people and make a name for yourself, We cannot do that. And just because it is not your thing now, that does not mean it cannot be your thing soon. We are not trying to reinvent the game, just elevate it. Ibn has informed me that your father, Rasul Akbar, a very great, well-respected man, has frowned upon you dealing with me and others. And I do understand if you choose to turn this offer down. However, if you are your own man, which I think you are, you will at least consider it. Pray on it and maybe step out on faith."

Nieem gave Kalif the small plastic bag filled with Captagon pills dipped in heroin. All he asked was for the young hustler to test them out and see if he found that there was money to be made. On the way out of the restaurant, Kalif locked eyes with Ibn. Still no words passed between the two of them. Once back in his truck, Kalif stashed the pills. Before pulling off, he thought long and hard about whether he should reach back out to his father.

# Chapter 19

It was a new day. The sun was shining bright. The birds were chirping, and Kalif had just awoken from some of the best sleep he'd had in what seemed like months. He didn't know if it was because he had the entire king-size bed to himself or if it was the promise of making more money than he had the day before. After taking a piss, he cleaned himself and prepared to pray. Praying would normally take him no more than ten minutes, but Kalif spent well over an hour in deep thought and prayer.

Today he would start his fast, something all the mental professionals he'd ever seen had advised against. Kalif need to be on his medication not some days, but all days. And when taking those pills, he needed food in his stomach for them to be effective. It was no secret to most, and it was becoming more apparent to others, that Kalif was on the verge of becoming more unhinged as the weeks went by. Jada had attempted to keep him levelheaded, and now that she was gone, all bets were off. Still, Kalif kept his eye on the prize. He asked Allah to guide his hand in the next steps he would take. He asked Allah to rid his mind of impure thoughts and unholy urges. Kalif pleaded with Him to remove justifiably any persons that meant him no good or would bring him harm. Even though he was estranged from his family, he prayed for grace for them as well.

Once off the prayer rug, Kalif retrieved the bag of CDs from the nightstand. As he held the bag up, he imagined the implications of Nieem's claims. He wondered if what he was holding would indeed get him and his boys off of craps and keep them there. After removing his cell from the charger, he called Amir. When he received a text saying that Amir was in class until eleven, Kalif then hit up Pit Boy. He asked him to get the fellas together and meet him on the block around noon. Pit Boy informed Kalif that he could consider it done.

Now that that was in motion, Kalif had to handle the next bit of business at hand. Snatching his duffel bags off the top rack of the closet, he repeated what Jada had done the day before. He placed as many of his belongings as he could into the three oversized bags. After realizing they would not be enough, he carried those to his truck and then found the housekeeper, who was making her rounds. Always happy to see Kalif, who tipped her weekly, she smiled when she saw the good-looking, generous young man approaching. Kalif asked for several garbage bags and told her that he was moving on. Although she was sad to see her favorite extended-stay resident go, she wished him well.

Once back in the room, Kalif picked up where he had left off and gathered the remainder of his items. Of course, he found some things that belonged to Jada. He could have been an asshole and simply discarded them, but that was far from his style. And doing that would bring him no great pleasure. He wasn't mad she was gone. In fact, he was indifferent. He placed those things in a separate bag and threw that bag in the rear of his truck, with the others. When he swung by his house, which she was no doubt now staying in with her homegirls, he'd drop off the bag. After settling up with the front desk, he jumped into his vehicle.

From Sterling Heights, he drove into what would be considered the center of downtown Detroit. Kalif had to make a quick stop at the Thirty-sixth District Court. After clearing the metal detectors, he stood in line to pay a few tickets that were nearly due. When that task was completed, he pulled out of the parking lot and headed toward Metro Airport. He had nothing against Jada. And although she had never given him any reason not to trust her, Kalif felt it was wise to switch up where he was laying his head up. He knew women were emotional creatures and would put salt in the game at any time, even if they were unprovoked. When he was least thirty-eight to forty miles in the opposite direction of the old hotel, he wisely chose another hotel chain altogether. Then he paid the front desk to register him under an alias, claiming to be the stepson of one of the Pistons. Of course they obliged. Once he had all the bags transferred from his truck to room 217, he checked his cell for the time. It was almost noon.

Pit Boy was posted, as were Li'l James and Keys. Amir was on his way. Each wondered what was going on that had Kalif wanting to meet up. It had been well over a month since they'd all gotten together in one place, so this had to be about money. Or at least they hoped it was. A few minutes went by, and Amir was now waiting as well. Pit Boy checked the time as he led his dogs around the back to their kennels. By the time he had put food in all their bowls and given them water, Kalif was pulling up.

"What up, doe fellas?" Kalif called.

"What up, doe boss man? What it do?" Keys said. He was the first to give Kalif a fist pound.

After all the formal bullshit was done between the five men, it was time to put the business at hand on the floor. They all headed into Pit Boy's basement and then stepped over dog toys and a few huge bags of dog food as they made their way over to an old oak table in the corner. Once they were all seated, Kalif pulled out the plastic bag Nieem had given him. He tossed it into the middle of the table so that all of them could see it.

"So yeah, I know traditionally we've always tried to stay away from pushing drugs, especially pills, to make our money. And before y'all get started, I felt the same way when the hustle was brought my way," Kalif told them. "Everybody out here with pills and shit. But this is different. Much different. This shit gonna separate us from the rest of them lames."

Amir reached for the bag. After opening it, he examined a few of the pills. Kalif encouraged the others to do so as well. Just as he had never seen a pill like this, they were lost too.

"Dawg, what are these?" Li'l James asked after sniffing them and holding a few up to the light.

"Yeah. What's these markings?" Pit Boy rocked back and forth in his chair, almost falling backward.

Kalif let the suspense build up long enough. Then it was time for an explanation of the kind of pills these were. "So, y'all, take y'all phones out. Go to Google, or whatever y'all use to search with, and type in these letters. C-a-p-t-a-g-o-n. Then read. I'ma wait."

Kalif dumped the rest of the pills out of the bag, then watched the other men. One by one, each of his crew members raised his head, with a smile and a look of astonishment on his face.

"So, um, yeah. What y'all think?" Kalif gave each of them a look. "Oh yeah, I almost forgot. Each pill is dipped in a low grade of heroin. A two-for-one high," Kalif said, repeating what he'd been told.

After fielding question after question, Kalif asked for the general consensus about the pills. His crew members assured him that they were about to elevate their game. Even Amir, who was super hesitant about dealing drugs of any sort, was on board. Kalif reassured them that he had a solid, helluva connect, and that if he came up, they were going to come up as well. The deal right now was for them to split up the pills in the tester bag and then pass them out to people they knew who were hooked on them Percs and any other pills. Those addicts would be their targets. If they liked the crazy, courageous, and addictive high that the articles the crew had all read promised, then securing more bags would be forthcoming. The pill underworld game and the city would soon belong to them.

As they dispersed to put the product in the streets, Pit Boy pulled Kalif to the side. He told him that Jewels had come on the block the night prior, trying to be slick. "Yeah dawg, I don't know what's going on with you and ole girl, but her cousin was trying to pump a nigga for information."

"Oh yeah?" Kalif shook his head and ran his hand across his face, glad he had switched rooms.

"Yeah, but you already know me. Even if I knew shit, number one, it ain't none of my business. And number two, it ain't none of my business to tell. So instead of getting what she called herself coming for, I sent the bitch back with her mouth tasting like my dick and nuts."

Both of them laughed, but Kalif still didn't speak about Jada. As far as he was concerned, the only thing on his mind was getting on with Nieem. Anything else was and would be a distraction.

# Chapter 20

*Investment* was the word of the day. Kalif had set his crew in motion in one of his ventures, and now he had to deal with the other. He made a few calls and told all the workmen who were not already at one of his houses to meet him there. With the possibility of lots of money on the horizon, it was time to pick up the pace of this project, complete it, and then move on to the next one. The basement bathroom at this house needed to be completed, as well as the rear deck and patio. And Kalif wanted a new two-car garage built, but that would be later on down the line, just in case he decided to keep the house and not flip it as he and Ibn had originally planned.

When he arrived at the two-story brick dwelling off of Dexter, Kalif was elated to see that the front landscaping was finished and the left portion of the roof had new shingles. After he pointed out this and that, the numerous workers had a clear understanding of what was expected of them and the time frame they had to get it done. He assured them that bonuses were possible if they came in before the deadline.

Kalif took notice of not only nosy-ass Jewels's car in the driveway but Jada's as well, which reminded him of something. After popping his car's rear hatch, Kalif grabbed the plastic bag that contained her things. Using the key, he let himself inside the house. He was placing the bag on the dining-room table when he overheard voices upstairs. Without saying a word, he went back out just as quickly as he'd come in. Kalif's business there was done. He jumped back in his truck and drove off, hoping to make afternoon prayers at the Wayne State mosque.

As she stared out the top window and watched Kalif drive off, Jada's heart broke a little bit more. Not only had it been over twenty-four hours since she vacated the hotel room, and he'd not called or texted her once to check on her, but now he had just been here at the house and had not said a word to her. She knew full well that he'd seen her car parked up in the driveway. She couldn't believe it. This had to be some sort of bad dream.

When she'd seen him pull up, she had automatically assumed he was coming to beg her to come back. Snatching the bonnet, the one that he used to complain about so much, off her head, Jada had run to check herself out in the mirror. The workmen there had talked to Kalif, and she hadn't been able to make out what they were saying. But she'd known when the voices stopped. She heard someone unlock the dead bolt on the black steel security gate. Jada ran to the other side of the bedroom, sat on the edge of the bed, and pretended she was looking through her cell. She waited for Kalif to call out her name, but he didn't. She stared at the door, waiting for it to swing open, but it didn't. Jada was dumbfounded about what was taking him so long to make himself known. She tiptoed to the window, not wanting him to hear her footsteps on the wooden floorboards. When she got there, she was amazed, pissed, and salty. Kalif was getting back in his truck. And a minute later he drove away. Her feet seemed to be stuck to the floor. Her legs felt wobbly, and her mouth dry. He was really gone. He really didn't give a fuck about her. Jada wanted to scream and shout. She wanted to tear something up. Instead, she threw herself on the bed and cried until she could cry no more.

Jewels and TayTay wanted to stay out of it. TayTay was an emotional wreck herself and was much too weak minded to help the next person. And her cousin had tried to gather intel the night before and had ended up with nothing but a sore throat to show for all her efforts. The rest of the crew members were off doing their own thing and were barely there anyway. After figuring out that she had to be her own support system, Jada finally stopped the tears.

Nursing a headache, she took a few Motrin and turned on the shower. Making sure the water was as hot as she could possibly stand it, she stripped down, stepped inside the shower stall, and stood underneath the three-nozzle showerhead. She stayed in there until the water turned cool, but her mind still wasn't right. She could not fathom how, after all the time she had spent on Kalif and all the devotion she had shown him, he didn't have it in him to at least ask why she'd left. *That arrogant-ass, crazy lunatic. He ain't shit! All he cares about is fixing these low-budget hood houses. I should burn this bitch to the ground!* Part of her wanted to call him and curse him smooth the fuck out. But Jada fought her own emotions so that she could refrain from doing that. She had to have some pride left if she wanted to look herself in the mirror.

Distraught, she had to do something to make herself feel better. With her hair still damp and with no makeup on, she threw on a baseball cap and a tracksuit. Without a second thought, she decided to go to the mall and actually buy something extravagant instead of stealing it. Whenever Kalif had needed some extra money for whatever, she'd given it to him. This time she'd jack her funds off on herself and herself alone. Not saying a word to Jewels or TayTay, she left the house. When the workmen tried speaking to her, out of character, Jada ignored them and walked straight to her car.

With nothing in particular in mind to purchase, Jada slowly strolled through the mall. She stopped to get a few chocolate chip cookies and munched on them while window-shopping. Still upset, from time to time she had to fight back the tears, but she tried to remain strong. Having just finished off her second cookie, she heard her name being called. Looking over to the other side of the mall, Jada thought she had to be dreaming or having a nightmare. Before she could really focus, the girl said her name once more and this time headed in Jada's direction. Surrounded by a group of her friends, the girl greeted her. "Hello, Jada. I thought that was you. It's me, Stacy, Hakim's girlfriend. Remember? I'm out here looking for a prom dress for our big day. What about you?"

*Oh my fucking God! Not this troublemaker. Not now, of all times.* Jada was stunned. She'd seen the young girl only briefly, so how Stacy could remember her name right off the bat or even place her face was beyond her. "Yeah, I remember who you are." Jada had to force herself to speak. The last time she'd seen the girl, she'd wanted to slap her face, and not much had changed. The headache Jada thought the Motrin had cured was back, and this time it was twice as painful. *I swear I hate this li'l bitch. I don't see why Kalif was all in your face anyway. Look at you, trying to be all like you white or some shit. Talking all proper.*

"Sis, you look so different, I barely recognized you. I can call you sis, right? I mean, after all things considered, huh?" Stacy had a huge smile on her face, which showed her braces. "And I hope y'all can make it to our prom send-off."

*Good ho. I ain't here for your man-stealing ass to recognize. And fuck you, Hakim, and that funky prom! I hope somebody Carrie your ass!* The normally high-profile diva caught a glimpse of her reflection in one of the store windows. She was so depressed from what Kalif had done earlier that she looked a hot mess and hadn't even realized it. A far cry from how she had been put together the afternoon they met. Jada wanted to fade into the darkness. "Yeah, well, I gotta go. I was just running in here to get something real quick."

"What? Some cookies?" one of Stacy's friends interjected smartly, trying to be funny.

While the other girls in the small group giggled, Stacy did not. "Y'all shut up. Jada, I'm sorry about that. It's just that you have some crumbs on your shirt and a small bit of chocolate or something on your front tooth."

Jada looked down. Stacy was right. She did have cookie crumbs on her shirt. After brushing them off, she used her tongue to clean off her teeth, hopefully. Watching her do all that, the young girls giggled once more at her expense. However, this time Jada was not having it. This time she got enraged and ready to fight.

"You know what? Y'all some rude little bitches!" she barked.

Dressed preppy like Stacy, each girl turned her nose up at Jada, as if she was no more than filth. Something in her snapped. It was like they were all Kalif five times over, saying she was not good enough to be with him.

Stacy tried again to be the peacemaker and diffuse the situation, but for Jada, this only made matters worse. It reminded her that Stacy was the real reason that she wasn't with Kalif anymore, and that she was out here in public, looking crazy.

"Look, we gonna go," Stacy told her. "Tell Kalif I said hello and I hope I will see him . . . oh, and of course you real soon. Take care." Stacy rushed her friends away before Jada had a chance to respond.

*No, this little bitch didn't just tell me to tell my man hello. Who in the fuck do she think she is? Her and her stanking friends standing around, making fun of me, like I'm the joke. I knew I hated that ho off rip. If Kalif wasn't all up in that bitch face and her in his, shit would still be the same. She fucked up my entire life and future. Now little Miss Perfect out here bragging about some dumbass prom. Shit! We'll see if she even make it to that stupid shit! If my life gotta be fucked up, hers gonna be too! I'm done getting fucked over!*

Jada snapped. Her mind was gone. She had needed help for some time now, but she had never sought it out. While she had been so busy helping Kalif with his mental health, she'd failed to maintain hers. Being paranoid was a condition both Jada and Kalif suffered from. And now it was rearing its ugly head. An emotional wreck, she was focused on revenge for something that she imagined took place. When her cell rang several times, Jada didn't even bother to see who was calling. She was busy, on a mission.

Trying her best not to be seen, she followed Stacy and her friends throughout the entire mall. Once they left the mall, she followed them all to Stacy's car. Then she climbed in her own car and followed Hakim's beloved, flirtatious girlfriend as she dropped each of her homegirls off. After the last one got out at a mini mansion in Palmer Woods, Stacy was in the car alone. Jada wanted to make her move. As they drove past the old State Fairgrounds, they went across Eight Mile. Woodward Avenue was crowded, and Jada almost lost sight of her mark. She stayed at least two cars behind as Stacy got on I-696, heading east. In Jada's twisted mind, this was it. This was when it was going down. When Stacy exited the freeway, Jada would ram her car from behind, causing it to flip over. If the devil was on Jada's side, the young girl would not survive.

Stacy got over into the far right lane. Seconds later, she put on her blinker. Jada saw the red flashing light and got ready to make her move. She checked all her mirrors, knowing she'd have to have perfect timing so that she wouldn't kill or injure herself while trying to take Stacy out of the game. Jada got all the way over, cutting off a late-model Grand Prix with rims. Now only one car behind Stacy, Jada had to make this thing appear to be an accident. *Five, four, three, two . . .* Her countdown had almost reached one when a state boy came out of nowhere, lights flashing, ruining Jada's plan. His flashing lights caused everyone to slow down and merge to get out of his way.

Aggravated that her original plan had failed to work out, Jada became even more adamant about making Stacy pay. Now top side, she continued to follow her to her house. As Stacy turned into her driveway, Jada slowly crept by, eyeballing her hard. As she turned around at the end of the block, she watched Stacy go inside the ranch-style house. Totally deranged by this point, she quickly figured out what her next move would be. First, she went to the Dollar Store. Once there, she grabbed two huge plastic containers with screw-on tops. Then a gas can.

After she left the store, Jada headed in the direction of a gas station. Conniving, she parked her car a block from the station and walked over, with the gas can in hand. When she got to the gas station, she asked the attendant for three dollars' worth of gasoline. As part of her act, she claimed, loudly enough for other customers to hear, that she'd run out of gas. Almost in tears and looking disheveled, she announced she had no more money than the crumpled bill in her hand. Jada then fake begged the cashier and a few customers to help her out.

"Sir, excuse me, but can you please help me out with a few dollars? Or at least take me back to my car?" Jada asked one white man, but she was quickly cut off by his agitated wife, who got out of their vehicle and answered for her husband.

Others disregarded her pleas for help as well. Jada made sure to tell some of them thank you, anyway, and give them a smile. She then headed over to the pump and filled the gas can, along with both plastic containers.

With ill intentions on tap, her bad day was about to get better. She returned to the house she'd seen Stacy go into, and then she parked a few doors down. She didn't care who was in the house. It was what it was. If there were more casualties than Stacy's rotten ass, so what? After making sure there were no prying eyes watching, Jada removed the gas can and the two containers from the car and tiptoed onto the front porch of the house. She poured gasoline all around. Then she headed to the side door, which she doused with gasoline. Next, she walked around to the rear door and saturated it as well. The remainder of the strong-smelling, highly flammable chemical she let drip down on the hood of the vehicle Stacy had driven. Dumbly, she sat all three now empty containers she'd used on the rear stairs of the house.

After removing a red lighter from her back pocket, Jada grabbed a bunch of sales flyers that was lying near the trash cans. She lit one after the other, until she had four in total, and then she tossed one at each door to the house. As flames licked the doors, she threw the last lit flyer on Stacy's car. Then she took off running back to her car before Stacy's house became engulfed in flames.

After driving around the corner, Jada pulled over and finally looked at her cell phone while she waited for Stacy to be burned alive. Her cousin had called, but Jewels would have to wait. Jada had important business on the floor right now. In Jada's twisted mind and way of thinking, if the youngster Stacy was gone, Kalif would come and beg her to return to his side. As she sat in the car and nibbled on the last chocolate chip cookie she had in her bag, she wondered what Kalif was doing. It took a special type of crazy to recognize crazy. That was why she had always felt they were the perfect match. Seconds later, Jada was geeked when she heard fire trucks off in the distance. Stacy's house was ablaze.

*Yeah! Burn, bitch! Burn! Burn to the fucking ground with that funky ho inside!*

# Chapter 21

The feedback on the Captagon Dip, aka CD, the guys had received was more than impressive, just as Nieem had promised it would be. Each one that came on the block had a wild story to tell. Keys bragged that the handful of pills he'd passed out in the East Seven Mile and Van Dyke neighborhood and in parts of Black Bottom had had the addicts running around behaving as if they couldn't get hit by the cars they bravely walked in front of. When they'd been outside of the liquor store, begging for spare change, they hadn't taken no for an answer and had run up behind people. They also had ignored the requests to stop leaning on people's cars that were parked in the lots, and they'd thrown hands with each other until they were exhausted. Keys had just looked on in amazement at how fast the new magic moneymakers had caught on. He reported that he'd been around the way for only ten minutes or so before the pills kicked in. The high had been instant, just like the customers liked.

Li'l James and Pit Boy had experienced much the same reactions when spreading their portion of the testers in Southwest Detroit, Downriver, and the Cass Corridor. Amir had hesitantly given his to drug addicts he knew that stayed in the homeless shelter in Highland Park. Unlike the others, he hadn't waited for the addicts to give him a personal report. He had just sat in his car a little ways down and had watched the madness soon erupt.

Not to be left out, Kalif had put in work too. With the majority of the Captagon pills in his possession, he'd headed to the Brightmoor area of Detroit. While it was not heavily populated with working residents—or with any residents, period, for that matter—the ones that did live or hang out there were perfect. Not trying to hide what he was doing, Kalif had pulled up and set up shop. After passing out every pill, he'd told them he'd be back around sometime tomorrow if they wanted to get at him.

Now that their traps were set throughout the various parts of the city, it was time to sit back and hope they were onto the next big thing. If they got in on the ground floor, no matter how many wannabe imitators came along, trying to move heavy amounts of their come-up drug, they would be the originators and would make the majority of the revenue.

While the guys sat around chilling and just kicking it, Kalif's cell rang. After taking it out his pocket, he looked at the screen. *Damn. It's my pops.* He still had not returned Rasul's call from the night before. And at this point, given that what he had on the table was on the verge of skyrocketing, he doubted he ever would. Instead, Kalif shot Rasul to his voicemail, which wasn't even set up, on purpose. *Right about now, I ain't trying to hear that negative shit he gonna say. Especially since he still out in the streets, doing low-key bullshit hisself. It don't matter if it's old game or new game. Game is game.*

"Still no damn answer. I swear, that boy is gonna be the death of me. If I say go left, his ass goes right. If I say go up, you can best believe he's going down. I just don't understand him. I done tried working with him since he was little, and the outcome has always been the same. Kalif going against the grain." Rasul was venting to his best friend, Abdul. The two had met up for dinner not only so they could discuss in person what S. P. Black had told Rasul, but also so that Rasul could reveal to Abdul that he'd packed some of his belongings and moved out of the house and away from Fatima.

"Come on now," Abdul replied. "You know Kalif gonna be Kalif, so stop beating yourself up about it. You've always done the best you could where he was concerned. Allah knows your true heart for that boy, so that's enough. And as for Fatima . . ." He paused.

Rasul lowered his head, not wanting to hear the speech that was forthcoming. "Go ahead, man. I'm listening."

Abdul went on. Not only did he repeat the laws of Islam and what it said in the Koran about breaking up the family, but he also reminded Rasul about what he already had considered. "Fatima is still younger. Younger than us both. So she will remarry. Do you really want another man raising your daughters? Kalif and Hakim are both grown, but you got babies, girls no less."

Rasul didn't say a word. He just reached for his coffee, sat back, and thought about what his longtime friend had said. But for now, he and Fatima were broken.

# Chapter 22

Jada was ecstatic and still very much zoned out. It was as if she didn't understand the true implications of what had just happened. As she sat listening to the fire trucks and ambulances get closer, she felt as if she'd served justice on the young, worrisome tramp in training that had ruined her chance at happiness. The sirens were on the very next block. She could easily tell. Jada was beside herself. For her, it was as if it was Christmas, New Year's, Easter, and her birthday all rolled up into one.

*This is what she gets. Now maybe next time she will think twice about being all up in the face of the next female's man. That side chick jump-off shit might fly with some bitches, but I ain't with the man-sharing shit, in the dark or otherwise. Well, I guess my job is done here.*

Satisfied she had made her point, the crazed arsonist started her car and drove off. As she passed by the flashing lights that filled Stacy's block, once again she prayed that death was in the air. In much better spirits than when she had left the house, Jada went through the McDonald's drive-through and ordered a vanilla milk shake. She wanted an ice cream, but as always, their machine was down, so the milk shake would have to do. After she had eaten all those cookies and burned a bitch alive, a cool treat was exactly what she needed. Sipping on the straw, she drove back to the house and pulled up in the driveway. She parked her vehicle exactly where Kalif had seen it last. Most of the workmen were still there. After the way she had given them the evil eye at the beginning of the day, this time each man ignored her as she approached. But Jada was back to her old friendly self.

"How's everyone doing this evening? How y'all feeling?" she asked as she pranced by without a care in the world.

The men just nodded hello as all four of them took notice of the strong smell.

One worker asked if the others smelled it. "*Hueles eso*?"

Another replied that he did and that it smelled like gasoline. "*Huele a gasolina*."

"*Y por qué huele a eso*?" asked the first worker who had spoken.

"Look, don't ask why she smells like that," their foreman barked. "Just *regresemos al trabajo*. Okay? *Eso no les concierne*! You understand? It's none of your business! Just hurry up. It's almost seven."

With the exception of their foreman, the Mexican workers were all undocumented. The foreman often advised them to keep a low profile to avoid the possibility of Immigration being called. When Jada went into the house, their heads went back down, and they continued to work.


Very much in need of another shower, Jada jumped right out of her clothes. She simply tossed them in the corner of the bedroom, as if she was immune to their strong smell. Upon noticing the time, she grew sad, realizing it was going on forty-eight hours and still she had received no calls or texts from Kalif. But knowing that she had solved one of the roadblocks that was stopping him from wanting her once again, Jada was content. After turning the knob in the shower all the way to hot, she waited for steam to fill the bathroom. Her hair was already a mess from her first shower, so there wasn't much more damage that the water could do. She placed one leg in the shower, decided that the temperature was just right, and then climbed all the way in.

As she stood under the water, she broke down. All Jada White had ever wanted was Kalif, and for Kalif to want her in return. In her mind, that dream wasn't too much to ask for. She'd done each and every thing he'd ever asked of her, and even more. Her loyalty to him in his quest to be a boss had gone unchallenged. She'd stolen for him, robbed for him, fought for him, and now killed for him. There was nothing Kalif could ask of Jada that she wouldn't do. For months and months, she had been by his side in bed and had not even had sex. She'd waited in vain for him to make a move one night in the bed they shared. And the fact that he still had not called was evidence that her love had been no more than a waste of time.

Leaning against the wet marble walls of the shower stall, she trembled and got chill bumps, although the water was still hot. Jada's body slid to the tiled floor. Burying her face in her hands, she mourned the loss of being Kalif's ride-or-die. All she'd done for him was out of love. Why could he not see that? Why could he not accept that? And most importantly, why could he not return that same love and devotion? Hysterical, she couldn't calm down. But strangely, Jada shed not one tear of remorse for the pandemonium she had caused at Stacy's house. That type of emotion Jada was not built for.

Once out the sensitive state of mind she was in, Jada lay across her bed, with the belt on her robe tied tight. She felt that when she went to sleep, it would be for hours. She was exhausted. But before she went to bed, she had to check and see if her handiwork had paid off. After taking the remote from under the pillow, where she always kept it, she turned on the television. Before she could get to changing channels, her cousin came in the house and yelled out her name as she climbed the stairs.

"Jada! Jada! I know you hear me calling your punk ass."

For the first time in the forty-eight hours since parting ways with Kalif, Jada had a genuine smile on her face. Even when times had been crazy while she was growing up, Jewels had always made the worst situations better.

"Girl, I'm up here in my damn bed, chilling. But what up, doe?"

"What up doe is all this, bitch," Jewels said as she entered the room. She dropped an armful of clothes with the tags still on them on top of the bed. "Me, Euri, and Nia hit a dope-ass lick. I tried to call your ass so you could get on, but you ain't pick up or at least get back with me. So yeah, it was fuck you the long way. Let a bitch get all she can."

As she went through some of the expensive clothes, Jewels was distracted. But then she started waving her hand in front of her face. She frowned. "Girl, what in the entire fuck is that shit? It smells like straight-up gas in this motherfucker. Your room is lit!"

Jada laughed. "Dang. You right. My bad. It's my clothes over there in the corner, the ones I had on today. I probably need to throw them in the washing machine."

"Washing machine? Hell to the naw! You need to burn them stanking motherfuckers. Which probably won't be hard, as strong as they smelling," Jewels saw a wet towel on the floor and threw it over Jada's tracksuit. "How your ass get that shit like that anyhow?"

"Shhh. Be quiet. The news coming on." Jada turned up the volume on the television.

The first story was about a suspicious house fire that had left one elderly woman dead and her granddaughter fighting for her life. Then Channel Four News went live and showed the severely damaged home in the nearby suburb of Madison Heights. With smoke still visible in the rear area of the dwelling, officials permitted the cameras and reporters to get only within thirty feet of the front door. The neighbors who were interviewed had nothing but nice things to say about the woman who had lost her life and her young caregiver and granddaughter. At this point, they were not certain, but the authorities believed arson played a part in the tragedy.

Jewels knew her cousin all too well, and the way Jada was looking at the TV screen was almost a dead giveaway. "Jada, I asked you a question, and you still haven't answered it. I said, How did you get that gas on your tracksuit?"

Jada smirked devilishly, pointing the remote at the television. "That's how."

Jewels was speechless. She was stunned. She couldn't believe her ears or what her eyes had just seen on the television. If what her cousin had said was indeed true, then Jada was more than a hustler, a go-getter, and a con

woman. She was now a murderer too. Praying that what
Jada claimed was no more than a bad joke, Jewels asked
her once more about the tracksuit, this time demanding
the truth. "Look, crazy girl, stop fucking around with
some serious bullshit like that. How ya clothes really get
soaked?"

Jada sat all the way up on the bed. With her knees
pointed to the ceiling, she casually explained what she
had done. "Oh my God, is you going deaf or something?
I ran into that little bitch Stacy that was all up in Kalif
face. Her and her girls called theyself clowning me, so I
burned the ho up. Case closed. Well, I guess I burned her
and her old granny up. Case closed!"

Jewels had known since they were kids that her cousin
had problems, but she had never thought they were the
kinds of problems that would cause Jada to do something
as wild and crazy as burning people alive. Since Jada
wasn't thinking clearly, Jewels would have to do it for
her. The first thing she did was run to the linen closet
and get a pillowcase. After stuffing the strong-smelling
clothes inside the pillowcase, she rushed down the stairs
and out the back door. Then she lifted the lid on the
barbecue grill and tossed the pillowcase inside. After
drenching it with lighter fluid, she started a fire. Flames
leapt up, and the clothes started to burn. With bandos on
most of the block, there was no one to question her as
to why she was grilling at such a late hour. Once the fire
burned out and the grill cooled off, Jewels would drag it
down the alley, dump the ashes in one vacant backyard,
and discard the grill itself in another.

After rushing back upstairs, she lifted both of Jada's
windows so the room could start to air out. She then
sprayed damn near an entire can of air freshener in the

room. After that she asked for her cousin's car keys so she could park her car down the block.

Before she left the room, Jewels said, "Did anyone see you do that shit? I mean, you know if they can ID you, it's only a matter of time before they come this way." She then thought about herself and all the stolen goods inside the house. "Oh shit. Damn, bitch. You done messed around and made us all hot over some dick you ain't never had, not once. And you do realize they said that old woman is dead, don't you? Dead as in ain't coming back and your ass going to jail!"

"Girl, bye. Ain't nobody about to go to jail."

In the middle of Jewels's next rant, Jada reassured her cousin that she had not been seen at the scene of the crime and that Jewels could relax. But hours later, Jewels was wide awake, looking up at the ceiling fan and thinking she heard police cars pulling up, with officers ready to kick the door outta the frame. Jada, on the other hand, was snoring, sleeping just like an innocent baby.

# Chapter 23

The crack of dawn and Kalif were no strangers. Like clockwork, he was up for morning prayer and, since he was fasting now, a light workout. For Kalif and his team, there was no question about their newest mission. They wanted to rock out with the CD pills. From all accounts, they'd be semi rich by summer's end, all driving good. Kalif's only hope was that Allah would protect them and bless their hustle.

After his workout, Kalif placed a call to Nieem, who he trusted was up for Fajr as well. When Nieem answered, Kalif excitedly informed him that he wanted to meet as soon as possible. Nieem did not want talk on the phone in great detail, so he asked Kalif to swing by the gas station right away, before the sun came all the way up. Promptly, Kalif did as requested. When he pulled up at the gas station, there was no signs of any panhandlers, which was good for them and their well-being, not his. Before he got out of the truck, his cell phone rang. When he held the phone up, he saw that it was Jada calling.

*Well, I guess she is finished playing them female games and is ready to explain why she felt the need to run away like a thief in the night*, he thought. "*I'ma hear her out, because I want her to make some money with this CD shit too. She deserves to win. She done put in work in the trenches. But now is not the time for me to listen.* He let the call go to voicemail and made a mental note to call her back later.

After he was welcomed into Nieem's office with open arms and an Islamic greeting, Kalif let it be known that the testers he and his crew had passed out were fire and already had the streets talking. Nieem was pleased, and so they discussed the terms of their new arrangement at great length. Neither Nieem nor Kalif wanted any misunderstandings to hinder them when things got to pumping. Most great things folded over a slight misunderstanding, something that should have been brought to the table before the venture even started. There would be none of that. This association between the two men would run smoothly and would be beneficial to all involved. Nieem offered his suggestions on how to distribute the product, but Kalif had his own ideas on how to get the job done. Realizing that Kalif or his people would be the ones on the front lines, Nieem yielded and accepted Kalif's blueprint.

"Now we need to find common ground on the price. One we can both live with," Nieem then announced. He was pleased with how things had gone so far, and he expected this part of the deal to be cut and dry.

"I guess it's pretty much up to you to tell me how much you want a pill, and then I can tax in the streets what I need to make sure my people eat and it's worth their risk," Kalif replied. He took out his cell and hit the calculator app. "So, um, how much?"

Nieem wanted to get Kalif's foot in the door. He liked Kalif and wanted him to do well. In reality, the pills he had access to were plentiful and were extremely cheap to make. Even after having them shipped in from Syria or

Saudi Arabia, where they were going for five to twenty dollars a pop, he was only paying pennies on the dollar. So anything over one dollar meant he would at the very least double his money. However, no matter how much he liked Kalif, he wasn't going tell him that. At the end of the day, this was still business. "So since we are just getting going, let's say that you give me two dollars a pill. How does that sound to you?"

Kalif was elated right off the bat. He was expecting the cost would be way more than that. And if he was going through a middleman, and a black one at that, the price he would get would be triple the cost. "Okay. That's cool with me. Definitely not a problem on my end."

"And I know you have your own plan how to get them out into the streets, but as your business partner, can I make a suggestion?"

"Of course." Kalif was eager to hear what Nieem had to say.

Nieem went under his desk. He then placed a box of off-brand tampons in front of Kalif and asked him to open it. Although puzzled as to why, Kalif played along and did as he was asked. Once the box was open, Kalif then took out one of the tampons. Nieem then instructed him to tear off the wrapper. Awkwardly, Kalif peeled off the thin paper around the tampon.

"What the fuck," Kalif exclaimed as pills spilled everywhere.

"Yes, son, in the future open each one over a shoebox or a deep bowl. It's much easier to contain them that way."

Kalif was amazed as he tried his best to scoop up the small pills. "This is crazy."

"So my suggestion is this. For a short time only, you offer one pill for eight dollars and two for twelve dollars on a quick flip. If you do sell them one by one, that's a six-dollar profit on each pill after my cut. Each box has forty tampons, with a hundred fifty pills inside each tampon. That's twelve thousand dollars a box you will owe me. You can figure out your cash on your end later. As long as I get my payment each week, I'm good."

Kalif still thought the play and the possibilities were good. There was no front money, just making money. "All right, then." He reached for the box, ready to hit the streets.

"No, no, this is not for you. My people are waiting in the front for you. I have a whole case of twenty-four of these boxes ready for them to carry to your truck for you. That's two hundred eighty-eight K in total you will owe me when this is completed. Just make sure you store them in a cool place." Nieem reached for his cane so he could stand to his feet and shake Kalif's hand and thus seal their new partnership. "Don't let me down."

"I won't, Nieem. And thanks for the vote of confidence. Now let me go out here, hit the streets, and make us both some money." Kalif's head was always held high when he walked. But now his stride would be different. He'd just officially crossed over on his way to becoming a true legendary kingpin of Detroit. It was his time to shine. This was a moment he'd been waiting for, for a very long time, practically since birth.


Jada was wide awake. She was used to waking up while Kalif said his morning prayers, and she knew this would be a habit hard to break. Having come back to her normal self, she thought about what she'd done the day before. Whereas she hadn't been concerned about her actions then, she was now. She had not had this type of episode for years and was in denial. Now that she was no longer hyped, the thought that she was solely responsible for an old woman's death was fucking with her.

It wasn't her style to let anyone get under her skin and get a reaction, but Stacy and her friends had caught her at the wrong time, when she was feeling hurt and vulnerable. Kalif had her going crazy, the way he was ignoring her, as if she meant no more to him that a speck of dirt on the ground. She didn't know what it was about him that she loved so much. After all, he was self-centered, self-serving, and had never once shown her affection she yearned for. Now, if the truth came out about the fire, the bottom line was that her cousin Jewels was right. It would not only make the entire household as hot as the Fourth of July, but it would mean that Jada had thrown away her entire life and probably her freedom in the process.

Jada was fucked up and had fucked up. She wanted to call Kalif for advice on what to do next, but she knew from his actions that he had stopped giving a damn about her. Swallowing her pride, she decided that she had nothing to lose by calling him. Despite it all, he was the only person whose opinion she trusted, and she knew he would advise her well on what she should do next. After picking up her cell, she dialed Kalif's number. His phone rang and rang as she held her breath in anticipation of hearing his voice. But she was met by his voicemail. Knowing how many times the phone rung, she surmised that he'd disregarded her call on purpose.

After watching the sun come all the way up, she turned on the morning news. Jada prayed the reporter from the night before had been mistaken. That the old woman had actually pulled through and even that Stacy's bitch ass was okay. After a few words about the threat of heavy rain showers today and a commercial break, the local news was up. The tragic deadly fire was again the top headline story. When she saw the house on the TV screen, Jada felt such guilt that it was as if her head might explode. Then a picture of the deceased elderly victim flashed across the screen. Next, an interview with the fire chief indicated that not only had it been determined that the cause of the fire was arson, but that they also had a person of interest they wanted to interview. The news reporter promised to make the images of that person available to the general public as soon as possible.

Jada didn't know what to do or say next. The only thing she could do was pray that this person was not her, even though deep down inside, she knew she was cooked.

# Chapter 24

Jada was depressed. Like her cousin was the night before, she was terrified each time she heard a car drive down the street or noticed sounds she didn't recognize. As careful as she felt she had been, she knew she hadn't been in her right mind when followed Stacy and then set her house on fire. Pacing back and forth in her bedroom, Jada went from window to window. Finally, she stopped and looked out. She was far from a dummy, and she felt in her heart that she was going to go to jail in the long run. Not wanting to spend the rest of her life locked up, Jada started devising another plan, a plan of freedom and escape.

After taking from under the bed the same duffel bags she had packed her belongings in back at the hotel, a panicked Jada gathered a few more items. Then she put the bags near the door. She went over to her secret stash, retrieved all the money she had saved the past few months, and put it in her purse. The two glass mason jars she saved loose change in were also placed by the door. Not knowing how much cash she would need on hand while she was on the run, Jada grabbed the purple Crown Royal bag she kept her jewelry in. She'd pawn it all if necessary for her survival.

*Okay. Damn. Think, Jada. Think! What else do a bitch need to get? Shit. I know I'm forgetting something.*

Her eyes quickly scanned the room for anything else she needed or wanted. She knew there was no way she'd ever return here, so it was now or never. After she walked out the front door, this house would be a wrap. If the police eventually found out it was she who had started the fire that had burned up the old lady, sooner or later they'd find their way to the crib where she laid her head. So she knew she had to hide and hide well. Like Kalif had always told her, "Never, ever help the police do they jobs. Let the lying motherfuckers work for it and earn they paychecks."

With her bags in hand and a bonnet on her head, Jada went out in the hallway and dragged her bags to the top of the stairs. Then she ducked back inside her bedroom and got her purse, which she zipped up, but not before stuffing inside it a few bags of ultraexpensive Malaysian weave and a few of her favorite wigs. Back in the hallway, Jada was interrupted by Jewels's bedroom door opening. And then TayTay's too. Both women glanced at Jada, and the looks on both of their faces gave the impression that they'd seen not one, but two ghosts.

"Why y'all looking at me like that?" Jada squeaked. "I can't stay here. What if they find out it was me that did that dumb shit?"

"Girl, you ain't gotta worry about maybe if they find out, 'cause they have found out. Well, at least they think they have." Jewels had tears forming in her eyes. Her heart was breaking for her cousin, as she knew what Jada had to face.

TayTay finally chimed in, just as shocked as Jewels was. "Jada, why would you do something like that? I can't believe it!"

"Okay, y'all. I know I fucked up. I know I did. But that's why I'm about to be out before that shit hits the fan. My bags are packed and everything."

Jewels took Jada by the hand and led her back into her bedroom. TayTay was close behind, shaking her head. "Cuz, you might wanna sit down for this," Jewels told Jada. Then she fell silent.

Wide eyed, the wannabe fugitive waited for Jewels to say more. When she didn't, Jada blurted, "Well, what's the deal? I gotta get going."

Jewels showed Jada her cell phone. "Do you see this? It's all on the news and on damn Facebook. It ain't hard to make your damn face out in this photo. My phone been ringing ever since this shit was posted a few minutes ago. They all telling me this picture look just like you!"

Reality set in. Jada could do nothing other than agree. It was indeed a picture of her at the gas station out near Stacy's house. She had her baseball cap pulled down some, but those who knew her could easily identify the person in the picture. Between the news and social media, she had to come to terms with the fact that there was nowhere she could run and hide. She was that person of interest the police wanted to talk to. Jada, Jewels, and TayTay all cried, knowing all three of their lives would be forever changed, just as Stacy and her old granny's lives had been.

About twenty minutes later, Jewels called a lawyer they would always use when they got knocked for shoplifting, and he suggested that they meet him at his office. Jada knew he would advise her to go voluntarily to the police station and clear things up. After the call, Jada dragged her bags back into her room, and then the young fire starter braced herself for the inevitable. She deactivated both her Facebook and Instagram pages. She then gave all her money to Jewels for the lawyer's fees. After that, she ran hot water in the tub, with plenty of bubbles included, and submerged herself. Closing her eyes, she exhaled, enjoying what would probably be the last bath she took for many years to come.


Hakim was devastated. He had been at the hospital damn near all night, surrounded by Stacy's family and friends, all of whom were in shock. This type of thing was inconceivable. It was dreadful enough that a fire had claimed the life of Granny Erma and had Stacy fighting for her life, but finding out that the inferno was not an accident was more than anyone could take. Everyone racked their brains, but no one could come up with a person would be so mean spirited and cruel as to commit such a heinous act.

Exhausted and drained, the weary boyfriend finally made it back home. After receiving a call about the fire from one of Stacy's friends the night before, he had run out the house with one shoe on and the other in his hand. He'd raced across town to the hospital, several times coming close to getting into an accident, trying to make it to Stacy's side as soon as possible. As he'd bolted through the doors of the emergency room, Hakim had thought about verses from both the Koran and the Bible. He just wanted God to bless them with a miracle and spare Stacy's life. When he'd found out that she was at least stable, but still unconscious, Hakim had rushed home to shower, change clothes, grab something to eat, and then he had headed back to be at Stacy's side. He'd stayed at the hospital until nearly dawn, and now he was back home again. He walked into the kitchen and found his mother there.

"Hey, son. How is she?" Fatima asked as she held one of the twins closely in her arms.

"Mom, it's bad. It's really bad. Her grandmother is gone. She didn't make it. And Stacy's hands are burned really badly. And her leg. You know she has asthma, so of course, her breathing is an issue from all that smoke she inhaled trying to get her grandmother out. Man, I just can't believe it!"

"I can't imagine how Stacy is feeling . . . and her family. I'm praying for all of them for their loss. It's been all over the news, on every channel, since last night. They said they have a person of interest and will be releasing their picture this morning sometime."

"I know. The police was down at the hospital, interviewing everyone."

"Well, go get some rest. You look like you really need it. We'll know more soon."

Hakim took his mother's advice and grabbed a few hours' sleep. When he came back downstairs around noon, he found Fatima in the living room. She turned on the news. Of course the fire was still the lead story. Pictures of the house, Stacy's grandmother, and Stacy in her cap and gown, seeing how she was only weeks away from graduating and going to the prom, flashed on the TV screen. The next picture they showed had Hakim dropping his jaw. He squinted. He was puzzled. He thought back to the other day in the backyard. This person of interest was almost a carbon copy of the girl Kalif had had with him that day. Sure, this female on television had on a baseball cap and no makeup, but she still looked familiar.

"What the hell? Mom, do you see this? That's that girl!"

"What girl, Hakim?" Fatima stared at the picture on the television screen.

"That same ratchet girl Kalif had with him the other day. That's her. I'm sure it is! I'm confused. Why would she even know where Stacy lives? And why would she have a problem with her? I don't understand."

Since Fatima had stayed upstairs during Kalif's surprise visit and had not gotten a close look at Jada, she assumed that Hakim was mistaken. But before she could tell him that, Hakim received a text from one of his classmates. It was a screenshot from a Facebook post. Underneath the same picture Hakim and his mother had just seen on television were comments about how the alleged arsonist looked like someone named Jada. That solidified it for Hakim. His brother's girlfriend had set Stacy's house on fire. And Hakim could only think that Kalif had put her up to doing it, since he still blamed Stacy for urging Hakim to denounce Islam, which he loved so much.

"I knew I wasn't going crazy. See? That is her," Hakim said as he showed his mother his phone. They both didn't know what to say.

Fatima went and put the baby down. When she returned, she had her phone in hand. Let me call Rasul and tell him what his "do no wrong" Kalif has done now!"

Hakim didn't want to hear anything his father had to say. He already knew Rasul was going to defend Kalif, no matter what, so what was the sense of hearing it once more? "Mom, forget Dad. He abandoned you and the girls, and for what? For that murdering, lying Kalif, who should not have been in this house in the first place, not even when he was a baby! He's no brother of mine and never will be. He's poison. You think I don't hear you crying every night over Dad being gone because of Kalif? Instead of Granny Erma being dead and Stacy being so messed up, Kalif should be in that hospital bed. Or, better yet, dead!" After removing from his back pocket a card a detective had given him last night, Hakim disappeared upstairs to make a call.

Fatima knew Hakim was correct, but she called her estranged husband just the same. She wanted to speak her piece, even if he didn't want to hear it or accept it as the truth. When he picked up, she said, "Hello, Rasul. We need to talk." The mother of his children wasted no time in telling Rasul about what had happened to Stacy and her grandmother and what part his adored Kalif had played in it.

"I'm not saying Kalif is an angel. I know he's far from it. But burning down that girl's house, acting like he's public enemy number one? Come on now, Fatima. You reaching. You already made it clear you could care less about him, but don't just start making up shit because you bitter. That's not a good look for you."

Just as Hakim had predicted, his father didn't believe it. He promised to check into the incident, but it was obvious to Fatima that he had just chalked it up to rumor and gossip, not facts.

# Chapter 25

After everyone had gathered on the block, they all went into the house. Eager and ready to put in work, Kalif placed a few of the boxes of tampons in the center of the table and asked everyone to take a seat. When he had one of his guys open a tampon, the crew was just as bewildered as Kalif had been when Nieem showed him. After all the jokes about which one of them had turned bitch and was on their period, Kalif revealed the play. When the count was done, Pit Boy, Li'l James, Keys, and even Amir had their package together, their ticket noted, and were ready to hit the streets and make money. Li'l James and Keys were the first out the door. Their cell phones were hot. They'd been ringing off the chain since yesterday. No sooner had they put the testers out, along with their numbers, than customers were at their heads, wanting to get more. Amir left shortly after them, as he had a class to get to. He had told Kalif he'd get on his grind later in the day. The one good thing about this hustle was these pills didn't have expiration dates. So they were good as far as that was concerned.

Just as Pit Boy and Kalif were about to part ways as well, Kalif got a call from his pops. He'd been low key avoiding him for days. But now that he was completely plugged in and had the work in his possession, he had no problem picking up. Pit Boy fell back, giving his homeboy some privacy. He went outside to feed his dogs. Kalif picked up and greeted his father as every good Muslim should. Then they got right to it.

"Hey, Dad. What's going on?"

"Damn, son. You a hard person to get up with."

"Yeah, well, I've been really busy."

"I know. I heard you stopped by the house, looking for me."

"Yeah, I did, but you probably already know how that turned out."

"Yeah, I do."

"But don't worry, Dad. I promise I won't go back over there, looking for you. It ain't no thang."

Rasul was silent for a few moments before he made his next statement. "Well, son, truth be told, there's not a reason to. You see, your mother and I have parted ways. I'm no longer staying there."

Kalif was at a loss for words. He hadn't seen this coming in a million years. "Wow, Dad. I don't know what to say."

"Well, son, if it's Allah's will, things will work themselves out. But that's not why I'm calling you now. And it's not about the situation that you had going on with that kid Ibn. He already gave me his word he wouldn't drag you into no mess. So I'm good with that."

"Oh yeah, dig that." Kalif let his father think whatever he wanted to think. And truth be told, Ibn hadn't broken his word.

"See, your mother just called me, talking out the side of her neck about you."

"Again? I mean, what else is new?"

"Well, this was about some girl that you brought by the house. Her name is Jada. And, by the way, I hope she's Muslim."

Kalif laughed at what his father was implying and then set him straight. "First of all, she's not. But she's just my homegirl. No one I'm trying to marry. And secondly, yeah? So what that she was with me? What's your point?"

"Well, your mother and brother seem to think she has something to do with Hakim's girlfriend's house being set on fire. And get this. They think you put her up to it."

"Say what? Are they both crazy? Are you talking about that lame girl that was over at the house the other day? The one that's got Hakim's nose wide open? Come on now!"

"Yes, I assume so. They say it's all over the news and social media, but you know I don't fool with that propaganda."

Kalif had had enough of his mother's and his little brother's bullshit. If it wasn't one thing with them, it was another. But this was over the top, even for them. "Man, them two be doing the most. Jada don't even know that girl. Neither do I. And why in the hell would we care if her house was on fire, or anything else dealing with her pagan ass?"

Rasul and Kalif ended their conversation, with each promising to make time later in the week to sit down together and break bread. Rasul called Fatima back to tell her once again she was wrong about their son. And Kalif called Jada, but she did not answer. When Pit Boy returned to the basement, Kalif retold the story his father had just told him. Pit Boy then hit Jewels up, but she did not answer, either. Then he went on Facebook to see if there was any mention of some fire the night before. It didn't take long before he, too, was staring at Jada's picture. Dismayed, he showed it to Kalif.

*Damn. I know that girl been acting crazy, but not that damn crazy.* Kalif was perplexed. For now the streets would have to wait. They jumped into Kalif's truck and headed over to his house, the one where the girls were staying. The drive was silent, as Pit Boy read all the Facebook comments bashing Jada to himself. Both Kalif and Pit Boy had been involved in all kinds of crimes. They had done and seen it all, but this shit—burning an old woman alive—was some kind of different.

When the astounded pair arrived at the house, it looked calm from the outside. Nothing seemed out of place, and the work crew had yet to arrive. Everything was everything. When they got on the porch, they were met by TayTay. She'd been smoking weed heavily and drinking shots of Rémy, and it was only a little after noon. Tears filled her eyes, and there was misery in her heart.

"Where she at?" Kalif blurted out, pushing past TayTay.

"Yeah, and where the fuck is Jewels? I been calling her ass!" Pit Boy snapped.

The trio stepped inside the house, and TayTay sadly brought them up to date. She informed them that they had just missed Jada and Jewels by minutes. She told them that they, too, had seen the news reports, as well as the stuff plastered on social media. And she revealed that Jada and Jewels were meeting with a lawyer so Jada could surrender herself for questioning at the Madison Heights Police Department. Pit Boy asked TayTay if Jada had really done what she was accused of doing. At that point what the fellas feared may be true was confirmed. Kalif was dumbfounded. None of Jada's erratic actions the past few days made any sense to him. He was lost, and apparently, so was she.

# Chapter 26

Li'l James was in the streets, making a name for himself and their crew. When he returned to the same neighborhood he'd posted up in with the testers, he found that people were bragging about the high they had had. And the ones that had missed out were wondering how they could get on. No sooner had Li'l James parked his car around the corner and stepped into the drug-polluted area than he was mobbed. After letting everyone know that he was out of testers and that it was now a "cash and go" thing jumping off, not one person complained. The ones that had the money wasted no time paying the price. The misfortunate ones that didn't rushed to get on their petty grind so that they could cop before the new hot pill CD was sold out and Li'l James was gone. Most weren't new to the game of getting high. From experience, they knew a bag would be super strong and potent one day, then weak as baby aspirins the next. Getting on when the play was right was like a job to drug addicts.

"I got them CDs. I got them CDs on deck," Li'l James repeated damn near until his voice grew hoarse. As he sold one pill there and then two, three, and four the next go-around, he watched not only the amount of pills he'd had on him get depleted, but then the stash he had left in his car as well. Exhausted, but with pockets on bump, Li'l James decided that this was one of most lucrative licks, if not *the* most lucrative one, that Kalif had put him and the rest of the fellas onto.

The next day was the same in terms of the amount of business Li'l James did, and so was the day after that. Though he tried to be on time, even if Li'l James was a few minutes late to the corner, the customers would be lined up and waiting for the old-school, "back in the eighties" way.

"Yo, young blood, you gotta know you got the best thing going over this way. You done shut the whole neighborhood down, from Woodward all the way over damn near to the Motor City, with this right here," a customer with a runny nose told Li'l James that third day on the corner. He was in need of a haircut, and when he grinned, he showed all five of his rotten teeth. "If you let me get one or two of them thangs on credit, I can run 'em your way. Put me on the payroll. Them other guys from the East Side with them Percs and even five-one-twos from last week was garbage. They down the way, getting no money! You killin' out here, young blood. You killin' 'em."

Li'l James told the man he'd think about it, but for the time being, if he didn't have cash, he needed to push on. If he started that "I'ma owe you" bullshit with him, he ran the risk of the rest of the heads thinking he was some sort of sucker or was green to the game. A few hours later, after putting in work, he was headed home. He had to get some rest if he wanted to stay alert in the days to follow. The streets was no place for a dude who was hustling not to be on point.

Keys was a morning person. It was nothing for him to hit the block before 8:00 a.m. So being posted, ready to take care of business, before the next man was second nature to him. When it came down to handling anything, Keys was the first person you'd want on your team. He was loyal and had no problem being the fall guy, if need be. He was the only one out of the crew that had been to prison. Not the Wayne County Jail or over on Dickerson, where lames acted like they were doing hard-ass time when they were doing only sixty days, but prison, the penitentiary. Keys was no ho. He had stood tall and had served his time. When he'd been released, he had linked back up with Kalif, and now he was down for whatever.

Keys didn't mind one bit all the small-time capers his homeboy had been putting them up to. They were keeping money in his pocket, but just like he'd been locked up for real, Keys had a whole kid he had to take care of. And that meant he needed extra dough. The baby mama had not pressed the issue when it came to trying to get him to pay child support. Not because she was a good girl, but because she was the complete opposite. The rumor around the way was that Keys's infant daughter was no more than a toss-up hood baby. And if the shady female allowed him to get a blood test, her scam would be discovered. Rumors meant nothing to Keys. He was a stand-up dude and had bonded with the child. So in his eyes, it was what it was. She was his daughter, his pride and joy, and no one could tell him differently.

Having spent half the day on the Mile, near Van Dyke Avenue, he'd made more money off this new product than he ever had when selling crack or Ecstasy or any other illegal substance. In Keys's eyes, Captagon would be the thing that would help him to move his mother out of the hood and make sure his child stayed in baby Jordans. At one thirty in the afternoon, he closed shop in that location and headed even deeper east. Although he'd been born near Canfield and McDougall, he hadn't lived on that side of town since he was three years old. His hood was Linwood, and he claimed nothing else. After he pulled up on his old block, he parked his late-model blue minivan in front of the vacant lot where his birth home used to stand. On foot, he headed up the block. In a span of a few hours, Keys had covered a good two miles or so up and down the busy streets, getting his package off. There was definitely not a shortage of interested buyers looking for a new blast.

Throughout the day he had been met with a few hard stares from the neighborhood drug dealers. That part was to be expected. After all, he had appeared out of nowhere and was putting a serious squeeze on their cash flow. He knew if some random snowball nigga popped up in his hood, he and his boys would be on that same tip. But Keys was in his own world and was staying focused. His job was to make money, not friends. He minded the business that paid him. Nothing more and nothing less.

It was mid-afternoon when Amir got out of class. With his final grade depending on one more test, he hadn't put slanging these new pills high on his list of things to do. He'd been involved in most, if not all, the various crimes the crew had committed, but selling drugs had never been his thing. He'd heard enough horror stories from his old man and Rasul to scare him straight ten times over and keep him from getting off into that line of work. And up until now, Kalif hadn't been on that tip, either. Countless times they'd both turned down making runs with their fathers. At the end of the day, getting money was all good and well. Amir loved going shopping and loved the hoes that came along with stuntin'. However, being an accountant was his endgame, and he was determined to avoid getting knocked for dumb shit if he could help it.

Working smart, Amir picked up his little cousin on his mother's side. His cousin was always bugging him, trying to get put on, so he jumped at the opportunity when he got Amir's call. Once on Manchester, Derek got out of the car as his big cousin parked in the lot near Captain Jay's Fish & Chicken. Derek had a plastic sandwich bag filled with CDs in his hand, and the same dudes from the homeless shelter that Amir had blessed the day before recognized Derek by the Michigan State hoodie he was wearing and the U of M fitted cap. They told Derek they rooted for both teams, as well, and that was the code that they wanted to get served.

Amir ate chicken wings with lemon pepper and watched his money grow from afar. If Derek got arrested, then that was on him. He wanted to be down so bad and in the game, and sometimes spending the night on a hard bench with a bunch of other niggas was the price you had to pay.

# Chapter 27

Kalif had a huge ticket pending with Nieem. This being their first venture, he wanted to make sure he paid him in a timely fashion. Each of them knew that out of the gate, things would go slow. Building a strong clientele or even an empire took time. Nieem was not the type to be pushy, but he wanted to see how hard his young associate would work to make some initial payment for the fronted Captagon. The older man kept his ear to the ground and made it his business to keep up with the goings-on in the hood. He and his Middle Eastern friends would laugh that black people's lives and their daily over-the-top drama were better than television.

As Nieem was watching an episode of Hood TV, he came upon some news that even he found disturbing. A young woman had deliberately set a house on fire, knowing that an old woman was inside. That was far from the truth, but it still sounded awful. From some of his sources, he discovered that the young killer had been closely affiliated with Kalif. Of course, Nieem found that to be troubling. However, he didn't want to drop his hand that he had people keeping tabs on Kalif. In his culture, as well as in his religion, they respected their elderly. They did not burn them up before their time. But the girl who had set the fire was in jail, and Kalif still owed him money. Those payments were what were most important to him, not who Kalif had been sleeping with. Nieem would just sit back and see how everything played out.

Weeks flew by, and each Thursday, like clockwork, Kalif would drop off the prearranged amount at the gas station. With Pit Boy doubling up the amount of CDs he was moving in Southwest Detroit and Downriver, he had brought someone else, a guy named Juan, into the fold, just as Amir had done. Juan had worked in a restaurant in Mexicantown, and he had bought pills for some of the white customers that often stopped by. He'd been doubling up on the price he got. Not one person had complained about the Captagon Dip being too expensive, because the explosive high was well worth triple to them. One day Juan had gotten caught serving a white boy out in the parking lot, and his manager had fired him. Ironically, Pit Boy had been there with Juan's re-up. Instead of advising him to beg for his job, he had offered Juan an alternative: grab a new territory and set up shop.

Juan had taken him up on the offer, and soon he had added Delray to their roster of areas of Detroit they covered. Now Juan made more money going balls to the wall with CDs than he had when he was sneaking around. Kalif liked Juan and his determination to go hard. So even though he had a strong hold on the Brightmoor area, he gave that part of the city to Juan to handle. Doing that freed Kalif up to keep the count up and the money right, and to drop off the product anytime Li'l James, Pit Boy, Keys, or Amir was running low. That part of Kalif's quest for power was going better than planned.

However, since he hadn't taken his meds consistently for well over a month, Kalif was struggling to stay sane. Suffering from headaches, nighttime shivers, and delusions, he was getting worse as the days went by. He was completely paranoid and watched everyone, believing they were out to get him. He was even suspicious of waitresses at restaurants and the housekeepers at the various hotels he transferred to weekly. If Kalif was deep into his zone, everyone was suspect. The only thing that gave him peace was prayer. Sometimes he'd be on his prayer rug for hours. It didn't matter the time or the place. If Kalif felt the need to pray, he'd shut it all down at the drop of a dime and do so.

Since Jada was not there to help him manage that part of his life, he was lost. He had never realized how major a role she played in keeping his eye on the prize. Since Kalif had been off the mind-altering prescriptions for so long on a consistent basis, when he attempted to take a few, he would feel much worse physically. It was as if his bloodstream was rejecting the chemical. Doing that would put him on his ass for days, something he couldn't afford to do if he wanted to keep up his financial bargain with Nieem. Even with his mental illness, he knew maintaining that pipeline of product was the only way he could stay cranking in the streets. His name was ringing in the underground, and being young and naïve, he thought that was a good thing. A more seasoned vet in the game knew quiet money always spent better. But Kalif would learn that in time on his own. If not, the Feds certainly would teach him.

# Chapter 28

The request for news interviews kept coming. Advised by her lawyer not to speak to anyone without him by her side, Jada happily stayed quiet. Since walking into the police station nearly a month ago, she had been treated like pure filth. The detectives had video of her in the gas station, with a gas can in hand. Of course, that station was located only blocks from Stacy's home. So that definitely put Jada in the area at the time the fire was started. But her lawyer had argued that although she had met the victim briefly—of course a furious Hakim had called the police to confirm that meeting—she had had no reasonable motive to commit such a heinous act of violence. It made no sense. Jada claimed that it was just a coincidence that she'd run out of gas in that neighborhood.

Hesitant witnesses had corroborated her story, saying that she had indeed run out of gas and stood out in front of the station, with a gas can in hand, asking for assistance. The white man's wife had even given a statement, saying that Jada asked her husband if he could take her back to her car and have a look at it. The clerk at the gas station had confirmed that he sold her three dollars' worth of gas, because she had only that much money in her pocket. And he'd added that Jada had asked him if he could maybe take money off of her EBT card in trade for some gas or maybe a tow truck. Taking all those things into consideration, the district attorney was having a hard time connecting a person who had been so adamant about needing assistance with an act of arson that had resulted in murder.

During one meeting with the police, Jada's lawyer had been emphatic about this point. "Come on now. This is becoming a witch hunt of sorts. Although my client was in the general area, that does not make her guilty. Yes, you have her on video at the gas station. So what? You also have her on there practically begging people to help her. She was even trying to use her own personal government assistance card to get help. What kind of dumb criminal would beg people to help her burn down a house? I guess she was going to get that woman's husband to help her light the match!"

The prosecutors' office knew they couldn't make a solid case with the evidence they had so far. So they put the word out that they wanted to speak with any of the neighbors that might have security cameras. But fortunately for Jada, the residents out there felt safe and secure enough not to need such cameras. And she had also been wise enough to drive a few miles, pull into another gas station, and tell the clerk that she had only three dollars of gas from down the way to make it this far. Closer to the hood, more people were generous, and then and only then was she able to get at least nine dollars' worth of gas. By the time that was happening, Stacy's house was already in full blaze mode. Even though they couldn't make felony charges stick at the moment, police still came to pick her up, because she had an outstanding warrant for two shoplifting charges, which she'd have to serve time on. So now Jada was behind bars.

"Have you seen Kalif lately?" Jada asked her cousin solemnly through the thick plastic divider separating the two of them.

"Yeah, actually, I saw him the other day. He stopped by the house to give me the money to pay the water bill. He said next week he'd drop off the money for DTE. And, girl, he wasn't looking right. He looked like just not hisself, I guess."

Jada already knew what that meant. No stranger to Kalif and his mood changes, she could only assume he was all the way off his meds, and that was never good. She wished she could talk to him or lay eyes on him. But she knew that was out of the question. Kalif wasn't coming nowhere near anybody's jail. And taking her calls was out of the question as well. They both knew those calls were being recorded. So for the time being, Jada would have to be content with the money he was giving to Jewels to put on her books. When she got out, if she ever got out, Jada knew she would have to explain why she did what she did. Maybe he'd accept her weak explanation for snapping, or maybe not. But for now her beloved Kalif had not left her for dead, and that was all that mattered.

Hakim was beyond pissed. He'd placed call after call, trying to ensure that his brother's girlfriend was brought to justice for what she had done. Even though there were no eyewitnesses who had actually seen her start the fire that killed Stacy's grandmother and left Stacy with permanent scars, he knew Jada was guilty. Just as he knew his brother had definitely been the mastermind behind the crime. For years Hakim had believed his sick-in-the-head brother had been jealous of him. He reasoned that because their mother had put Kalif out in the streets for jumping on him, Kalif wanted revenge. A normal person would just talk shit or want to throw hands again. But Rasul and Fatima's youngest son had found out long ago that nothing was normal about Kalif. They all had. He had been born pure evil, and putting Jada up to the work of the devil was more of his black-hearted handiwork.

During his latest phone conversation with a detective who was working the case, Hakim could not hide his frustration over the fact that Jada had yet to pay for what she had done to Stacy and her family. "Detective, how can you tell me she is going to get away with this? You just telling me somebody can come out to your city, burn down a house, burn someone's grandmother to death and damn near kill the next person, and she's gonna be free," Hakim seethed, ready to tear something up. "What kind of system is that? I don't understand. She didn't even have a reason to be out that way. Y'all just gonna let her and my brother get away with murder? 'Cause even though he wasn't actually there, I know he put that girl up to it. He thinks everybody his puppet. I'm telling you, it's both of them. They both need to be locked up or dead too!"

Regretfully, the detective told the irate young man that sometimes bad things happened to good people. And in most instances, given enough time, criminals who thought they had got away with committing a crime would get bolder and would commit another, and then they would get caught. But for Hakim, that time could not come soon enough. He wanted justice and would get it one way or another. He made up in his mind he'd have satisfaction in the long run.

After hanging up from that call, he eagerly placed another. And after ending that conversation, he was now hopeful Kalif would finally pay. With a sneer of contentment, he went back into the hospital waiting room to rejoin Stacy's family. His girlfriend was having her second round of skin grafts, in an attempt to recover her once normal life. When they got a chance to speak, Hakim wanted to be able to tell Stacy that the people responsible for ruining their senior year, causing her so much pain, and taking her grandmother's life would be held accountable soon.

# Chapter 29

With racks upon racks being made daily, Kalif was hiding money not only in the rafters of his attic but also in the rear part of the storage lockers he would rent and fill with old furniture and clothes from the Salvation Army as a play off. He was also careful not to dress in anything other than paint-covered overalls, so as not to attract any unwanted attention. Knowing people would steal if given the opportunity of a come up, he didn't want or need any of the storage facility workers to get any wise ideas. He wasn't a murderer, but when you dealt in the street life, that could easily change if you were pushed.

The more money he made, the more unhinged Kalif seemed to become. One minute he was in good spirits; the next he was bouncing off the walls. At one point he spent three days and nights straight in a mosque out near Inkster, reciting the Holy Koran cover to cover from memory. The only break Kalif would take was to use the bathroom and maybe drink a bottle of water. And that brief interruption came at the urging of the imam. During those times when Kalif was bouncing off the walls, Amir would step in and step up. He made sure that everyone had their packages and that the money was straight. Low-key Amir was happy to take on that responsibility, because he had discovered that the streets were just not for him.

Kalif's entire crew had been observing Kalif go through changes. He was talking to himself and would often speak in tongues. All of them were worried, but they knew not to step to their boy. Kalif's temper had been explosive from the beginning, but now with the CDs taking the city by storm, he was under more pressure than ever before. Although he dreamed about being important and garnering the respect of other legendary players who were in the streets, banging, this life was far from easy. Whenever he stepped on the block, he would be surrounded. People wanted this and that. Begged for credit. Cried about their past-due bills. And complained that their checks were short. Kalif was overwhelmed. But it was too late to put the genie back in the bottle.

No longer in the shadow of Rasul, Kalif was nearing kingpin status in the eyes of the task force that had been assembled to curtail Detroit's crime, which had catapulted to epidemic proportions. The task force had zeroed in on a few different organizations that were making more noise than all the other mom-and-pop wannabe drug dealers. Kalif and his crew were now neck and neck with the BBM, aka the Black Bottom Mafia, which had been a problem on the East Side of the Motor City for a few years strong now. The task force captain and his men all were amazed at how this CD pill had seemingly taken over the town in such a short time frame. Unfortunately, the leader of the BBM was wondering the same exact thing, as his workers' money grew shorter each week.

There was nothing much in the way of homes still left standing in the neighborhood. Mack and Manistique was almost a ghost town. However, Brutus made sure that the house his grandmother owned still stood tall. He didn't care that there were at least five vacant lots on one side of the house. He was in the neighborhood now because he had ordered all the fellas of the BBM to appear at a mandatory meeting in his grandmother's living room. Normally, the big man himself would not drive down from his home out in Clawson. But this situation with the CDs was getting out of hand. He'd put both his crew leaders on top of making sure the "new kids on the block" failed, but they kept coming up short. It didn't matter to the drug addicts who they spent their money with. They were loyal to the high and nothing else. So even if the BBM threatened them, intimidated them, and promised to have a better and stronger product the following week, it didn't matter. The addicts were in the business of getting high right then and there.

"Okay, so yeah. Y'all got me down here on some bullshit," Brutus remarked as he stood near the fireplace. "Y'all motherfuckers let some young lames from the West Side come and run y'all off from getting that money. A nigga like me can't even watch Netflix and chill, because y'all acting straight pussy. If you or you or you"—Brutus pointed at several different workers—"ain't about that life no more, let me know. Ain't no hard feelings, but just get the fuck on and stop making the team look bad. We get money over here on the East Side."

Brutus went on. "Back in the day, I wish a nigga or bitch would step foot on our shit we done pumped up, thinking they gonna sell jack shit. Naw, we was some soldiers back then. But y'all don't know how to stand tall with it. Dressing in them old gay-ass tight pants, which are sagging all off y'all asses. What about when the police get on y'all? You stupid young niggas can't even run when y'all dressed like that."

The crew captains stood over in a corner. Arms folded, they snarled while nodding their heads in agreement with Brutus. Equally disappointed in the workers' sales, or lack thereof, each one was called up to explain why they thought their ticket money was short. They cited the same reason repeatedly, no matter which sector of the city they were speaking of. With a heavy concentration on the East Side of Detroit, that was where the BBM made the bulk of their money. And to the boss man's surprise, that was the area that was taking the biggest hit from the competition. Infuriated with what he was hearing, he knew something drastic had to be done if he wanted to continue living the carefree lifestyle he'd been enjoying for the past few years.

"Most of you motherfuckers lay y'all's heads this way, and y'all letting this go down. Some lames from off Linwood and Dexter. I'm ashamed for you," Brutus said. He stood to his feet, tired of holding court and school with the modern-day, new-breed, lean fiends he had so-called hustling for him. "It's like this here. The shit with them youngins and that CD bullshit stops today. Cutt and Mutt, y'all true savage warriors? Y'all ready to step in and step up?"

Out of the shadows of the room, the deranged pair moved toward Brutus. Since they had been down with the BBM since damn near day one, their drastic services were needed and called upon only when there were no other options and when words or negotiations were no longer effective. Cutt had been given that nickname because a bullet had grazed his head during a shoot-out, leaving a long and very visible raised wound. Hair had ceased growing on that part of his head, so he got stares no matter where he went.

His counterpart and partner in mayhem, Mutt, earned his name daily. Tragically, he had been born a mutant, since he had only three fingers and half of a thumb on one hand. Despite his bright skin, he always looked dingy, and the sandy-colored locks he'd been growing since grade school were matted and oftentimes gave off an unflattering smell. One thing was for sure, and two things were certain: if that pair of the worst Detroit had to offer was on your head, you might as well say your prayers, because the angel of death was not far behind.

Brutus had a small-size duffel bag brought from his truck. After opening it, he set a few racks on the mantel of the fireplace. "This right here is a bonus for any of y'all that can get our money back right over near Midtown and the Cass Corridor. Get some runners and run a few two-for-one specials. If you have to get physical with a few motherfuckers trying to go against the grain, then so be it. Make that shit profitable again, or y'all done working for me." Then he took out more than double the amount of racks he had removed, and handed them directly to Cutt and Mutt. "Look, them other areas of the city is just extra, like it's whatever. But over this way? East? The Black Bottom? This us all day! So do what y'all need to do. I don't wanna have to come back down here because we getting punked where we made the streets famous. Handle that!"

As a frustrated Brutus stormed out of the house and drove off, each worker knew he had a job to do. And if they wanted to keep drinking lean, popping Percs, Xany and—though they kept quiet about it—CDs, and tricking with the hoes, then they'd step their game up. Period. Cutt and Mutt went off on their own to devise a plan of action that would earn them those racks.

# Chapter 30

Kalif was temporarily in his right state of mind. As he and his main-tier people sat around the table, they all discussed their plans for the day. The re-up had just come in from an elated Nieem, and the guys were all in great spirits overall. Amir had received his final grades. Pit Boy's dog had just delivered her litter. Li'l James had added more money to his stash to get his mother out of the hood. And today was Key's daughter's birthday party at Chuck E. Cheese's, which he definitely was looking forward to. And Keys hoped his friends would show up and show love, despite their dislike for his no-good baby mama.

After opening several boxes of the tampons, Amir did the honors of separating their portions into huge piles. After the final count of the infamous, highly addictive pills was complete, all the fellas knew what their tickets were. They varied depending on how each area of town had been buying the week prior. Whereas Li'l James and his crew were doing much better than Pit Boy and his, Keys and his boys posted up on East Side were bringing in more revenue than them both. Keys had earned those bragging rights by always being first on the scene, before most of his workers, and by always being the last to leave.

With several other workers added to the original group of friends, Kalif's workforce had grown not only in numbers but also in popularity in the streets. Whenever one of them would step foot on any set, the crowd of drug addicts would follow, leaving in the dust other playas attempting to get their hustle on.

Ready to face the day, the group of close-knit friends parted ways, each headed in a different direction.


The sun had barely come up. The streets had yet to get busy. But shear madness never rested or slept. Cutt and Mutt had been up all night. Popping pills and drinking lean was their normal activity, whether they were on the clock or not. Both new-age, modern-day drug addicts, the two of them had been plotting their hunt for days. Extra high and feeling invincible, they knew that this morning they would execute their plan to earn the money Brutus had blessed them with. If their scheme went as intended, they'd be back at the trap house they laid their heads at, celebrating by getting even higher.

"Yo, my nigga. He right on time," Mutt told Cutt.

"Yeah, I see. This shit gonna be easy as a motherfucker."

"You think so?" Mutt moved his wild dreads out of his face.

"Nigga, I know so. He ain't gonna know what hit his ass. He gonna go running back to the West Side and never, ever come back this way. Not even if bitches giving away free pussy all day and night to whoever pulls up," Cutt said, reaffirming how easily they would be earning their bread.

Watching Keys park his minivan, Cutt took out his gun. Although using it was not the plan, he still put one up top. Mutt then followed suit. After laying on Keys for days, the crazed, pill-polluted pair had quickly discerned that their soon-to-be target was a creature of habit. He'd pull up down at the end of the block and drink a coffee. One by one, his always late crew members would show up and cop their package from him and exchange a few words. Once he'd touched base with all of them, then Keys would leave for a couple of hours. After following him three or four times, Cutt and Mutt had discovered that he would always go park a few miles away, on various side streets off of Mt. Elliott. There, it seemed to them, he would count money, talk on his cell, and take a piss in the alley if need be.

Now, as Cutt and Mutt watched, one by one, Keys's crew members showed up. They all followed their regular routine, and after Keys had put his people in full motion, he pulled off the block. Cutt and Mutt quickly jumped in their beater and followed, but not close enough to be noticed. Keys, a true creature of habit, bent a few corners. This time he parked on Theodore. After giving Keys no more than five minutes to get started on his customary way of doing things, the bloodthirsty duo made their move. Undetected, guns drawn, each man crept up on the sides of the van. Preoccupied by the conversation he was having on his cell, Keys was caught off guard. There was nothing he could do, nothing he could say. Cutt was at the driver's side. Mutt was at the passenger's side. Both had their weapons pointed at Keys's head.


"Look, girl. Damn! Stop fucking stressing me the hell out," Keys yelled. "I already told you I got the shit covered. All you gotta do is bring li'l mama and her friends to the place. Grab whatever tables you want, and we good. Just make sure you get enough space, because all my homeboys coming to."

Keys was getting pissed as he reached for a half-eaten bag of hot Better Made Potato Chips. He was aggravated. It was bad enough he felt his daughter was too young to be having a birthday party at expensive-ass Chuck E. Cheese's in the first place, but since early this morning, his worrisome, greedy baby moms had been on him. He'd already bought all his baby's gifts. They were wrapped and in the rear of his van. He'd gotten her not one, but two outfits to wear on her big day. And when he shut down for the day, which would be earlier than usual, he'd then swing by and pick up her over-the-top custom cake, which her mother had insisted on. Keys didn't care. Not really. He'd do anything for his princess. However, his baby moms was doing beyond the most. Now she was pestering him to bring her a couple more dollars so she could get her hair done.

"All right. Damn, girl. Just hold up and let me figure some shit out. I'ma get back with you in a few. But don't forget what I said about grabbing enough tables for later." Having developed a severe migraine, thanks to that nonstop nagging he'd endured, Keys ended the call and briefly closed his eyes, regretting he'd even fucked with her in the first place.

When he reopened his eyes, he was shocked. *Oh shit! What the fuck?* His eyes widened, and his migraine immediately grew worse.

The doors to the older-model van were already unlocked. After opening the passenger's side door, Mutt got in the van and ordered Keys to drive. There was no way Keys could not do as he was told. He had got caught slipping when he was arguing with that rotten-mouthed bitch. His boys had always said she was bad luck for him. And this proved just that. After putting the van in motion, he did as instructed. Cutt was trailing behind. The game plan was to go to a more secluded area and rough Keys up. Maybe break both his legs, putting him out of commission for some time to come. Or maybe even severely pistol-whipping him. They'd decide that when the time came.

Keys never said a word. His mind was working overtime. Far from being a ho, he knew he was gonna make a move. But it was only a matter of picking the right opportunity to do so. Keys was not too familiar with the East Side; however, like every other Detroiter, Keys did recognize where he was when his dreadlocked captor had him pull over. The old Packard Automotive Plant had been shut down for decades, but it still stood as an iconic city landmark. The walls that were still intact had been covered in multicolored graffiti and gang signs. And litter covered the broken-up floors. Remains of steel rails and cinder blocks were everywhere in the once well-constructed building, as were illegally dumped old tires.

"Kill the engine and get your big, goofy punk ass out of this van," Mutt demanded, holding his gun as steady as he could, knowing he was still buzzing strong from the few pills he'd popped earlier.

Keys did as he was told, still not saying a word. Then the unannounced passenger's partner joined them. Now with two guns on him, Keys knew getting away would be twice as difficult, but he wasn't going out like nobody's little bitch. He wasn't cut like that, period. Standing more than a few inches taller than both of the other men, Keys knew if they didn't have weapons, he'd beat a few pints of blood outta both they weird-looking asses. But the fact was, they did have those guns, so his next play would definitely have to be his best if he wished to survive.

"All right, homeboy. It's like this. You and your people can't be coming over here on our side of town, stepping on niggas' toes like shit's a joke," Mutt growled. He mean mugged Keys as Cutt cosigned.

"Yeah, we ain't no lames this way. We let your bitch ass get a li'l money, but you done went too far with the bullshit. You got our peoples screaming on us, so yeah, nigga, we at you!"

"So this is how this right here about to go. First, start your ass to walking up in this motherfucker." Mutt waved his gun, motioning to a huge area in the building where a wall had collapsed. "You gonna go on a little sightseeing tour with me and my boy. We wanna show you some shit."

Cutt laughed, still high as hell, thinking shit was funny. "Yeah, West Side bitch, come get some of this East Side hospitality."

Keys was no fool, far from it. He knew if he allowed these funny-style idiots to march him up inside this building, it'd be lights out for him. If he wanted to come out of this hole and see his baby girl's face once more, he knew now would be his time to react. Catching the overconfident Cutt and Mutt slipping, arguing about who was going to get Keys's watch and diamond stud earring, the West Side warrior made his move and bolted. Not knowing which way was which, Keys ran down a short side street, made a quick left, then another left, and then a right. The more he ran for his life, the more his heart rate increased. He was out of breath and confused. He felt turned around, as if he was going in circles. This way was wrong. This way was blocked. And the other way would take him right back to Mutt and Cutt, or so he believed. And sadly for him, he was correct. If you had not grown up in this neighborhood, you'd have no way of knowing which blocks were dead ends and which streets would lead you right back to the automotive plant's perimeters.

Staring down the barrels of both guns, Keys ended up inside the back area of the building. This was a better location than Cutt and Mutt had originally wanted to be in. After being told more of the same about why the pair was on a mission to do him harm, Keys had a chance to catch his breath a bit. When the father of one did catch his breath, he did not utter a word. He did not ask for mercy. He wasted no more time. He swiftly bum-rushed the bigger of the two men, which was Cutt, and tried his luck. Having totally caught Cutt off guard, Keys was successful. He knocked the gun from Cutt's hand. Mutt saw his boy being manhandled, and of course, he reacted automatically by pulling the trigger. The sound of the single gunshot seemed to echo throughout the deserted structure. Cutt stumbled backward, trying to catch his balance, as Keys fell to his knees.

With blood gushing from a gaping hole in the rear of his skull, Keys struggled to keep life in his body. He wanted nothing more than to pick up that over-the-top cake and make it to the party. However, the angel of death cruelly appeared. Keys tragically succumbed to the gunshot wound, and his upper body slumped over. Showing no signs of remorse, the pair of murderers removed Keys's watch and earring, the ones they'd already argued about. After running through his pockets for any cash and his new iPhone, they left him facedown in a pile of garbage.

After Mutt and Cutt emerged victorious from the rear of the Packard Plant, one drove Keys's van a few blocks away, and the other followed. They then casually abandoned the vehicle, just as they had Keys's lifeless body, but not before stealing his remaining re-up of CDs and all his daughter's birthday presents, which were wrapped and ready to go in the rear hatch, just waiting to put a smile on her innocent face.

# Chapter 31

Four o'clock came. Then five, then six. There was still no sign of Keys. Which meant there were no presents on the gift table, other than the few his baby mom's trifling friends had brought. And there was no birthday cake. The child's mother was livid, to say the least. As she placed call after call, her voicemails became more and more disrespectful. The text messages were also off the chain. She had no idea that Keys no longer had possession of his cell. His killers did, and they were sitting back, getting high off the extra-potent CDs, laughing, and reading all her messages to their deceased victim. Time and time again, she walked up to Kalif, Pit Boy, Amir, and Li'l James and bombarded them with questions about whether they'd heard from their homeboy, but they had not. Even though they would lie for Keys if he asked them to, he had not. They were being honest. Keys was ghost.

By six o'clock, the crew had started to worry. They had gathered over on one side of the large table. Not showing up to some birthday party was one thing, even if it was his daughter's. Yet Keys had not returned one call since that morning. Kalif had texted him the emergency code after a few of Keys's workers said he hadn't come back to drop off more product or collect the ticket money.

At 6:10 p.m. the crew left the birthday and piled into their cars. As a caravan, the worried friends pulled out of the parking lot and headed east. En route, Kalif called the police station's main number for inmate booking and even a few hospitals to see if they had Keys. He came up empty on both fronts. When the guys got to the area that Keys held down, they were met by his workers. Kalif collected the money from them and told them to go ahead to the crib. He'd call them the next day if there was work. Heads lowered, confused, the workers parted ways. Then the guys in the crew got back on the road. On the way home, they drove down Mt. Elliott, heading to I-94. When they went past East Grand Boulevard, Kalif turned his head to the right and looked over at the shut-down El Capri Bar, which his father used to talk about. He had no idea his missing friend lay dead right down the street. Days later, the world would know.

Kalif was beside himself when he got the news that Keys's body had been found, as was everyone who knew Keys. It was if their lives were moving in slow motion. Keys had been through various trials, hardships, and tribulations. But Keys was strong. He was a fighter. If there was a way for him to come out on top, he always found that way. But this time had been different. This time someone had got the drop on him. Everyone knew there was no good reason for Keys to be inside that old, dilapidated eyesore of a building. After his van was located a few blocks away, it took no brain surgeon or private eye to figure out he had been forced inside the Packard Plant in some sort of fashion. And with the fatal shot being delivered to the back of his head, it was also discerned that whoever Keys's final executioner was, the person had feared Keys to some degree.

Everyone was grieving in their own way, and Kalif was no different. Completely off his meds, he'd gone to a dark place in his mind, seemingly never to return. He could not be reasoned with. He was becoming more reckless and more deliberate with his rage. A few days after Keys was found, Kalif went back to his house where the girls were staying and sat on the couch. For some time now, Jada had been crossing his mind. He never did find out why she had just up and left him, but one day maybe he might.

Hearing noise in the living room, TayTay came down the stairs, clutching a bottle of Jack Daniel's in her hand. She was still in bad shape mentally. Having liquor courage, she dared Kalif to take a swig of her magic potion, something she'd never do when in her right mind. Kalif was gone. He was having delusions as he thought about his life in general. He couldn't help but wonder what it would have been like if both his parents hadn't been murdered in cold blood, much like Keys had been. The next thing he knew, not only had he snatched the bottle out of TayTay's hands, but he was turning it up. Even though he'd broken almost every rule set forth in Islam, drinking was not one of them, until now.

Dizzy and dazed, Kalif then pulled the equally buzzed TayTay to him. Dick rock hard, he ripped at her booty shorts and moved them to the side. Sticking his tongue down her throat, Kalif roughly shoved his manhood deep inside of her. Their bodies were locked together. It was the first time either one of them had felt raw passion in some time. Hours later, the two would awaken, embarrassed and ashamed over what had taken place. TayTay ran upstairs to take a shower, hoping to wash off the guilt she felt from betraying Jada. And Kalif went out the door, headed to the mosque. Just as he was pulling out of the driveway, Jewels pulled up. She waved at Kalif, but either he didn't see her or he was ignoring her. Either way something seemed strange. When she went in the house, TayTay was still in the shower. Jewels rolled her eyes, hoping TayTay had not broken the girl code.

After ensuring Keys had a proper burial, his friends, all pallbearers, swore they'd avenge Keys's death someway, someday. Back on the grind in other areas of the city, Kalif let Keys's sector fall for the time being. He shifted his workers toward the west. But as the days went by, nothing else weighed heavily on Kalif's troubled soul but retaliation. Knowing the streets had a habit of revealing the truth; Kalif sent Jewels, who was still suspicious of him, and Nia and Euri on a mission. He knew that the crews on that side of town that were getting money would be instantly drawn to the girls at the club. In a matter of days, he had his answer: the BBM, aka the Black Bottom Mafia. Taking the vital information back to his team, Kalif announced that they were going to war. He warned them that anyone that wasn't built for the shit that was about to jump off needed to bow out now. The room grew silent. Keys was all they manz, and the BBM would pay much sooner than later. Eye for an eye, blood for blood.

With murder on his mind, Kalif went to speak to Nieem. Not expecting to see him so soon, the older man still welcomed his top moneymaker with open arms. He had heard through the "hood news grapevine" what had happened to Kalif's people, and offered his condolences. Kalif excepted Nieem's heartfelt words, but then he told him his true agenda for the unscheduled visit.

"I need to put my hands on some more guns. We ain't holding enough for what I need to handle."

"More guns?" Nieem asked, puzzled, as he rubbed his hands together.

"Yeah, more guns. There's no way in hell I'ma let them motherfuckers get away with doing my boy like that. They started it, so fuck all that. I'm good with finishing it. I want they asses to feel this shit coming they way!"

Nieem was silent as he considered how to put what he wanted to say next in a way that did not give the impression that didn't care about the boy's death. Kalif looked and sounded as if he was losing it, but who was Nieem to pass judgment. That was God's job. He could only give advice. "Listen, my young friend. I understand your desire for revenge. And I cannot lie and say I felt otherwise when in my youth. But now I have to think. I have to calculate my steps and actions. You, too, will learn this in time."

"Yeah, well, when that time comes, maybe I'll learn that lesson. But right about now, I need to put my hands on some guns. Some of that off the chain rebels fighting in the bush type of shit y'all be having in the desert. That shit a guy can easily modify, and with it, he can kill an entire mob if he need to."

Nieem had linked up with Kalif to make money. Not to sponsor a mini war in the city. With Keys's death, Kalif's money flow had slowed down, and Nieem understood that was to be expected, as Kalif and the others were mourning their loss. But selfishly, he wanted them to be grown-ass men, shake that shit off, and get back to business as usual, which was moving product and making money. Yet he could see and hear that Kalif had other

plans to execute before that could take place: he wanted
to wage an all-out war with the BBM. With the pressure
on him to deliver and do this favor, Nieem reluctantly
arranged for a small shipment of unmarked firearms to
be made available to Kalif. When his young visitor left,
Nieem could do nothing but ask Allah to protect Kalif
and guide his actions.

# Chapter 32

During the next few months, the streets of Detroit ran bloodred. They were on fire and were not in line to get extinguished any time soon. In direct retaliation for Keys's untimely death, Kalif made sure two members of the BBM felt the pain of burying their own. The BBM was a long-established organization, with members posted not only on the East Side, where most of the third-generation crew hailed from, but also scattered here and there on the West Side. Kalif had been doing his homework. With the aid of some of his young brothers at the mosque, Kalif had been able to reach out and touch those members of the BBM who felt they were untouchable or were living under the radar.

But Kalif knew that if you were in a bloody war being played out in the city streets, there were no rules for either side. No regulations. And definitely no time-outs. If you were dumb enough to get caught slipping while shopping at CVS in Midtown, leaving the MGM with your grandmother, browsing at Greenfield Plaza or Eastland Center, or enjoying a comedy show at the Fox Theater, you deserved your fate. Just as Keys had had to meet his Maker by not staying focused, you had to face the possibility of joining him. Traveling in pairs, and even in groups, had become second nature to those involved in the deadly underground conflict. If you were out selling drugs or even buying them on some corner, your life was most certainly in jeopardy.

While the war was being waged, the only ones making steady money in Detroit were the undertakers. When Cantrell on Mack Avenue folded after infant remains were found stashed in the rafters, their low-income welfare funerals and cremations were split between Swanson, Stinson, and Cole, the "big three" funeral homes in Motown. Those places were making money hand over fist.

Eventually, clergy from one side of the crime-ridden city to the other came together to call for an end to the violence and bloodshed. Unified, they took their message of peace to the media, in hopes that their once great town would have a healing. Mothers had lost sons. Children had witnessed siblings being shot. Females had buried baby daddies, and all because of that jealous Willie Lynch mentality that had been instilled in the hood. If you didn't have it, then tear down the next man that did, by any means. In most cases, in Detroit that meant open murder.

During the bloody war, Kalif was picked up and brought in for questioning about a few heinous killings. Knowing to keep his mouth shut, he made no statements and let his high-priced lawyer earn his fee. And that he did, as Kalif walked out the doors of the police station a free man not once, but twice. Knowing that his oldest son was deeply involved in several killings, the tight-knit families in the mosque asked Rasul if he could speak to his son about maybe arriving at some sort of truce with the other drug gangs that slaughtered people at will, including the BBM. Rasul had still not returned home to his wife and family, but he was making biweekly visits.

He had promised Fatima years ago that he would always take care of her and provide for her. That word he would never break. During his visits, Rasul bonded with his twin daughters, who were growing up faster than any man wished his daughters to do.

However, his and Hakim's relationship was completely severed, as was Hakim and Kalif's. Hakim refused to speak to his father, even out of respect. Knowing he could beat the young man into showing him the respect he deserved and had earned, Rasul let it be. He still prayed daily that both his sons would be able to make amends with each other, as well as with him. The dedicated parent knew Kalif was headed in one of two directions, prison or death, so he hoped to intercede before either of those happened.

During one of Rasul's visits, Hakim was in the kitchen ear hustling, which he'd been doing a lot of lately, and he overheard Rasul begging his older brother to meet him at an abandoned warehouse, a place where they used to purchase fruit when they were small children. It was down near Fort Street. Hakim tucked that information away.

Ever since Stacy's condition had improved a little bit, she had refused to deal with Hakim, ultimately blaming him for the tragedy that had taken place, for which no one had yet been brought to justice. Hakim was heartbroken and devastated. So much so that he had refused to accept any of the out-of-state college scholarship offers. He had expressed to his mother that he needed to take a term off to get his head straight and to work on a few personal projects. Fatima knew her son had been stressed, all things considered, and she hadn't pressed the issue.

# Chapter 33

Rasul was the first to arrive at the deserted warehouse. Initially, he sat in his truck and thought. Despite his persistent efforts to get Kalif out of the game, he knew his oldest boy was correct when he called him out for being two-faced. How could he warn Kalif about the pitfalls of the game when he was still out in the streets, even if it was out of state, trying to avoid them himself? After he pondered that very fact, he made up his mind that after all this time of putting in work for his people, who operated according to a much different system of valor and loyalty than the new generation, Rasul placed a call. It was one he thought he'd never make. After a brief conversation, he made it clear that as of that moment in time, he'd no longer be handling business of any sort. He was officially retiring from the game so he could raise his daughters in peace and show his son a better way . . . both of his sons.

Nearly twenty minutes had passed, and Kalif had yet to show up. Not ready to throw in the towel, Rasul got out of his vehicle and went inside the cold building through the side door, which hadn't had any locks on it for years. The sun shining through the broken glass was the only light the building had to offer. Walking around, the still proud father reminisced about all the wonderful times he'd shared there with his sons. They would

pick out fresh produce, then go slaughter a lamb for special Islamic occasions. Just as Rasul decided that Kalif
had stood him up, he heard the side door swing open,
then closed. Kalif had come. He was a little late, and
Rasul could easily see he had not been on his medication
for quite some time, but he had shown up just the same.
Rasul opened his arms to welcome his boy. Mentally
drained, but still willing to stand and fight on principle,
Kalif embraced his father in return.

Their heartfelt talk went on for ten minutes before the
father and son heard the warehouse's side door swing
open and closed once more. Rasul and Kalif didn't
have to say a word. Their eyes spoke for them both.
Simultaneously, they pulled out their guns, ready to team
up and prepared to do battle. With guns drawn and aimed
at the door, they waited. But they quickly lowered those
guns when Hakim emerged from the shadows. His father
and older brother were not expecting to see him, and they
wondered why he was there. That much was apparent
from their expressions.

"So I guess, as always, this is a private party with
just you and Kalif. The way you always wanted it to
be. Just you two," Hakim snapped.

Not in the mood for the younger boy's "cry me a
river" antics, Rasul tried to calm Hakim down before
Kalif reacted and did what he always did when feeling
attacked, which was to attack back, but with no rules,
rhyme, or reason. But it was too late. His sons had locked
eyes, indicating both were ready to take it to another
level. First, came the hatred, followed by the accusations,
then, of course, by the blame. Years of animosity spilled
out on the warehouse floor. Trying his best to bring an
end to the brothers' furious name-calling and threats of

violence, Rasul stepped in between his irate, emotional sons, one adopted, one biological, but loved equally. Just when he thought he had them calmed down, Kalif asked the most explosive question he could.

"So yeah, where's that li'l bitch the devil himself couldn't burn the fuck up at? She still got you being a sucker or what?"

It was as if the next few minutes moved in slow motion, bringing the impromptu family reunion to a close. Suddenly, Hakim produced a handgun, which he had tucked in the waistband at small of his back. Rasul recognized it as one he had stashed back at the house. He knew it had a hairline trigger, and he had stopped carrying it years ago. He warned Hakim to put the gun down, but his youngest son was defiant, as he had been for close to a year. He raised his arm and pointed the jankey firearm in his brother's direction. Kalif had been out in the streets for months, at war with hustlers and real, official killers. So he was quick on the draw and ready to put in work, brother or not.

"Yeah, all right, nigga. What your bitch ass gonna do? You produced that motherfucker, so don't just stand there being straight pussy. Be on it," Kalif taunted.

Hakim was fed up with Kalif thinking he was the only one that could act crazy and lash out. He had no real intention to use the gun, but once again, Kalif had pushed his buttons, and he resented that. "Look, just admit you was the one that put Jada White up to setting Stacy's house on fire. Just say you did it!"

"Nigga, what? Is this what this bullshit about?" Kalif hissed with rage. "Man, like I said months ago, fuck you, fuck her, and oh yeah, fuck her dead granny too!"

Rasul had had enough as he shoved each son back. He wanted peace. Purposely or not, the gun Hakim was holding went off. One fatal shot rang out. The earsplitting sound seemed to repeat itself as the bullet found a new home in Rasul's left temple.

"Born to die. The angel of death is certain. Allah, spare me long dwelling on the threshold of final judgment. Take me quick. Do with my soul what you see fit. I'm not worthy," the dedicated father slowly muttered before being welcomed home to paradise.

The person each boy had idolized at one point or another as the greatest man to ever live was now dead. Hakim dropped the gun in his hand, but not before Kalif deliberately let off one round himself and robbed his father's killer of his life too. If ever there was a time Kalif needed to be medicated, it was now. Kneeling down, Kalif used his hand to close his father's eyes, which were wide open, with tears running out of them. He then started to cry himself.

Despite everything tragic and solemn he'd been through, it'd been years since he'd shed real tears. Even when he'd found out Keys was gone, no tears had dropped. But this was his father. This was his hero. This was the one person that believed in him when no one else did. This was the man that had saved his life when he was an infant and had never stopped embracing him. He was gone. Rasul was gone, and now Kalif was officially alone in the world. Praying over his father's deceased body, Kalif knew what he had to do next to ensure he wasn't implicated in any wrongdoing.

He called Nieem. Almost immediately, making good on his second huge favor, Nieem sent over a few men who were dressed as painters and drove a white van.

When they entered the building, they found Kalif in tears, praying over his father one last time.

"Hello. Nieem sent us," said the older of the two men.

"Yes, I know." Kalif reluctantly stood to his feet, wiping his face. "Listen, this is my father. Treat his body with respect and dignity. Nieem reassured me that although he will have to be buried in an unmarked grave, he will at least be properly prepared to enter paradise."

The men, both Muslims, gave Kalif their word that their Muslim brother would receive the highest reverence.

"Okay, what about this body here? Nieem said this is your brother. Should we bury them each the same?" said the man who had first spoken.

On his way out the door, Kalif looked over at Hakim with disgust before replying. "Naw, that ain't my damn brother. Never was. That's just my father's son. And he's a nonbeliever. You can just toss him into the Detroit River. He'll be good there."

# Chapter 34

It was a sad day. Kalif had been driving around all day. He had not eaten and had not had a clear thought since seeing the white van leave with his father inside. Not in the mood to speak to anyone, he had been avoiding all calls. But when Pit Boy kept calling back to back, Kalif knew something must have popped off. When he finally picked up, Pit Boy told him he may need to swing by his crib as soon as possible. Jewels was there, straight clowning. Pit Boy said he'd already laid hands on her twice, but the bitch was like her cousin Jada, relentless.

Getting himself as together as possible, Kalif headed in that direction. When he pulled up, it was just as Pit Boy had said. Even from out in the street, Jewels could be heard going ham. He was in mourning but could not share that information. So he kept it to himself and just tried to boss up the best he could. He climbed out of his truck and started walking toward the front door. When he was just a few feet from the truck, Jewels came bolting out the door, making all sorts of accusations. Pit Boy was behind her, ready to smack the fire outta her mouth once more if she didn't shut the fuck up.

"So you fucked that stanking, loose pussy bitch? My cousin sitting in jail behind you, and you out here fucking her girl like it ain't shit!" Jewels raged.

Kalif was drained and not in the mood for this. "Look, girl."

"Naw, 'look, girl,' my ass. Everybody be running around here, scared of your ass, but I ain't. You need to keep shit real and just admit you fucked TayTay and that's your baby!"

Kalif was even more confused now, as was Pit Boy. This was the first time during Jewels's ongoing rant that she had revealed that part. "Who having a baby? And what the hell you mean, mine?"

"Stop playing games and fronting. Did you put your dick up in her or what?" Jewels got extra bossy, as if this was her house and she was running shit, not the other way around.

Not one to lie about his dick, Kalif finally said he did and asked Jewels why she cared so much. He then reminded her that when her Jada went to jail, they were no longer cool. She'd left him. Lastly, he had to put her in her place and remind her that just because he and Jada was tight like that, they had never been physical and he was free to put his dick anywhere he wanted to, even up in TayTay's stanking, loose pussy, as she'd stated.

Before things got further out of hand, Jewels took another huge garbage bag of her belongings out of the house and stuffed it in her car. She and the other girls had used that house for quite some time now, selling stolen goods out of it. Before driving away, she threw her set of house keys into the bushes out of spite. Pit Boy retrieved them as Kalif went inside and then upstairs to speak to TayTay. Up until now what had happened between them had been left unspoken. So, of course, Kalif wanted to know why she had revealed it now. And, of course, he wanted to know about this baby thing.

TayTay was locked in her bedroom, where she spent the majority of her time. When Kalif knocked, she immediately swung the door open and apologized. She was nursing a black eye courtesy of Jewels's fist making contact with her face. One other thing that Kalif couldn't miss was TayTay's protruding belly. Now in tears, she confessed that she must've gotten pregnant that day the two of them messed around. She swore she'd been with no one else, and it was true. She was carrying his baby. TayTay then lowered her head in shame, awaiting the verbal and maybe physical fallout from Kalif. But there was none. In fact, the only thing he wanted to know was when she was due. When he found out, he did the math.

He was going to be a father. In his mind, Kalif could not help but believe Allah had blessed him with a seed to replace the love of Rasul. It was God's will, so he would embrace it. On that very day, the father to be moved all the way into the house he owned and had been paying the bills on for someone else to live in.

# Chapter 35

Even though Kalif had endured more than his share of bumps, bruises, and hardships along the way, he was finally a true force to be reckoned with in the streets. His crew was back on their CD grind, and money was back to coming in heavy and regular. But make no mistake. The beef with the BBM was going on stronger than ever. And in Kalif's eyes, there would always be a murder waiting to jump off where they were concerned.

Still, Allah had been blessing him. And this time he felt the blessing was better than ever. Li'l James had been in a dice game the evening prior. Sadly, he had lost his money. But what made it a blessing was the fact that Li'l James had caught one of the BBM fellas slipping. Kalif's homeboy had quickly spotted him because of the gaudy chain he was rocking, with the letters *BBM* sprinkled in diamond dust. Thinking it was all good, because it was early morning, the guy had dropped some female off at the Amtrak station. Unfortunately for him, he wasn't strapped. Li'l James, however, had stayed with a gun ever since the war started. When the man attempted to return to his car, he was cut off, a gun was shoved in his dental, and he was ordered to get inside the rental Li'l James was pushing. Like Keys months and months ago, the man had been ambushed. He would soon become another statistic in the beef of all beefs. But not before

Kalif and company asked a few questions and demanded a few answers.

With several of his anxious crew members gathered together and passing around a gallon of Hennessy, Kalif, cell in hand, waited patiently to receive an text. He'd sent a throwaway worker to the other side of town. Having gotten word that their sworn enemies were posted at a certain stash house located near the old Kettering High School, the often deranged leader had to make sure the information was indeed correct. Not trying to tip his hand, he couldn't run the risk of being made. And even though everyone that worked for him was capable, Kalif didn't have to take or ask for volunteers for this job. This time around, the man's task was fairly simple: creep on the address he was given and take pictures of all the vehicles in the driveway and parked out in front of the house. All he had to do then was text them to the Obama burnout, nothing more and nothing less.

It was 5:23 a.m. and still no word from old boy. If they wanted to make an early morning move, he'd have to get at them sooner rather than later. Yet while the others remained restless as they finished their community bottle, Kalif was patient. The crew had been down at Greektown Casino all night, keeping their "go time" energy up. But Kalif's energy had been up for trouble ever since Keys's murder. But now he continued to be calm. He'd prayed this morning to be protected from all his enemies and to be granted grace. So of course, he moved differently than the nonbelievers that surrounded him. His need for revenge and his taste for blood would come on Allah's time, not on his own.

Seconds soon turned to minutes, and then Kalif received the notification he had been waiting for. He downloaded each picture, and the reality of the situation quickly became evident. The informant was telling the truth, but still hard to die on point and principle.

"Before daybreak, it's gonna be some dead BBM bitches," Kalif vowed with certainty before stepping over to the washing machine. Ready to put in even more work, he snatched up the dark brown handle of the meat cleaver. With it down at his side, he felt like the angel of death was speaking to him. *Fear not being in the land of the living. But fear the painful scorch of hellfire that awaits you.*

The members of the nine-man crew, who had been handpicked to murder when need be, moved back toward the walls of the basement. Kalif slow strolled along the path they had made for him. He then focused on the man they had duct-taped to an old lawn chair, and the next play was obvious to everyone present. As he got closer to the visitor, Kalif's grip tightened on the handle of the meat cleaver. When they were only two feet from each other, they locked eyes, the predator and his prey. A stone-faced Kalif was not bothered by the other man's gaze. He knew the tortured BBM member wanted mercy in return for snitching. And even though he had ratted out his own people and had put Kalif and 'em up on game, unfortunately, there would be no mercy. Retaliation for being on the wrong team and for killing his homeboy, and others since the war had begun, would be swift.

They were working against the promise of daybreak. After thanking the BBM member for his service, Kalif raised the meat cleaver. There was no hesitation on his part. The future was now. With one strong swing of the blade, it was done. Kalif hit his mark. Blood splattered on Kalif's face and forearm and on some parts of the wall. Kalif looked down. The man's neck had a huge open wound, and his head was dangling to the side, much to his executioner's delight. Kalif showed no remorse, and neither did the others in the basement, who'd been down this deadly road before. For them, it was business as usual. After watching the man's body slump over, Kalif dropped the bloodied meat cleaver to the floor and proclaimed victory.

It was still rather dark outside, but that didn't slow Kalif down. And the normal busy traffic on Davison was not a factor. Kalif looked over at the passenger seat, at his high-powered weapon and the 9 mm that was keeping it company. In true gangster fashion, he had filed the serial numbers off both weapons. Unlike his boys behind him, Kalif had opted to ride alone. Always in deep thought, he had tunnel vision for what was about to take place. Concentration was boss as he drove through the city, heading east. Since there was no music playing to distract him, his adoptive father's final words before his untimely death ran through Kalif's mind.

*Born to die. The angel of death is certain. Allah, spare me long dwelling on the threshold of final judgment. Take me quick. Do with my soul what you see fit. I'm not worthy.*

He couldn't come to terms with the fact that the man he had once looked upon as his hero was gone. The only man that Allah had put on this earth to believe in him was no more. Kalif would forever be plagued with guilt over Rasul's ultimate sacrifice. From the moment he had witnessed his father take that fatal bullet to the head and had realized his life had been spared, Kalif had been no more than a shell of a man, one of the walking dead. But for what? Kalif knew he didn't deserve having been conceived, let alone having a life. That thought haunted him and always would.

Navigating around countless potholes, he and his squad kept the vehicles tight, as if they were in a parade. As they jumped onto the Lodge Freeway, then connected with 94 East, it was almost "go time" for the band of would-be assassins. After they exited at Harper Avenue, the blue-colored metal K greeted them. They made a few right turns, passed a cluster of vacant lots, and then made a sharp left at a huge abandoned house. The clock was ticking.

When the ill-intentioned caravan reached their destination, Kalif's heart raced. Not out of fear, but in anticipation of snatching the next man's soul. After he came to a stop, Kalif flung the driver's side door open. One foot on the ground, then the next, he took a deep breath, ready to do battle. His team did the same. Like a boss, Kalif was the one to lead the charge. And like a warrior, he was prepared to die first. As he let off a barrage of bullets, the street-ordained kingpin of Detroit mumbled his same earlier thoughts with each step he took.

"Born to die. The angel of death is certain. Allah, spare me long dwelling on the threshold of final judgment. Take me quick. Do with my soul what you see fit. I'm not worthy." Kalif prayed for the best but would bravely accept the worst. This madness was the world he had been born into and the life he embraced.

The battlefield was harsh. But this morning's attack was written in the stars to happen. The bloody certainty of demise had been building not for days and weeks, but for months. And now especially, since Kalif, Li'l James, Pit Boy, and Amir had been told back in the basement by the rat that Cutt and Mutt, who were indeed the hired guns who had left Keys facedown, would be in the house. It was their hope that if nothing else, Cutt And Mutt would feel the pain of death this morning.

With bullets flying in every direction, bodies were dropping left and right on both sides. Minutes into the battle, Kalif took a slug in his upper shoulder. It burned. It was hot. But it didn't slow him down. And when he saw his boy Li'l James take a direct hit to the chest, Kalif moved even faster to get the job done, fueled by the rage inside him. Ten minutes later, many inside the house lay dead on the floor. Only a handful off BBM members were out of the house and still firing shots at Kalif and his crew. But one by one, Kalif and his guys picked them off, and the gunfire slowed down, then ceased. Police sirens could be heard approaching.

Kalif was certain that cowardly members of the BBM had hidden themselves somewhere around the house, and he wanted to continue until every single one of them was dead and buried, but he knew he had to retreat if he hoped to remain free. Nursing his shoulder wound, he rushed to his truck while yelling out for the rest of his team to do the same. Glancing back, he instantly mourned for Li'l James, who had yet to move an inch since taking one in the chest. Whenever his people had the chance to claim their fallen comrade, Kalif would make sure he was buried as a G. He owed that much to his homeboy, who'd been rolling with him almost since day one.

The strong-willed, murderous caravan headed back to the West Side a few vehicles light. Just when Kalif thought no one else was badly injured, he looked in the rearview mirror and saw that Pit Boy was no longer behind him. He hit up Pit Boy's cell, and one of the other loyal warriors answered the call and said they were pulling up at the emergency room entrance at Detroit Receiving Hospital. He informed his boss that Pit Bull had taken at least one in the stomach and two in the arm. And he needed medical treatment immediately. Kalif knew his wound could and would be treated at home. He couldn't run the risk of being directly associated with the bloody mayhem that'd just gone down. Praying for Li'l James's soul and Pit Boy's recovery, he pushed on and headed home to regroup.

# Chapter 36

The leader of the police task force was heated. This crime scene was worse than any of the others he'd worked since he'd gotten on the task force. The faces of some of the deceased and badly injured looked familiar to him, but others didn't. But one thing was for sure: the Wayne County Morgue would be full today. One by one, the leader had his second-in-command take pictures of each victim. He was immediately alerted when one of the deceased stood out from the others. As two cops stood over Li'l James, the task force leader looked down at him and easily recognized him as one of the infamous Kalif's top-tier men.

Just to make sure, the task force leader took out his cell phone and placed a call. There was no answer. He hung up and called again. The response was the same. For months on end, he'd been receiving countless calls, texts, pictures, and other valuable information from Hakim Akbar, who had been attempting to build a solid case against his older brother. But now, just as had been the deal for a while, the brother turned rat-snitch informant was not picking up.

"No answer. Look, we'll get back with that guy later," the task force leader told his second-in-command. "Besides, we have enough to do now. Especially after all this bloodshed and bullshit! I want you to call down to the prosecutors' office. Tell them to have the judge sign an emergency warrant for everyone in both the BBM and that crazy, insane Kalif's crew. If they ain't dead, I want them all locked up by the time the sun goes down!" After giving that direct order, the task force leader felt elated. In a matter of hours, he'd have both Brutus and Kalif behind bars. Maybe sharing a jail cell, for his own amusement.

Distraught and in undeniable pain, Kalif grimaced while getting down out of his bullet hole–ridden truck at the house. Besides the physical pain he was in, his mental state was all the way gone. Even he knew he needed to be institutionalized to get some much-needed help. But Kalif was a proud black man and was now considered on kingpin status. He knew that getting help would never take place. He wouldn't allow it. Way too many people were counting and depending on him. As he headed up to the porch, his shoulder dripped blood. But he felt that if he took a hot shower, it would ease the pain and clean the wound out. Then he would simply bandage up the wound and figure out his next move for the days to follow. Not naïve, Kalif realized the streets were going to be hot, which meant that sales would be down. He knew that would sadden Nieem, but taking a loss from time to time was all part of the game.

Once inside the house, Kalif took each stair slowly. TayTay, who very pregnant and ready to deliver, was no doubt still in her bedroom, sleeping. Even though Kalif was living there now full-time, this was for the sake of his unborn child, nothing more, nothing less. With the pain intensifying, he decided he'd have to wake her up to